# Separate Flights

# Separate Flights

## ANDRE DUBUS

DAVID R. GODINE ⋅ Publisher ⋅ BOSTON

First published in 1975 by

David R. Godine, Publisher

306 Dartmouth Street

Boston, Massachusetts

LCC 74-25955

ISBN 0-87923-123-8 softcover

Printed in the United States of America


Acknowledgments: 'Over the Hill' was first published in *Sage*; 'The Doctor' (© 1969 The New Yorker Magazine, Inc.) in *The New Yorker*; 'In My Life' in *Northwest Review*; 'If They Knew Yvonne' (© 1969 University of Northern Iowa), 'Separate Flights' (© 1970 University of Northern Iowa), and 'Going Under' (© 1974 University of Northern Iowa) in *North American Review*.


Second printing April 1981

*To Suzanne, Andre, Jeb, & Nicole*

# Contents

*The name of 'Threads of the Virgin' is applied to certain tiny threads that float in the wind and on which a certain kind of spiders . . . take flight in the free breezes of the air and even in the midst of a violent storm. . . . But these spiders spin those floating threads out of their own entrails, delicate webs by means of which they hurl themselves into space unknown.*

Miguel de Unamuno, *The Agony of Christianity*

*Save me, thought the Consul vaguely . . .*

Malcolm Lowry, *Under the Volcano*

# We Don't Live Here Anymore

*Pity is the worst passion of all: we don't outlive it like sex.*
—Graham Greene, *The Ministry of Fear*

*Come see us again some time; nobody's home but us, and we don't live here anymore.*
—a friend, drunk one night

§ 1    THE owner of the liquor store was an Irishman with graying hair; he glanced at Edith, then pretended he hadn't, and said: 'There's my ale man.'

'Six Pickwicks,' I said. 'And a six-pack of Miller's for the women.'

'You hardly find a woman who'll drink ale.'

'That's right.'

We leaned against the counter; I felt Edith wanting to touch me, so I stepped back and took out my wallet. Hank had wanted to pay for all of it but I held him to two dollars.

'Used to be everybody in New England drank ale. Who taught you? Your father?'

'He taught me to drink ale and laugh with pretty girls. What happened to the others?'

I was watching Edith enjoying us. She is dark and very small with long black hair, and she has the same charming gestures that other girls with long hair have: with a slow hand she pushes it from her eye; when she bends over a drinking fountain, she holds it at her ear so it won't fall into the basin. Some time I would like to see it fall: Edith drinking, lips wet, throat moving with cool water, and her hair fallen in the chrome basin, soaking.

'World War II. The boys all got drafted before they were old enough to drink in Massachusetts, see? So they started drinking beer on the Army bases. When they came home they still wanted beer. That was the end of ale. Now if one of your old ale drinkers dies, you don't replace him.'

Outside under the streetlights Edith took my arm. In front of the news stand across the street a cop watched us get into the car, and in the dark Edith sat close to me as I drove through town. There were few cars and no one was on the sidewalks. On the streets where people lived most of the houses were dark; a few blocks from my house I stopped under a large tree near the curb and held Edith and we kissed.

'We'd better go,' she said.

'I'll bring my car to the Shell Station at twelve.'

She moved near the door and brushed her hair with her fingers, and I drove home. Terry and Hank were sitting on the front steps. When I stopped the car Edith got out and crossed the lawn without waiting or looking back. Terry watched me carrying the bag, and when I stepped between her and Hank she looked straight up at me.

We talked in the dark, sitting in lawn chairs on the porch. Except Hank, who was always restless: he leaned against the porch rail, paced, leaned against a wall, stood over one of us as we talked, nodding his head, a bottle in one fist, a glass in the other, listening, then breaking in, swinging his glass like a slow hook to the body the instant before he interrupted, then his voice came, louder than ours. In high school he had played halfback. He went to college weighing a hundred and fifty-six pounds and started writing. He had kept in condition, and his walk and gestures had about them an athletic grace that I had tried to cultivate as a boy, walking home from movies where I had seen gunmen striding like mountain lions. Edith sat to my right, with her back to the wall; sometimes she rested her foot against mine. Terry sat across from me, smoking too much. She has long red hair and eleven years ago she was the prettiest girl I had ever seen; or, rather, the prettiest girl I had ever touched. Now she's thirty and she's gained a pound for each of those eleven years, but she has gained them subtly, and her only striking change is in her eyes, blue eyes that I fell in love with: more and more now, they have that sad, pensive look that married women get after a few years. Her eyes used to be merry. Edith is twenty-seven and her eyes are still merry, and she turned them bright and dark to me as I talked. When Hank and Edith left, we walked them to the car, hugging and pecking them goodnight as we always did; I watched Edith's silhouette as they drove away.

'Come here,' Terry said. She took my wrist and pulled me toward the back door.

'Come where.'

'In the kitchen. I want to talk to you.'

'Would you let go of my wrist?'

She kept pulling. At the sidewalk leading to the back door I stopped and jerked my arm but she held on and turned to face me.

'I said let go of my wrist,' and I jerked again and was free. Then I followed her in.

'From now on we're going to act like married people,' she said. 'No more of this crap.' I went to the refrigerator and got an ale. 'Just like other married people. And no flirting around with silly adventures. Do you understand that?'

'Of course I don't. Who could understand such bullshit.'

'You're not *really* going to play dumb. Are you? Come on.'

'Terry.' I was still calm; I thought I might be able to hold onto that, pull us out of this, into bed, into sleep. 'Would you please tell me what's wrong?'

She moved toward me and I squared my feet to duck or block, but she went past me and got ice from the refrigerator and went to the cabinet where the bourbon was.

'Why don't you have a beer instead.'

'I don't want a beer.'

'You'll get drunk.'

'Maybe I will.'

I looked down at my glass, away from her face: in summer she had freckles that were pretty, and I remembered how I used to touch her in daylight, a quick kiss or hug as I went through the kitchen, a hand at her waist or shoulder as we walked in town; that was not long ago, and still she reached for me passing in the house, or touched me as she walked by the couch where I read, but I never did; in bed at night, yes, but not in daylight anymore.

'Why don't we talk in the morning. We'll just fight now, you've got that look of yours.'

'Never mind that look of mine.'

The pots from dinner were still on the stove, the plates were dirty in the sink, and when I sat at the table I brushed crumbs and bits of food from the place in front of me; the table was sticky where I rested my hands, and I went to the sink and got a sponge and wiped the part I had cleaned. I left the sponge on the table and sat down and felt her fury at my cleaning before I looked up and saw it in her eyes. She stood at the stove, an unlit cigarette in her hand.

'You and Edith, all these trips you make, all these Goddamn errands, all summer if someone runs out of booze or cigarettes or wants Goddamn egg rolls, off you go, you and Edith, and it's not right to leave me with Hank, to put me in that position—'

'Now wait a minute.'

'—something's going on, either it's going on or you want it to—'

'Just a minute, wait just a minute—two questions: why is it wrong for Edith and me to go get some beer and Goddamn ale, and what's this position you're in when you're alone with Hank, and what is it you're *really* worrying about? Do you get horny every time you're alone with Hank and you want Daddy to save you from yourself?'

'*No*, I don't get horny when I'm alone with Hank; I only get horny for my Goddamn husband but he likes to be with *Edith*.'

'We've been married ten years. We're not on our honeymoon, for Christ's sake.'

Her eyes changed, softened, and her voice did too: 'Why aren't we? Don't you love me?'

'Oh hell. Of course I do.'

'Well what are you saying, that you love me but we've been married so long that you need Edith too, or maybe you're already having her? Is that it, because if it is maybe we should talk about how long this marriage is going to last. Because you can move out anytime you want to, I can get a job—'

'Terry.'

'—and the kids will be all right, there's no reason for you to suffer if marriage is such a disappointment. Maybe I've done something—'

'Terry.'

'What.'

'Calm down. Here.' I reached across the table with my lighter and she leaned over to light her cigarette, cupping her hands around mine, and under her flesh like a pulse I could feel her need and I wanted at once to shove her against the stove, and to stroke her cheek and tousle her hair.

'Terry, you said those things. Not me. I have never wanted to leave you. I am not suffering. I'm not tired of you, and I don't need

Edith or anyone else. I like being with her. Like with any other friend—man or woman—sometimes I like being alone with her. So once in a while we run an errand. I see nothing threatening in that, nothing bad. I don't think married people have to cling to each other, and I think if you look around you'll see that most of them don't. You're the only wife I know who gets pissed at her husband because he doesn't touch her at parties—'

'The other husbands *touch* their wives! They put their *arms* around them!'

'Hank doesn't.'

'That's why she's so lonely, that's why she likes to tag along like your little lamb, because Hank doesn't love her—'

'Who ever said that?'

'Hank did.' Her eyes lowered. 'Tonight while you two were gone.'

'He said that?'

'Yes.'

'Why?'

'I don't know, he just said it.'

'What were you doing?'

'Well we were talking, how else do you tell people things.'

'When people talk like that they're usually doing other things.'

'Oh sure, we were screwing on the front porch, what do you care?'

'I don't, as long as I know the truth.'

'The *truth*. You wouldn't know the truth if it knocked on the door. You won't even admit the truth about yourself, that you don't really love me—'

'Stop that, Terry. Do not say that shit. You know why? Because it's not true, it's never been true, but when you say it like that, it is. For a minute. For long enough to start a *really* crazy fight. Do you understand that?'

She was nodding, her cheeks looking numb, her eyes frightened and forlorn; then I felt my own eyes giving her pity, washing her cheeks and lips with it, and when I did that her face tightened, her eyes raged again, and too quick for me to duck she threw her drink in my face, ice cubes flying past my head and smacking the wall and sliding across the floor. I rose fast but only halfway, poised with my hands gripping the edge of the table; then I looked away from her and sat down and took out my handkerchief and slowly wiped my face and beard, looking out the back door at the night where I wanted to be, then I brushed at the spots on the burgundy sweat shirt she had brought home for me one day, happily taking it from the bag and holding it up for me to see. Then I stood up and walked quickly out the back door, and she threw her glass at me but too late, the door was already swinging to and the glass bounced off the screen and hit the floor. Somehow it didn't break.

I crossed the lawn, onto the sidewalk that sloped down with the street; a half block from the house I was suddenly afraid she was coming, I felt her behind me, and I turned, but the sidewalk was empty and lovely in the shadows of maples and elms. I went on. If there was a way to call Edith and she could come get me. But of course no. I could go back and get my car, the keys were in my pocket, I could start it and be gone before Terry came running out with a Goddamn knife, if I drove to Edith's and parked in front of the house and looked up at the window where she slept beside Hank she would know, if I waited long enough watching her window she would know in her sleep and she would wake and look out the window at me under the moon; she would tiptoe downstairs and hold me on the damp lawn. I came to a corner and went up another street. 'Edith,' I whispered into the shadows of my diagonal walk, 'oh Edith sweet baby, I love you, I love you forever.' I thought about forever and if we live afterward, then I saw myself laid out in a coffin, the beard and hair lovely white. I stopped and leaned against a car, dew on its fender cool through my slacks. Natasha and Sean and I looked at Terry in her coffin. I stood between them holding their small hands. Terry's smooth cheeks were pale against her red hair.

When she told me she was pregnant she wasn't afraid. She was twenty years old. It was a cold bright Thursday in January, the sky had been blue for a week and the snow in Boston was dirty and old. We went to a bookstore on Boylston Street and bought paperbacks for each other, then we had steamers and draft beer in a dim place with paintings of whale fishing and storms at sea and fishing boats in harbor on the walls. For some reason the waiters wore leather tunics. In those days Terry always seemed happy. I can close my eyes any time and remember how I loved her and see and feel her as she took my hand on the table and said: 'After today I'll be careful about eating, and if I promise not to get fat and if I get a job, can I keep our baby?'

Now I started walking home. We were, after all this, the same Jack and Terry, and I would go to her now and touch her and hold her; I walked faster, nodding my head yes yes yes. Then going into the dark living room I felt her in the house like the large and sharpened edge of a knife. She was asleep. I crept into the bedroom and lay beside her, at the edge of the bed so we didn't touch.

Natasha and Sean woke Terry early for breakfast but I stayed in bed, held onto sleep through the breakfast voices then their voices outside, while the sun got higher and the room hotter until it was too hot and I got up. I went straight to the shower without seeing anyone. While I was drying myself she tapped on the door.

'Do you want lunch or breakfast?'

Her voice had the practiced sweetness she assumed when she was afraid: strangers got it, and I got it after some fights or when she made mistakes with money. For an instant I was tender and warm and I wanted to help her with a cheerful line (Oh, I'll have you for breakfast, love; just stick a banana in it and hop in bed); but then sure as time is a trick I was sitting in the kitchen last night, and the bourbon and ice were flying at me.

'I don't know,' I said. Through the door I could feel the tone of my voice piercing her. 'What do you have?'

'Just cereal if you want breakfast. But if you want lunch I could get some lobsters, just for you and me; the kids don't like them anyway.'

'No, I have to hurry. I'm taking the car in.'

*Linhart*, I said to my face in the mirror. *You are a petulant son of a bitch. Why don't you drag her in here and whip her ass then eat lobster with her.* She was still waiting outside the door; I pretended not to know, and went about drying myself.

'I could go to the fish market and be back and have them done in thirty minutes. Forty to be safe.'

'I have to get the car there at twelve.'

'You *have* to?'

'If I want the work done, yes.'

'What's the work?'

'Oil and grease.'

'That doesn't take long.'

'They're busy, Terry. They want it at twelve or not at all. They don't care how badly you want a lobster. But if you want one, get it now before I leave.'

'I don't want one by myself.'

'What, you mean it won't taste good?'

'Oh, you know what I *mean*,' in that mock-whine you hear from girls everywhere when they're being lovingly teased. I started brushing my teeth.

'Cheerios or Grape Nuts?'

'Grape Nuts.'

She went away. When I came dressed to the kitchen the table was set neatly for one: a red straw place mat, a deep bowl which had the faint sparkle of fresh washing, a spoon on a napkin, a glass of orange juice. She was upstairs with the vacuum cleaner. Over in the sink were the children's breakfast dishes, unwashed; beneath them were last night's dishes.

Terry is the toy of poltergeists: washer, dryer, stove, refrigerator, dishes, clothes, and woolly house dust. The stove wants cleaning and as she lifts off burners the washing machine stops in the wash room; she leaves the stove and takes another load of dirty clothes to the wash room; it is a white load, bagged in a sheet, lying on the kitchen floor since before breakfast. She unloads the washing machine and, hugging the wet clothes to her breasts, she opens the dryer; but she has forgotten, it's full of clothes she dried last night. She lays the wet ones on top of the dryer and takes out the dry ones; these she carries to the living room and drops in a loose pile on the couch; a pair of Sean's Levi's falls to the floor and as she stoops to pick it up she sees a bread crust and an orange peel lying in the dust under the couch. She cannot reach them without lying on the floor, so she tells herself, with the beginnings of panic, that she must do the living room this morning: sweep, dust, vacuum. But there are clothes waiting to be folded, and a new load going into the dryer, another into the washer. Going through the kitchen she sees the stove she has forgotten, its crusted burners lying on greasy white porcelain. In the wash room she puts the wet clothes into the dryer, shuts the door, and starts it, a good smooth sound of machine, the clothes turning in the dark. In fifty minutes they will be dry. It is all so efficient, and standing there listening to the machine, she feels that efficiency, and everything seems in order now, she is in control, she can rest. This lasts only a moment. She loads the washer, turns it on, goes back to the kitchen, averts her eyes from the stove and makes for the coffee pot; she will first have a cup of coffee, gather herself up, plan her morning. With despair she sees it is not a morning but an entire day, past cocktail hour and dinner, into the night: when the dinner dishes are done she will have more clothes to fold and some to iron. This happens often and forces her to watch television while she works. She is ashamed of watching Johnny Carson.

The breakfast dishes are in the sink, last night's pots are on the counter: hardened mashed potatoes, congealed grease. She hunts for the coffee cup she's been using all morning, finds it on the lavatory in the bathroom, and empties the cold coffee over the dishes in the sink. She lights a cigarette and thinks of some place she can sit, some place that will let her drink a cup of coffee. There is none, there's not a clean room downstairs; upstairs the TV room is clean enough, because no one lives there. But to climb the stairs for a sanctuary is too depressing, so she goes to the living room and sits on the couch with the clean clothes, ignores the bread crust and orange peel whispering to her from the floor. Trying to plan her work for the day overwhelms her; it is too much. So she does what is at hand; she begins folding clothes, drinking coffee, smoking. After a while she hears the washer stop. Then the dryer. She goes to the wash room, brings back the dry clothes, goes back and puts the wet load in the dryer. When I come in for lunch, the living room is filled with clothes: they are in heaps on chairs, folded and stacked on the couch and floor; I look at them and then at Terry on the couch; beyond her legs are the bread crust and orange peel; with a harried face she is drinking coffee, and the ash tray is full. 'Is it noon already?' she says. Her eyes are quick with panic. 'Oh Goddamnit, I didn't know it was that late.' I walk past her into the kitchen: the burners, the dishes. 'Jesus Christ,' I say. We fight, but only briefly, because it is daylight, we aren't drinking, the children will be in from playing soon, hungry and dirty. Like our marriage, I think, hungry and dirty.

While I ate the Grape Nuts, Natasha and Sean came in, brown arms and legs and blond hair crowding through the door at once, the screen slamming behind them. Natasha is nine; she is the love child who bound us. Sean is seven. Looking at them I felt love for the first time that day.

'You slept late,' Sean said.

'That's because you were up late, you guys were fighting,' Natasha said. 'I heard you.'

'What did you hear?'

'I don't know—' She was hiding whatever it was, down in her heart angry words breaking into her sleep. 'Yelling and swear words and then you left.'

'You left?' Sean said. He was simply interested, not worried. He lives his own life. He eats and sleeps with us, comes to us when he needs something, but he lives outside with boys and bicycles.

'All grown-ups fight from time to time. If they're married.'

'I know,' Sean said. 'Where's Mom?'

I pointed to the ceiling, to the sound of the vacuum cleaner.

'We want to eat,' he said.

'Let her work. I'll fix it.'

'You're eating,' Natasha said.

'I'll hurry.'

'Is that your lunch?' Sean said. 'Grape Nuts?'

'It's my supper.'

I asked what they had done all morning. It was hard to follow and I didn't try; I just watched their loud faces. They interrupted each other: Natasha likes to draw a story out, lead up to it with history ('Well see, first we thought we'd go to Carol's but then they weren't home and I remembered she said they were going—'). Sean likes to tell a story as quickly as he can, sometimes quicker. While they talked, I made sandwiches. It was close to noon but I lingered; Natasha was stirring Kool-Aid in a pitcher. In twelve minutes Edith would be waiting at the Shell station, but I stood watching them eat, and I hoped something would change her day and she wouldn't be there. But she would. An advantage of an affair with a friend's wife was the matter of phone calls: there was nothing suspicious about them. If Edith called and talked to Terry I'd know she couldn't see me this afternoon. I asked the children if they wanted dessert.

'Do we have any?' Natasha said.

'We never have dessert,' Sean said.

I looked in the freezer compartment for ice cream, then in the cupboard for cookies, sweets to sweeten my goodbye, and there were none. Sean was right: we never had desserts because I didn't like them and Terry liked them too much; she controlled her sweet tooth by having nothing sweet in the house.

'I'm sorry,' I said. I knew I was being foolish but I couldn't stop. 'I'm a stupid daddy. I'll bring some dessert home with me.'

'Where you going?' Natasha said.

'To get the car worked on,' my voice jumping to tenor with the lie.

'Can I go?' Sean said. He had a moustache of grape Kool-Aid.

'Me too,' Natasha said.

'No, it takes a long time, then I'm going to run with Hank.'

'We don't mind,' Natasha said. 'We'll watch you.'

There is not one God, I thought. There are several, and they all like jests.

'No you won't,' I growled, and went at her with fingers curled like talons, then tickled her ribs; her sandwich dropped to her plate, she became a fleshed laugh. 'Because after we run we're going to a bar and drink beer. It's what mean old men do.'

They were laughing. Now I could leave. Then Terry came downstairs, one of my old shirts hanging out, covering her shorts.

'I want us to start having desserts.'

'What?'

'Yay!' Sean said. 'Desserts.'

'We never have desserts,' Natasha said.

Terry stood looking at us, smiling, confused, ready to joke or defend.

'We're depriving the kids of a basic childhood experience.'

'What's that?'

'Mother's desserts.'

'Jesus.'

I wished she were the one going off to wickedness; I would stay home and make cookies from a recipe book.

'Well, I'm off.'

I kissed their Kool-Aid mouths, touched lips with Terry, and went out. She followed me to the screen door.

'Did you get enough to eat?'

'Sure. Not as good as lobster,' talking over my shoulder, going down the steps, 'but cheaper anyway.'

She didn't answer. In the car I thought adultery is one thing, but being a male bitch waging peripheral war is another, this poison of throwing gift-lobsters at your wife's vulnerable eyes, drying up her sweetness and hope by alluding to the drought of the budget. Which was also a further, crueler allusion to her awful belief in a secular gospel of good news: we were Americans, nice, healthy, intelligent people with nice, healthy, intelligent friends, and we deserved to eat lobsters the day after a fight, just as we deserved to see plays in Boston and every good movie that came to town, and when I told her there was no money she was not bitter, but surprised. She was also surprised when the bank told her we were overdrawn and she found that she had forgotten to record a check, or when someone wrote her about a bill that lay unopened in her desk.

When I got to the Shell station Edith was parked across the street. I told the man to change the oil and grease it.

'I'll go run some errands with the wife,' I said, thumbing over my shoulder at Edith. 'Then I'll come pick it up.'

He looked across the street at Edith.

'Keys in the car?'

I slapped my pockets.

'Yes.'

I wondered what twelve months of daylight would do to adulterers. In daylight it seemed everyone knew: the fat man in the greasy T-shirt nodding at me as I told him twenty weight and a new filter and grease, the women who drove by and glanced at me as I waited to cross the street, and the little suntanned boy, squinting up at me, pulling a wagon with his tricycle on the sidewalk beside her car. I got in and said: 'He knows too.'

'Who?'

'That kid. He knows where we're going.'

She drove through the city. It is built on the Merrimack, which is foul, and the city itself is small, ugly, and has the look of death, as a man with cancer does. The industry was shoes, but the factories have been closing. On the main street the glass-fronted stores, no matter their size, all have the dismal look of pawn shops or Army surplus stores. But urban renewal has started: on the riverbank they have destroyed some old gray wooden buildings; in their place a shopping center will be built, and then as we stop at the red light and look toward the river we shall see instead the new brick buildings with wide glass windows, and specials posted on the glass of the supermarket, and the asphalt parking lot with cars, shopping carts, and unhappy women. Our city is no place for someone who is drawn to suicide.

When Edith got to the divided highway I twisted around and opened the ice chest on the floor in the back. Already we had a ritual like husband and wife: it was for me to begin the drive by opening two beers, lighting two cigarettes. Today she had added something: two Löwenbräus, two Asahis, and two San Miguels angled up at me in the ice.

'She brings such presents,' I said, and kissed her cheek.

'Cold presents from a cold woman.'

An opener was in the glove compartment, under one of her scarves that was red and soft like pants in my hand. The Asahis opened with a pop. Edith glanced in the rear-view mirror, swallowed, then took the lighted cigarette from my fingers.

'I think I'll change to Luckies,' she said, smiling.

'Sure, do that. Why not just let him babysit for us.'

We avoided naming them: we said he, she, him, her.

'He'd be glad to.'

'Well *she* wouldn't, sweetheart.'

I told her about the fight; the sun was warm on my face and arm at the window, the air smelled of trees and grass, we were driving in rolling wooded country under a blue sky, and I was too happy to care about last night. I told it quickly.

'I think he wants to make love with her,' she said.

'Why?'

'Why? Because she's pretty and he likes her and he hasn't had any strange since Jeanne. Why do you think?'

'I mean why do you think he wants to?'

'The way he looks at her. And the way he looked when we came back from getting beer last night.'

'Guilty?'

'Sheepish. Does that bother you?'

'Not me.'

'Good. We can babysit for each other,' smiling, her eyes bright.

'She blooms, she blooms,' I said. 'And in May you were so hurt.'

'In May I was alone.'

I am surrounded by painful marriages that no one understands. But Hank understands his, and I think for him it has never been painful; the pain was Edith's, and she came to me with it in May, at a party. When she asked me to go outside I knew she had finally caught Hank, and because she is small and her voice soft I saw her as vulnerable, and I felt she lacked the tough spirit to deal with adultery. First I found Terry in the kitchen so she wouldn't miss me, then start looking about to see which woman was missing too. I told her where I was going and she understood too that Edith had finally caught on; she looked at me with that veiled excitement we feel in the face of other people's disasters. In the backyard, away from lighted windows, Edith and I sat side by side on a picnic table.

'You probably already know this, I guess Terry does too and everybody else: about Hank and that phony French bitch that somebody brought to our Christmas party—'

'Jeanne.'

'And they crashed that party.' She touched my shirt pocket for a cigarette. 'I forgot my purse inside. Bumming cigarettes, that's how I first got suspicious: he'd come home with Parliaments, I guess they lay around in bed so long he smoked all his, and now I don't know what to do, I can't stand to see him naked, I keep thinking of—shit: I ought to divorce him, I could do that but I don't really want to, but why shouldn't I? When he doesn't love me.'

She stopped. My arm was around her; I patted her shoulder, then squeezed her against my side. There was a time in my life when I believed I could help people by talking to them, and because of that I became a confidant for several people, most of them young girls who were my students. People told me about marriages, jobs, parents, and boyfriends, and I listened and talked a lot and never helped anyone at all. So now if someone comes to me I offer what I know I can give: the friendship of a listening face. That night I held Edith and listened and said very little. After a while she jumped down from the table and walked toward the shadows of the house. She was wearing a white dress. I was about to call to her when she stopped and stood smoking with her back turned. Then she came back to the table.

'You're good to me.'

'I haven't helped you any.'

She stood looking up at me. I got down from the table and held her, pressing her face to my chest and stroking her hair, then we kissed and she squeezed me tightly, her hands moved on my back, and her tongue darted in. We stood a long time kissing in the shadows.

'Come see me.'

'Yes.'

'Monday afternoon.'

'Are you sure?'

'Yes. Yes, I want you to. Come at one.'

Next day was Sunday, and all day while the sun was up I didn't believe Edith, and I didn't believe what I had felt holding her, but after dinner in the night I went for a walk and I believed all of it again, and that night in bed I lay awake for a long time, like a child before a birthday. After my twelve o'clock class Monday I drove to Edith's. When she opened the door I knew from her face that she had been waiting.

Now the place we were going to, the place we always went to after that first afternoon in her house, was a woods off a highway in

New Hampshire: down a wide, curving dirt road, dry and dusty, then she parked in the shade and I opened two San Miguels, got the blanket from the back seat, and we climbed a gentle slope, brown pine needles slippery underfoot. I timidly held her hand. I prefer adultery to be a collision: suddenly and without thinking alone with a woman, an urgent embrace, buckles, zippers, buttons. Walking up through the trees gave me time to watch Terry taking the lunch dishes from the table, stacking them on the counter by the sink, and with a distracted, troubled face starting to wash the dishes from three meals. At the knoll's top I lay the blanket under pines and a tall hemlock and heard behind me the buttons of her shorts; I turned and, kneeling, pulled the shorts down her warm brown legs. She took her shirt off and reached back for the clasp of her brassiere; then she lay on the blanket and watched me until I was naked, lying beside her with the sun shining over the crown of a gray birch onto my face.

'What'll we do in winter,' she said.

'In the car, like kids.'

'If we have a winter.'

I kissed her eyes and said: 'When fall comes we'll make love in the car and when winter comes we'll fog the windows and make love wearing sweaters and in spring we'll be back here on this blanket on this hill.'

'Promise me.'

'I promise.'

Then I was alone thinking of a year of deceiving Terry and Hank and the others whom you don't and can't watch out for because they're faceless and nameless, but they're always watching you. I could feel Edith knowing what I was thinking.

'I promise.'

'I know you do. No, lie down, love. I want to be on top. There. Hello, love.'

I reached up for her breasts and watched her face, eyes tightly shut, lips parted, and the long black hair falling across her right cheek, strands of it in her mouth, and she tossed her head, neck arching, and the hair fell back over her shoulder. Then I shut my eyes, and my hands dropped from her breasts and kneaded the earth. For a while we were still, then I opened my eyes to the sun and her face.

'I don't want to move yet,' she said. 'I want to sit here and drip on you.' Already I could feel it. 'Can you get the beer?'

I reached behind me and gave her a bottle and watched her throat as she swallowed. I raised my head to drink from mine.

'You're much faster now,' she said.

On that afternoon in May we went to the guest room, downstairs at the rear of the house, and after an hour I gave up. We had our shirts on and I was wearing socks.

'Are you sure you can't?' she said.

'I keep listening for Sharon to come down or Hank to walk in.'

'You're sure that's all it is?'

'That's plenty enough.'

We went outside and sat on lawn chairs in the sun. After a while Sharon woke up and came out and played at Edith's feet. I said I would see her tomorrow, at the shopping center north of town, just over the New Hampshire line; then I went home happy and Terry said: 'You must have had a good day in class.' I avoided her eyes until she turned back to the stove, then I looked at her long red hair and like singing I thought: *I will love them both*. I said I would go take a shower, and I went to our bedroom: the bed was unmade and a pair of her Levi's and a shirt were on the floor, and I had to step over the vacuum cleaner to get into the bathroom, where two wet towels lay on the floor but no clean ones in the closet, and I yelled at her: 'Could I have a Goddamn towel!' That night I read in the living room until she was asleep, and next afternoon Edith and I found this road and woods and hill, and that time it wasn't Sharon and Hank I saw with my closed eyes but Terry at home, and Edith kept working with me until finally I came in spite of thinking, it was like some distant part of me coming, like the semen itself had decided it was tired of waiting, and it spurted out just to give us all a rest. For two or three weeks I was like that, then all at once one day I wasn't, as though even guilt and fear could not survive the familiarity of passion.

Now Edith lay beside me and we drank beer going tepid and smoked lying naked in the sun.

'Don't let it get sunburned,' she said. 'You'll get caught.'

'Poor limp thing.'

'I'll keep the sun off.'

'No. I can't.'

'Yes you can.'

'I'm an old man.'

'You're my young lover. Your stomach's growling; have you eaten lunch?'

'Grape Nuts. I slept late.'

'You should live with me. I'd feed you better than that.'

'It's what I wanted. She feeds me what I want.'

'You taste like me.'

A squirrel darted up the hemlock. After a while I said, 'Wait.' I stroked her arm, then tugged it, and she moved up beside me. I was on her, in her, taking a long time, the sun on my back, sweating against her belly, listening to the monologue of moans.

'Did you?' I said.

'Yes. I want you to.'

Her tongue-moistened fingers went up to my nipples. She had taught me I had those.

'Oh love,' she said.

'Again?'

'I think so. Yes. God, yes.'

She took me with her and I collapsed on her damp belly and breasts and listened to the pounding of her heart.

'It felt like spurting blood,' I said.

'Did it hurt?'

'I couldn't tell.'

'My young lover.'

'I'm starving.'

'You have to run first.'

'Maybe I'll cop out.'

'No, you have to be strong, taking care of two women. Would you like to live with me?'

'Yes.'

'I'd like to live with you. We should all rent one big house.'

'And who'd mop up the blood?'

'There wouldn't be any blood.'

'She'd cut my throat.'

I got up and dressed and went down to the car for the Löwen-braüs, then back up the slope treasuring my hard climbing calf muscles; now I wanted to run. She was dressed, lying on her back, her hands at her sides, eyes closed, face to the sun.

'I wonder how we'll get caught,' she said.

'He'll smell you when I undress.'

'I mean Terry. If he caught us I wouldn't care, I wouldn't stop unless you wanted to. You probably would. You'd be embarrassed.'

'Maybe not.'

'You would. You keep trying to fit me into your life, but it's hard for you, and if you got caught you'd throw me out. But you're part of my life: you're what allows me to live with Hank.'

'Am I a what? I don't want to be a what.' I held up the Löwenbraü. 'This is one. It's what's going to make me belch for the first mile.'

'You're my lovely what.'

'Good old Jack, just part of the family.'

'Sure. You make me a good wife. If I didn't love you I'd have to love someone else. We married too young—'

'We all did.'

Once at a party Terry was in the kitchen with Edith and two other wives. They came out grinning at the husbands: their own, the others. They had all admitted to shotgun weddings. That was four years ago and now one couple is divorced, another has made a separate peace, fishing and hunting for him and pottery and college for her; and there are the Allisons and the Linharts. A deck-stacking example, but the only one I know.

'He needs us, Sharon and me, but he can't really love anyone, only his work, and the rest is surface.'

'I don't believe that.'

'I don't mean his friendship with you. Of course it's deep, he doesn't live with you, and best of all you're a man, you don't have those needs he can't be bothered with. He'd give you a kidney if you needed one.'

'He'd give it to you too.'

'Of course he would. But he wouldn't go to a marriage counselor.'

'You funny girl. After a long carnivorous fuck you talk about a marriage counselor. Who *are* you, sweetheart?'

'My name is Edith Allison and I'm the leader of the band. I wanted to go to a marriage counselor so he'd talk. Because he wouldn't talk just to me. He wanted everything simple: he'd been screwing Jeanne, now he'd stopped, and that was that.'

'What more did you want?'

'You know what I wanted. Remember me back in May? I still believed in things. I wanted to know where we were, what Jeanne meant. Now that I have you I know what she meant: that he doesn't love me. You love the person you're having the affair with. But it doesn't matter now, I can live with him like that, on the surface. He'll be busting out again soon. He's been hibernating with that novel since he broke off with Jeanne. Before long he'll look around and blink and screw the first thing that walks into his office.'

'Jesus. I hope somebody goes in before I do.'

'He'd probably do that too.'

'Now, now: bitchy bitchy.'

'Well, he screws his wife once in a while, so why not another man.'

'He screws you? Frigid like you are?'

'I try hard.'

'I hear you can go to St. Louis and screw for that man and woman who wrote the book. The one about coming.'

'Really?'

'Sure. They watch you and straighten out your hang-ups.'

'Let's you and I go. I'd like them to watch us. We'd make them hot.'

'You might get rid of your guilt. Do you good.'

'Why spoil my fun? Maybe you'd learn to come more.'

'What would a wee dirty lass like you have told a marriage counselor?'

'I was trying to keep from being a wee dirty lass. I'm glad now I didn't. What are you doing?'

'Touching you.'

'Isn't it getting late?'

'I don't know.'

'Can you again?'

'I don't know.'

We left our shirts on, a wrong move: they reminded us that time was running out. My back hurt but I kept trying; Edith didn't make it either, and finally she said: 'Let's stop.' Our shirts were wet. We gathered up the bottles, the cigarettes, the blanket. In the car she made up her face.

'What'll you do with the bottles?' I said.

'I think I'll burn candles in them at dinner. And if he notices—which he wouldn't—I'll tell him they're souvenirs from this afternoon. Along with my sore pussy.'

'He'll see them in the garbage. You know, when he empties it or something.'

She started the car and grinned at me, almost laughing.

'And then what, Charlie Chan?'

'He'll wonder why in the hell you drank six bottles of imported beer this afternoon.'

'Well, he doesn't deserve honesty, but a few clues might be nice.'

'Sometimes I think—'

It was possible she wanted him to catch her; you have to keep that in mind when you're making love with a man's wife. But I didn't want to talk about it.

'Sometimes you think what?'

'Sometimes I think I love you even more than I think I do. Which is a lot.'

'Which is a lot. Impotent as you are, you try hard.'

She turned the car around and drove slowly and bouncing out of the woods. At the highway she stopped and put on sunglasses.

'Light me a Lucky,' she said. 'My last one till—?'

I thought of the acting and the lies and, right then, if she had said we must stop seeing each other, I would have been relieved.

'I don't know, I'll call you.'

As she drove onto the highway both of us pretended we weren't eyeing the road for friends' cars. My damp shirt and chest cooled in the air blowing through the window.

'My pecker aches.'

'I'm going to keep the sitter another hour and take a nap.'

'Let me give you some money for her.'

'Another time. Mother sent me some.'

'The empties are in the chest.'

'I'll go by the dump.'

Summer school was in session, and walking downtown you'd see college girls licking ice cream cones. Once I was teaching *Goodbye, Columbus* and a blonde girl with brown eyes like a deer stopped me at the door before class and said: 'Mr. Linhart, what is oral love?' She was licking a lollipop. I looked away from her tongue on the lollipop and said fellatio; when she asked what that was I mumbled in the heat of my face that she ought to ask a girl. It took me a couple of hours to know she was having fun with me. After that I tried to talk to her but she had only wanted that fun; she had a boyfriend who waited every day in the hall outside our classroom, and seeing them holding hands and walking down the hall I felt old and foolish. That was three years ago, when I was twenty-seven.

On summer afternoons there were no classes, and the buildings were empty. Most days when I climbed the three flights of stairs in the old, cool building Hank would be working with his back to the open door; he'd hear me coming and he'd turn smiling, stacking and paper-clipping the manuscript. 'Hi,' he'd say, his voice affectionate like he was talking to a woman or a child. There are several men I love and who love me, all of us married, passive misogamists, and if we did not have each other to talk to we would probably in our various ways go mad. But our love embarrasses us; we show our affection in reverse: *Where you been, you sonofabitch? Look at that bastard, he wouldn't buy a round for Jesus Christ*—But Hank only did that if it made you feel better.

'Hi,' he said.

'You can't write, you fucker, so let's go run.'

'One Goddamn page.'

'In four hours?'

'Three hours and forty-six minutes. Let's go.'

I started walking downstairs before he asked what I had done with my day. Walking over to the gym he was quiet. By the flag-pole he lit a cigarette, then flung it to the sidewalk, crumpled his pack and threw it hard, like an outfielder; it arched softly, red and white in the sun.

'You just quit.'

'Goddamn right.'

'Which time?'

'For the last time.'

'You won't make it.'

'You watch. They're pissing me off. They're trying to kill me.'

'They have no souls.'

'Exactly.'

'So they're not trying to kill you.'

'Not the cigarettes. I mean the fuckers that make 'em.'

There were tennis players in the locker room. We had lockers next to each other and I glanced at him as he pulled up his jockstrap then gym shorts.

'Jesus, don't you ever get fat?' I said.

'I'm fat now.'

He pinched some tight flesh at the back of his waist.

'Bullshit,' I said.

I rarely believed that Edith preferred my flabbier waist and smaller cock. But sometimes I believed it and, when I did, I felt wonderful.

'You smell like beer, man.'

'I had a couple.'

'I'll carry you in.'

'Watch me go, baby.'

On the clipped grass behind the gym we did push-ups and sit-ups and side-straddle hops, then started jogging on a blacktop road that would take us into the country.

'Five?' I said.

'I oughta do ten. Run off my Goddamn frustration.'

'A page a day's not bad.'

'Shit.'

It was a hot, still day. We ran easily, stride for stride, past the houses where children waved and called to us and women looked up from their lawns or porches. I belched a couple of times and he grinned and punched my arm. Then the houses weren't close together anymore, the country was rolling and we climbed with it, pounding up the blacktop, not talking as we panted up hills, but going down or level we talked: 'Goddamn, there's that lovely orchard.' 'Hold your breath, mothuh, here comes the hog stench.' 'Jesus, look at that cock pheasant.' Then he was all right, he had forgotten his work, he was talking about shooting pheasants in Iowa, walking through frozen cornfields, the stalks lying brown in the sun. We ran to the top of a wooded hill two and a half miles from the gym and started back, still stride for stride: it would be that last two hundred yards when he'd kick. We ran downhill through sudden cool shade between thick woods; in fall the maple leaves turned orange and yellow and scarlet, and it was like peeping at God. Then on our left the woods stopped, and the hog smell lay on the air we breathed as we ran past the cleared low hills and the barn, chickens walking and pecking in front of it, then past the hog pen and the gray shingled house. A white dog came out from under the porch, barking; he had missed us on the way up, and now he chased us until he was almost at our legs, then we looked back at him and yelled 'Hey white dog!' and he trotted away, looking back at us over his shoulder, sometimes stopping to turn and bark. Running has taught me that most dogs are cowards. But there used to be a Doberman pinscher living on this road: he loped after us so quietly that we never knew he was there until we heard his paws on the road and we'd yell and turn on him and crouch to fight, watching him decide whether he wanted to chew on us. He always looked very detached; that's what scared us. Then he'd trot back down the road, dignity intact; we were glad when last year he moved away. All the other dogs were like the white one at the farmhouse. Past the farm there were trees again, pines motionless in the still air, and then to the right, up a long green hill, the apple orchard.

'You're a little screwed up this summer,' Hank said.

'Do I look it?'

'Yep.'

'Should've taught summer school.'

'Maybe not.'

'Thought I wouldn't this year. Needed a break, I thought. Now I need the money.'

'Need the work more.'

'Bothers me. You'd think a man would do something. All that time. Read. Even think. Noble fucking pursuits. I run errands. Makes me wonder what'd happen if I didn't have to make a living.'

'You'll never find out.'

'Good. Probably mean suicide. Man ought to be able to live with himself. Idly. Without going mad. Women do it.'

'Not so well.'

'Work is strange.'

'All there is.'

'This. This is good.'

'Best of all.'

We stopped talking and right away my head was clear and serene, I was lungs and legs and arms, sun on my shoulders, sweat seeping through the red handkerchief around my forehead, dripping to my eyes, burning, and I flicked it away with a finger. At the houses near the college he moved ahead of me, a pace or two. I caught him and ran beside him for a while, then he kicked and was gone; I stretched my legs, arms swinging, breath in gasps, and watched his back ten then twenty yards away as he sprinted past the gym and slowed and walked, head going up and down for air, hands on his hips. I walked beside him. He didn't smile at beating me, but I felt a smile as though in his rushing breath.

'Competitive bastard,' I said.

Then he smiled, and I believed then he knew I was making love with Edith and he was telling me he knew, saying, *You see Edith can't touch me and you can't either, what matters here is what matters to me and what matters to me is I will write and I will outrun you and I will outlive all of you too, and that's where I am.*

He didn't smoke, either. After the shower, a long time of hot water on the shoulders and legs and back muscles, then warm then cool, we drank Heineken draft in tall frosted mugs. We were alone in the bar, then a thin bald man came in carrying wrapped fish. Adjacent to the lounge was the dining room, where people ate fish from the sea and looked out at the dirty Merrimack; if you walked out of the lounge, across the hall, you went into the fish market. Before starting to drink, Hank and I had gone in and stood in the smell of fish, looking at the lobsters in a tank. I thought of Terry, but not with guilt; I had loved and run and sweated that out of me. I stood shifting my weight from one leg to another so I could feel the muscles, and I breathed my own clean smell with the salt water and fish, and resolved not to smoke for an hour, to keep the sharp sense of smell I always had after running restored innocence to my lungs; and I loved and wanted to embrace Edith and Hank and Terry, who in their separate ways made my life good. I felt at the border of some discovery, some way I could juggle my beloveds and save us all. But I didn't know what it was.

The man with the fish sat to our left, put his fish on the bar, and ordered a Schlitz. Betty was tending bar; she was a middle-aged blonde who had lived all her life in this town. She sat on a high stool near the taps and talked to the fish man. He looked at the Heineken sign over the mirror and asked if that was imported beer; she said yes it was. He said he'd never heard of it and she told him oh yes, it was quite popular, it sold ten to one here.

'Schlitz,' Hank said, so they couldn't hear. 'Some people like it better inside the horse.'

'Did you see her before she left?'

'Yeah, I saw her.' He gave me the foxy smile I got after he beat me running.

'To tell her goodbye?'

'Remember when I went to New York to see my agent?'

'Ah. I didn't know you could lie so well.'

He held out two dollars to the woman.

'We'll have a round, and give my friend on the end a Heineken.'

The fish man looked over at us.

'Well, thank you. Thank you very much.'

'Beats that horse piss Schlitz is bottling.'

Betty grinned. The fish man was embarrassed and he started to say something, maybe about Schlitz, then he just watched her filling the mug; when he tasted it, he said: 'Well, by golly, it does have something to it, doesn't it?'

He and Betty talked about beer.

'I've never spent the night with anyone but Terry.'

'Same old thing. Sleep, dream, wake up in the morning; piss; brush your teeth.'

'Have a cigarette, lover.'

'Hell no. Every time I want one I'm going to hold my breath for sixty seconds and think of the Marlboro man and the Winston ass-holes and all the rest of them, and that'll do it.'

'All right, I won't till you do. But you won't be able to stand Edith. I quit once for three days and Terry smelled like an ash tray.'

'Not *all* over. It was a good scene, though, in Boston. Hotel, took her to the airport in the morning, sad loving Bloody Marys. Then up in the air. Gone. Me watching the plane. Thinking of her looking down. Gone. Back to France. Maybe I'll go see her someday.'

'You love her, huh?'

'I was fucking her, wasn't I?'

'I guess it was tough breaking it off, her right down in Boston.'

'Jack.' Grinning. 'What made you think I broke it off? Why would I do a stupid thing like that?'

'Well, when the shit hit the fan Edith said you broke it off.'

'Course she said that. It's what I told her.'

'Have a beer, you sly son of a bitch.'

I held up two fingers to Betty and she slid off the stool.

'Wait,' the fish man said. 'I'll get this one for the boys, and— lemmee see—' he pulled out a pocket watch from his khakis, peered down in the red-lighted dark '—yeah, Betty, I'll have one more, then I'll be getting home and put my fish in the oven.' Hank cocked his head and watched him. 'Don't get it started, the wife'll come home and start looking around, wanting to know where's the dinner.'

'I don't blame her,' Betty said.

'Oh sure. She works all day too, and I get home a little earlier, so I put the dinner on.'

She gave us the beer and we raised our mugs to him and said thanks. He raised his, smiled, nodded, sipped. He picked up his fish, turning it in his hands, then lowered it to the bar.

'If I'm going to fry it I can start later, but when I'm baking like with this one, I need a little more time.' He looked through the door at two men going into the dining room. 'Someday I'm going to come in here and get me one of those fish platters. I'll be about ready for one, one of these days.'

Hank was watching him.

'Did you ever want to leave with her?' I said.

'Why?'

'You said you loved her.'

'I still do. You're nineteenth century, Jack.'

'That's what you keep telling me.'

'It's why you've been faithful so long. Your conscience is made for whores but you're too good for that, so you end up worse: monogamous.'

'What's this made for whores shit.'

'The way it used to be. Man had his wife and kids. That was one life. And he had his whore. He knew which was which, see; he didn't get them confused. But now it's not that way: a man has a wife and a girlfriend and they get blurred, you see, he doesn't know where his emotional deposits are supposed to be. He's in love, for Christ sake. It's incongruous. He can't live with it, it's against everything he's supposed to feel, so naturally he takes some sort of action to get himself back to where he believes he's supposed to be. Devoted to one woman or some such shit. He does something stupid: either he breaks with the girl and tries to love only his wife, or he leaves the wife and marries the girl. It he does that, he'll be in the same shit in a few years, so he'll just have to keep marrying—'

'Or stay monogamous.'

'Aye. Both of which are utter bullshit.'

'And you think that's me.'

'I think so. You're a good enough man not to fuck without feeling love, but it you're lucky enough for that to happen, then you feel confused and guilty because you think it means you don't love Terry.'

I looked him in the eyes and said: 'Have you been talking to my mistress?'

'Mistress pisstress. I've been talking to *you* for three years. I've been watching you watching women.'

I believed him. If he knew about Edith and me, it was because he'd guessed: they had not been talking.

'Am I right?' he said.

'I worry about Terry, that's true. Just getting caught, I mean. I worry about love affairs too: the commitment, you know.'

'What's commitment got to do with a love affair? A love affair is abandon. Put the joy back in fucking. It's got to be with a good woman, though. See, Jeanne knew. She *knew* I'd never leave Sharon and Edith. Commitment. That's with Terry. It doesn't even matter if you love Terry. You're married. What matters is not to hate each other, and to keep peace. The old Munich of marriage. You live with a wife, around a wife, not through her. She doesn't run with you and come drink beer with you, for Christ sake. Love, shit.

Love the kids. Love the horny wives and the girls in short skirts. Love everyone, my son, and keep peace with your wife. Who, by the way, is not invulnerable to love either. What'll you do if that happens?'

'That's her business.'

'All right. I believe you.'

'You should; it's true.'

'So why are *you* so uptight?'

'I'm not, man. What brought all this on, anyway?'

'I didn't like that look of awe in your face. When I said I spent the night with Jeanne, and never broke up with her. I love you, man. You shouldn't feel awe for *any*thing I do. I don't have more guts than you. I just respond more, that's all. I don't like seeing you cramped. Chicks *like* you, I *see* it, Jack. Hell, Edith gets juiced up every time you call the house. Other day Sharon said she wanted a jack-in-the-box, I thought Edith would fall off the couch laughing. Wicked laugh. Lying there laughing.'

'Jack-in-the-box,' I said, smiling, shaking my head.

He slapped my shoulder and we drained our mugs and left. 'Take care,' I said, passing the fish man. 'See you boys.' He raised his mug. Going out the door Hank turned left, toward the dining room; I waited while he talked to the hostess, nodding, smiling, reaching for his wallet. He gave her four dollars and waved off the change.

'What was that about?'

We walked to the front door and I started to go outside, but turned instead and went into the fish market.

'I bought him a fish platter.'

I went to the lobster tank, and an old man in a long white apron came from behind the fish counter.

'He'll be gone before it's ready,' I said.

'Told her to give him a beer too. He won't waste a beer. By the time he's done, there it'll be.'

'All right: cool.' I turned to the old man. 'How much are you getting for lobsters?'

'As much as we can,' winking, laughing, then a wheeze and a cough.

The chicken lobsters were a dollar seventy-nine a pound; she loved to eat, she'd say *mmmm*, sucking the claws, splitting open the tail. I asked for two and didn't watch him weigh them or ring them up. I couldn't; it was like when they call you in to pay for your crime: your father, your boss: the old humiliation of chilled ass and quickened heart. They were four dollars and fifty-two cents. I did not think about the bank balance until I bought the wine. On the way to Hank's I stopped at the liquor store and bought Pinot Chardonnay, Paul Masson: two-fifty. Seven dollars. Two on beer. Nine. I went next door into the A&P; Hank was waiting in the car, listening to the Red Sox in a twi-nighter. Eight at the service station: seventeen. I bought half pints of strawberry, chocolate, and vanilla ice cream, a bunch of bananas, a can of chocolate syrup, a jar of cherries, a pressurized can of whipped cream, but no nuts, there were only cocktail nuts, salted things. My children didn't know what a banana split was; I had told them the other day how the boys and I used to eat them after a movie, and if I could spend seven on Terry and me then certainly they deserved—was love no more than guilt? I have a girl so Terry should have a lover. We get lobster and Pinot Chardonnay so the kids should have this junk. The banana splits cost four dollars and twenty-eight cents. A twenty-one-dollar day, only two on something I wanted: the beer with Hank. Now I could slide back the door in my mind, look at the bank balance written there: forty-three dollars and eighty cents. I had glanced at it yesterday, I hadn't really wanted to see, but it sprang like a snake and got in my head and stayed there. Eight days before payday and a week's groceries still to buy. What now? Stop drinking? Stop smoking? So we could sit stiff and tight-faced night after night, chewing blades of grass, watching the food and milk and gas all going down down down. We had tried that once, for six weeks: nothing but red wine, a dollar and a quarter a half gallon. Nothing happened. The bourbon and gin and beer money never turned up; it jumped into the cash register at the supermarket, the service stations, it went to the utilities and telephone gangs, the landlord, it paid for repairs on a bad car, it went to people who sold bad shoes to children and to people who sold worse toys. It just kept going, and days before payday it was gone; when the last milk carton was empty, Terry put powdered milk in it and didn't fool the kids, and every day there was more space in the refrigerator and cupboard, and each day I woke wanting payday to come and hating the trap I was in: afraid of death and therefore resisting the passage of time, yet now having to wish for it.

'I spent twenty-one bucks today. What's the score?'

'Sox, 2-1. Top of the third. You broke?'

There were driving lanes in the big parking lot, but people drove through the parking spaces too; they drove in circles, triangles, squares, trapezoids, and other geometric figures, and I had to look in all directions at once.

'Not for a couple of days.'

'Here.' He took out his wallet.

'No, man. That's not why I said that.'

'Jesus, I know that. How much you need?'

'I can't.'

'Come on. Some day you'll come through for me.'

'I need about forty *bucks*, man. I'll go to the bank.'

He was holding out two twenties and Reggie Smith was catching a fly ball on the warning path.

'Edith got a check from Winnetka.'

'It won't last for shit if you support me too.' Thinking of the imported beer, the babysitter.

'We needed two hundred, so she asked for three and her mother sent five.'

'*Five?* No shit: you mean there are people in the world who can write a check for five hundred dollars and not break into tears? I'll pay it back a little at a time, okay?'

'Sure. Buy me a bottle some time. Buy me one round of *beer* some time, you cheap cocksucker.'

At his house he said to come in for a quick one. I was worried about the ice cream but he reached back and took it from the bag, so I followed him in. She was at the stove. She smiled at us over her shoulder; she had changed her shorts and shirt and had a red ribbon in her black hair. She looked as if she'd changed souls. She stirred a pot of something and looked in the oven while Hank put up the ice cream and opened two ales and a beer. Then she sat at the table and asked Hank for a cigarette.

'I quit.'

'Good luck, baby.'

I gave her one of mine, and took one too.

'Oh, a Lucky,' she said.

'See what you did. As long as he was with me he didn't smoke.'

'I like to corrupt.'

'You looked like a girl from the forties just then,' I said. 'Or early fifties. Taking the tobacco off your tongue. Except their fingernails were painted. You'd see that red fingernail moving down their tongues, and I used to love watching them.'

'Why?' Hank said.

'I don't know. I think it was watching a woman being sensual. You were a little hard on that fish man.'

'I know. Didn't seem so funny once I got in the car.'

'What fish man?'

I watched her listen to the story and I thought how she didn't know Hank and Jeanne hadn't ended till she went back to France. And whether he guessed or not he could never know what she was like out there on the blanket. Now she was just an attentive young wife, listening to her husband, her eyes going from him to Sharon with her coloring book on the floor. Still they had a marriage. He was talking to her about his day. She had got that money for them. Her dinner smelled good, and her house was clean. I felt it was my house too, and I remembered what I was like before I loved her, during that long time when I wasn't in love; I need to be in love, I know it is called romantic, it isn't what they call realistic, I am supposed to settle into the steady seasons, the ticking Baby Bens, of marriage.

'Hank, that was cruel.'

'I know. But he had no balls. Cooking, for Christ sake.'

At my back door I smelled spaghetti sauce. She was ironing in the kitchen and I looked past her at the black iron skillet of sauce on the stove. I didn't give her a chance to ask me how the day had been; I saw the question in her face as she looked up from ironing and reached for her drink at the end of the ironing board. Edith had not been drinking when Hank and I got there, and I wondered if other wives drank before their husbands came home.

'This guy gave me some lobsters,' I said, as the screen door shut behind me. 'I saved his daughter from drowning and he gave me all he had.'

'Oh let me *see*.'

She hurried around the ironing board and took the bag and looked in. I put the wine in the freezer compartment.

'Wine too?'

'Sure. And some stuff for the kids.'

I gave her the supermarket bag.

'Oh look,' peering in, taking out the jar of cherries, the whipped cream, the chocolate syrup. 'What a nice daddy.'

She took the ironed clothes on hangers upstairs, then put the ironing board and basket of waiting clothes in the wash room. I got the ball game on the radio and sat at the kitchen table with the *Boston Globe* while she looked for her big pot and found it and put it on the stove. I skimmed the news stories I couldn't believe while I told her Hank had written only a page, he had quit smoking, we had had a good run, drunk some beer, and he had loaned me forty dollars. She was happy about the money, but she said very seriously we must be sure to pay him back, ten dollars a payday till it was done. All this time I was following the ball game and getting through the news about Nixon and the war, getting to those stories I could believe: a man winning a tobacco spitting contest; a woman and her son drowning, taken into the sea by waves on the coast of Maine; the baseball news. I could also believe all stories about evil. I was accustomed to lies from the government and the press, and I never believed them when they spoke with hope or comfort. So I believed all stories of lies, atrocity, and corruption, for they seemed to be the truth that I was rarely told and that I was waiting for. I knew that my vision was as distorted as the vision of those who lied, but I saw no way out. When I finished the paper, I started to tell Terry about the fish man, but with the first word already shaping my lips, I stopped.

In a marriage there are all sorts of lies whose malignancy slowly kills everything, and that day I was running the gamut from the outright lie of adultery to the careful selectivity which comes when there are things that two people can no longer talk about. It is hard to say which kills faster but I would guess selectivity, because it is a surrender: you avoid touching wounds and therefore avoid touching the heart. If I told her the story, she would see it as a devious way of getting at her: the man's cooking would be the part of me she smothered; Hank's buying the seafood platter would be my rebellion. And she would be right. So I treated our disease with aspirins, I weaved my conversation around us, and all the time I knew with a taste of despair that I was stuck forever with this easy, lying pose; that with the decay of years I had slipped gradually into it, as into death, and that now at the end of those years and the beginning of all the years to come I had lost all dedication to honesty between us. Yet sometimes when I was alone and away from the house, always for this to happen I had to be away from the house, driving perhaps on a day of sunlight and green trees and rolling meadows, I would hear a song from another time and I could weep (but did not) for the time when I loved her every day and came up the walk in the afternoons happy to see her, days when I never had to think before I spoke. As we ate lobsters and drank wine we listened to the ball game.

And later, after the spaghetti dinner that wasn't eaten, we made love. We had watched the children, who were impatient for banana splits and so ate only a little and that quickly, sucking spaghetti, spearing meatballs, their eyes returning again and again to the door of the freezer compartment, to Terry slicing bananas, punching open the can of chocolate syrup. They were like men late for work eyeing the clock behind a lunch counter. They loved the banana splits, ate till I feared for their stomachs, then I went with a book to the living room couch, and Terry put the meatballs and spaghetti sauce in the refrigerator to be warmed again another day.

When she got into bed I pretended to be asleep but she touched my chest and spoke my name until I looked at her.

'I went a little crazy last night,' she said. 'I'm sorry.'

'Okay.'

'I shouldn't have got drunk.'

She found my hand and held it.

'Forget it,' I said.

'I've got to grow up.'

'Who ever told you grown-ups weren't violent?'

'Not with their husbands.'

'Read the papers. Women murder their husbands.'

'Not people like us.'

'Sailors' wives, is that it? Construction workers?'

'I don't mean that.'

'Maybe some people have enough money so they don't have to kill each other. You can have separate lives then, when things go bad. You don't have to sweat over your beer in the same hot kitchen: watching her fat ass under wilted blue cotton, her dripping face and damp straight hair. Pretty soon somebody picks up a hammer and goes to it. Did Hank make a pass?'

'Yes.'

'He did?'

'I said yes.'

'Well?'

'Well what.'

'What did he do?'

'None of your business.'

'All right, then: what did *you* do?'

'Nothing.'

'Come on.'

'He tried to kiss me on the porch, so I went inside.'

'Where?' Grinning at her. 'Here?'

'To the *kit*chen. To get a beer.'

'And he followed you in and—'

'Said he loved me and kissed me and said he didn't love Edith. Then I felt dirty and we went outside and sat on the front steps.'

'Dirty. Because he said that about Edith?'

'Yes. She's a sweet girl and she doesn't deserve that, and I don't want any part of it.'

'But until he said that, you felt all right.'

'We can stop this now. Or do you want to know whether his nose was to the left or right of mine?'

'Do you remember?'

'We were lying on the floor and he was on my right, so I'd say his nose was to the left of mine.'

'Lying on the floor, huh? Goodness.'

'I'd squatted down to get a beer from— Oh shut up.'

'I was only teasing.'

'You were doing more than that. You're glad he kissed me.'

'Let's say I'm not disturbed.'

'Well I am.'

She got out of bed for a cigarette and when she came back I pretended to be asleep and listened to her smoking deeply beside me. Then she put out the cigarette and started touching me, the old lust on quiet signal, and I mounted her, thrusting the sound of bedsprings into the still summer night, not a word between us, only breath and the other sound: and I remembered newly married one morning she was holding a can of frozen orange juice over a pitcher and the sound of its slow descent out of the can drove us back to bed. I could feel her getting close but I still was far away, and I opened my eyes: hers were closed. I shut mine and saw Edith this afternoon *oh love*; then I thought *she is thinking of Hank, behind those closed eyes her skull is an adulterous room,* and now he was here too and he had given me the forty dollars and it was Hank, not I, Hank who was juggling us all, who would save us, and now we came, Hank and Terry and Edith and me, and I said, 'Goodnight, love,' and rolled over and slept.

§2 ON a moonlit summer night, in a cemetery six blocks from my house, lying perhaps among the bones of old whaling men, in the shadow of a pedestaled eight-foot bronze angel, Hank made love to my red-haired wife.

At midnight I had left them on the front porch. Edith had the flu, and Hank had come over late for a nightcap; it was the day after payday and I gave him ten dollars which he didn't want to take. We drank on the front porch, but I was tired and I watched them talking about books and movies, then I went to bed, their voices coming like an electric train around the corner of the house, through the screen of my open window. I slept. When I woke my heart was fast before I knew what it knew. I lay in silence louder than their voices had been, and listened for the creak of floor under a step, the click of her Zippo, a whisper before it died in the air. But there was only silence touching my flesh, so they weren't in the house; unless making love in the den or living room they had heard my heart when I woke and now they were locked in sculpted love waiting for me to go back to sleep. Or perhaps they were in the yard and if I went outside I would turn a corner of the house and smack into the sight of her splayed white legs under the moon and the white circle of his wedging ass.

The clock's luminous dial was too moonlit to work: with taut stealth I moved across the bed, onto Terry's side, and took the clock from the bedside table: two-twenty. I waited another ten minutes, each pale gray moonlit moment edged with expectancy, until I was certain it was emptiness I heard, not their silence. And if indeed they were listening, I would cast the burden of cunning on them: I rolled over and dropped my feet thumping to the floor, and walked to the bathroom next to my room and turned on the light. I flushed the toilet, then went out through the other door, into the kitchen, the dining room, the living room, and stepped onto the front porch. The night was cool and I shivered, standing in my T-shirt so white if they were watching. His car was parked in front. Their glasses were on the steps. I picked them up: lime and gin-smelling water. Then I went to bed and waited, and I saw them under the willow tree in the backyard, the branches hanging almost to the grass, and I asked myself and yes, I said, I want the horns; plant them, Hank, plant them. I wanted lovely Edith now there with me and twice I picked up the phone and once dialed three numbers, but she would be asleep with her fever and there was nothing really to tell yet, I didn't really know yet, and after that I lay in bed, quick-hearted and alert, and waited and smoked.

At ten minutes after three he started his car. I ran tiptoeing to the living room window as his car slowly left the curb and Terry stood on the sidewalk, smoking; she lifted a hand, waving as Hank drove down the street. He blinked his interior light, but I couldn't see him, then his car was dark, just tail lights again, and then he was gone and the street was quiet. She stood smoking. When she flicked the cigarette in the street and started up the walk, I ran back to the bedroom. She came in and crossed the living room, into the dining room and bathroom. She stayed there a while: water ran, the toilet flushed, water ran again. Then in the kitchen she popped open a beer and went to the living room; her lighter clicked, scraped, clicked shut. When she finished the beer she plunked it down on the coffee table and came into the bedroom.

'Where've you been?'

She got out of her clothes and dropped them on the floor, and lies cracked her voice: 'I woke up and couldn't get back to sleep so I went out for a walk.'

She went naked to the living room and came back shaking a cigarette from her pack and lit it and got into bed.

'Terry.'

'What.'

'You don't have to tell me that. I woke up at two-twenty.'

She drew on her cigarette. Still she had not looked at me.

'You bastard. Did you ever go to sleep?'

'Yes.'

'I wish I could believe that.'

'I was tired.'

'You could've brought me to bed.'

'You could've come with me.'

She threw back the sheet and blanket and got out of bed and went fast, pale skin and flopping hair, out of the room. She came back with a beer and got into bed and covered up and bent the pillow under her head so she could drink.

'I'm lonely, that's why. I'm a woman, I'm sorry, I can't be anything else, and I need to be told that and I need to be made love to, you don't make love with me anymore, you fuck me; I sat on the steps with him and he held my hand and listened to me talk about this shitty marriage because all you ever see is the house, you don't see me, and he said let's go see the bronze angel, we've never seen it in the dark, and I was happy when he said that and I was happy making love—'

So she had really done it, and I lay there feeling her wash down me, from my throat, down my chest, my legs, then gone like surf from the sea, cold like the sea.

'—and I lay afterward looking up at her wings and for the first time since leaving the porch I thought of you and for a moment under her wings I hated you for bringing me to this. Then that went away. I wanted to go home and seal up the split between us, like gluing this shitty old furniture, I wanted to clap my hands for Tinker Bell, do something profound and magic that would bring us back the way we used to be, when we were happy. When you loved me and when I never would have made love with someone else. And all the way walking home I wanted to hurry and be with you, here in this bed in this house with my husband and children where I belong. And right now I love you I think more than I have for years but I'm angry, Jack, way down in my blood I'm angry because you set this up in all kinds of ways, you wanted it to happen and now it has and now I don't know what else will happen, because it's not ended, making love is never ended—'

'Are you seeing him again?'

'No.'

'Then it's ended.'

'Do you think making love is like *smo*king, for Christ sake? That if you quit it's *o*ver? It's not just the act. What's wrong with you— it's feeling, it's—'

She drank, then sat up and drank again, head back for a long swallow, then she lit a cigarette from the one she was smoking.

'It's what,' I said.

'Promises.'

'You promised to see him again?'

'I didn't say anything. Opening my legs is a promise.'

'But he must have said something.'

'I wish you could hear your voice right now, the way it was just then, I wish I had it taped and I'd play it for you till you went to a shrink to find out why your voice just now was so Goddamn oily. You *like* this. You *like* it. Well hear: it took us a long time to get to the cemetery because we kept stopping to kiss and when we did walk it was slow because we had our arms around each other and his hand was on my tit all the time and when we got to the angel we didn't look at her, not once, we undressed and got down on the ground and we fucked, Jack, we fucked like mad, and I was so hot I came before he did; the second time I was on top and it was long and slow and I told him I loved him and you, you poor man, you sick cuckold, look at your face—Jesus Christ, what am I married to?'

'Will you stop?'

'Why should I? You ought to be knocking my teeth out now. But not you. You want to watch us. Is that it? Is that what you want, Jack?'

I sat up and was swinging at her but stopped even before she saw it coming, and my hand opened and I pointed at her eyes, the finger close, so close, and I wanted to gouge with it, to hit, to strangle, the finger quivering now as I tried not to shout beneath the children's rooms, my voice hoarse and constricted in my throat: 'Terry, you fuck who you want and when you want and where you want but do not do *not* give me any of your half-ass insights into the soul of a man you've never understood.'

Then she was laughing, a true laugh at first or at least a smile, but she lay with her head back on the pillow, throat arched, her shoulders and breasts shaking, and prolonged it, forced it cracking into the air, withering my tense arm, and I got out of bed so I would not even touch the sheet she lay on.

'Oh God: half-ass insights into the—what? The soul of a man I've never understood? Oh my. You poor baby, and it's so simple. You think you're a swinger, free love, I can fuck whoever I want, oh my how you talk and talk and talk and it all comes down to that one little flaw you won't admit: you're a pervert, Jack. You need help. And I'm sorry, I really am, but there's nothing I can do about it. I made love with Hank tonight and he wants to see me tomorrow—or this afternoon really—and when I finish this beer I'm going to sleep because the kids'll be up soon and you're not known for getting them breakfast—'

'I'll do it. Forget it, I'll do it.'

'Fine. Do that. That's one thing you can do. You can't help me with my other problem any more than I can help you with yours. See, I'm a big girl now and I knew what I was doing tonight and I don't know if I can very well say tomorrow—today—well gee Hank that was last night but this is now and gee I just don't want to anymore. I mean even you with all your progressive and liberal ideas will have to admit that even adultery has its morality, that one can cop out on that too. So I have things to figure out.'

'Yes.' I started leaving the room. 'Do what you can.'

'Oh, that's good.' I stopped at the door but didn't look back. 'That's what all my good existential friends say whenever I want advice: Just do what you can. Well, I will, Jack, I will.'

I went to the kitchen and drank an ale and when Terry was asleep I went to bed.

Next morning I woke first, alert and excited, though I had slept only four hours. Everything was quiet except birds. I got up and dressed, watching Terry asleep on her back, mouth open; I stepped over her clothes on the floor, and going through the living room picked up her beer can and brought it to the kitchen. In the silence I could feel the children sleeping upstairs, as if their breathing caressed me. I went outside: the morning was sun and blue and cool air. I drove to a small grocery store and bought a *Globe* and cigarettes. Then I drove to a service station with a pay phone and parked but didn't get out of the car. It was only five minutes of nine on a Sunday morning, and they would be asleep. Or certainly Hank would. But maybe she wouldn't, and I drove to their street: all the houses looked quiet, theirs did too, and I went past, then turned around in a driveway and started back, believing I would go on by; then I stopped and walked up their driveway to the back door and there she was in the dim kitchen away from the sun, surprised, turning to me in her short nightgown, a happy smile as she came to the door and pushed it gently so the latch was quiet. I stepped in and she was holding me tight, and I stroked her soft brushed hair and breathed her toothpaste and soap.

'Are you all right now?'

'The fever's gone. Was it fun last night?'

'They made love.'

She moved her head back to look at me and say, 'Really?'; then she was at my cheek again. 'She told you?'

'She didn't want to, but I knew, I had waked up. They went to the bronze angel.'

'Are you jealous?'

'No.' She was holding me, rubbing her cheek on my chest. Her kitchen was clean. 'They might see each other today. If they do, we can get together.'

'We'll have the kids and they'll have the cars.'

'Shit.'

Water started boiling; she let me go and turned off the fire. Then she was back.

'How are you?' I said.

'Still weak, that's all. I told you the fever's gone.'

'I mean about them.'

'Fine. I think it's fine. He'll be asleep for a long time.'

'He might wake up.'

'We'd hear him, we'd be right under the bedroom. He always goes to the bathroom first.'

'Sharon,' I said.

'She'll sleep too.'

We started for the door; she stopped and put instant coffee in two cups and poured water. Then we crept through the house to the guest room.

When I left, after drinking the coffee that was still warm enough, Sharon was coming downstairs. Before getting into the car I squinted up at the bedroom where Hank slept.

At home I didn't go in; I sat on the back steps to read the sports page. I could smell Terry's cigarette, then I heard her moving and she came outside in her robe, hair uncombed, and sat beside me and put a hand on my shoulder. I nearly flinched.

'I was scared,' she said. 'When I woke up and you weren't there. I thought you had left.'

'I did. To get cigarettes and a paper.'

'What took so long?'

'Driving around looking at the bright new morning.'

'Is it?'

I looked up from the paper and waved a hand at the trees and rooftops and sky.

'Blink your eyes and look at it.'

'Your beard's beautiful in the sun. It has some blond and red in it.'

'I got that from you and the kids.'

'I thought you had left me.'

'Why should I?'

'What I said.'

'That's night talk.'

'I know it. Just as long as you know it. I was being defensive because I was scared and when I'm scared I get vicious.'

'Why were you scared?'

'Because I have a lover.'

'Is that what you've decided?'

'I haven't decided anything. I made love with Hank so I have a lover, no matter what I do about it. You really don't care?'

She had the right word: care. So I must get her away from that. The way to hunt a deer is not to let him know you're alive.

'I care about you. It's monogamy I don't care about.'

'You've said that for years. I've waked up with that whispering to me for years. But a long time ago you weren't that way.'

'A long time ago I wasn't a lot of ways.'

'I couldn't let you do what I'm doing.'

'Are you doing anything?'

'I don't know yet.'

'But you want to.'

'If I knew that I'd know something.'

'Why don't you know it? I know it.'

'How?'

Her hand was still on my arm; I was scanning box scores.

'You stayed out there with him because you wanted to and I think you came home planning to see him today and tomorrow and tomorrow and tomorrow, but when you found out I knew about it then it got too sticky. Just too bloody sticky. To all in one night leave monogamy and then have to carry it out with your husband knowing about it, staying with the kids while you—'

'Oh stop,' her voice pleading, her fingers tightening on my shoulder. 'Shhh, stop.'

'Isn't that so?'

'I don't know. I mean, sure I wanted to, and I like Hank very much; in a way I love him, and I love you and nothing's changed that, what's with Hank is—' she squeezed my shoulder again and looking at the paper I heard the fake smile in her voice '—it's friendly lust, that's all. But it might not be marriage, living like this.'

'We're married. You and I are married. So it has to be marriage.'

'It might not be for long.'

'I wish Boston were a National League town. You mean you're afraid you'll run off with him?'

'*No. My God* no. There are all sorts of ways for a marriage not to be a marriage.'

'You're just afraid because it's new.'

'If I kept on with Hank you'd want a girl. You'd feel justified then. Maybe even with Edith, and wouldn't *that* be a horror.'

'Seems strange to me that while you're deciding whether or not to make love with a man you call your lover, you're thinking most about what *I'll* do.'

'That's not strange. You're my husband.'

'It is strange, and it's beneath you. This is between you and Hank, not me.'

She took a pack of cigarettes from the carton I'd bought and sat smoking while I read.

'Are you hungry?' she said.

'Yes.'

'Pancakes and eggs?'

'Buckwheat. Are the kids up?'

'No. I think I'll take them to the beach today. Do you want to go?'

'I want to watch the game.'

'I think I'll tell him no.'

'Is that what you want?'

'I don't know. I'm just scared.'

'Because I know about it?'

'Because there's something to know.'

She went inside. I read the batting averages and pitching records, then the rest of the paper, listening to her washing last night's pots and dishes. Then she started cooking bacon and I sat waiting, smelling and listening to the bacon, until I heard Natasha and Sean coming downstairs. We ate for a long time, then Terry lit a cigarette and said, 'Well,' and went to the bedroom and shut both doors. I could hear her voice, but that was all. Natasha and Sean were upstairs getting dressed; when Terry came back to the kitchen she went to the foot of the stairs and called them and said to put on bathing suits. 'We're going to the beach!'

'The beach!' they said. 'The beach!'

'How did you get it done?' I said.

'He answered. He'd said he would. I asked how Edith was and he told me.'

'That was the signal?'

'Yes.'

'Poor Hank. And what if you had decided to see him?'

'I wouldn't have called.'

She had been smoking a lot all morning. Now she started making a Bloody Mary.

'Do you want one?'

'No. How's Edith?'
'All right. Her fever's gone.'

For some years now I have been spiritually allergic to the words husband and wife. When I read or hear husband I see a grimly serene man in a station wagon; he is driving his loud family on a Sunday afternoon. They will end with ice cream, sticky car seats, weariness, and ill tempers. In his youth he had the virtues of madness: rage and passion and generosity. Now he gets a damp sponge from the kitchen and wipes dried ice cream from his seat covers. He longs for the company of loud and ribald men, he would like to drink bourbon and fight in a bar, steal a pretty young girl and love her through the night. When someone says wife I see the confident, possessive, and amused face of a woman in her kitchen; among bright curtains and walls and the smell of hot grease she offers her husband a kiss as he returns from the day sober, paunchy, on his way to some nebulous goal that began as love, changed through marriage to affluence, is now changing to respectable survival. She is wearing a new dress. From her scheming heart his balls hang like a trophy taken in battle from a young hero long dead.

I wheezed again with this allergy as I stood on the lawn and watched Terry and Natasha and Sean drive off to Plum Island. They had a picnic basket, a Styrofoam cooler of soft drinks and beer, a beach bag of cigarettes and towels, and a blanket. They left in a car that needed replacing. This morning's lovely air was now rent apart by the sounds of power mowers. One was across the street, two blocks down to the right; the man behind it wore a T-shirt and shorts and was bald. The one to the left was on my side of the street, behind shrubs, and I only saw him when he got to the very front of his lawn, turned, and started back. I sat on the grass and chewed a blade of it and watched the bald man. I wondered what he was thinking. Then I thought he must be thinking nothing at all. For if he thought, he might cut off the engine that was mowing his lawn and go into the garage and jam the garden shears into his throat.

Yet once in a while you saw them: they sat in restaurants, these old couples of twenty and twenty-five and thirty years, and looked at each other with affection, and above all they talked. They were always a wonder to see, and when I saw them I tried to hear what they said. Usually it was pleasant small talk: aging sailors speaking in signals and a language they have understood forever. If I looked at most couples with scorn and despair, I watched these others as mystified as if I had come across a happy tiger in a zoo; and I watched them with envy. *It can be faked*, Hank said once. We were in a bar. The afternoon bartender had just finished work for the day, his wife was waiting for him in a booth, and they had two drinks and talked; once they laughed aloud. *There are two kinds of people*, Hank said. *The unhappy ones who look it and the unhappy ones who don't.*

Now I went inside and upstairs and turned on the ball game. Hank's marriage wasn't a grave because Hank wasn't dead; he used his marriage as a center and he moved out from it on azimuths of madness and when he was tired he came back. While Edith held to the center she had been hurt, and for a few days when she started guessing that Hank was not faithful I didn't like being with them: you could smell the poison on their breaths, feel the tiny arrows flying between them. Now she had a separate life too and she came home and they sat in the kitchen with their secrets that were keeping them alive, and they were friendly and teasing again. It was as simple as that and all it required was to rid both people of jealousy and of the conviction that being friendly parents and being lovers were the same. Hank and Edith knew it, and I knew it. I had waked happy, believing Terry knew it too, and now after her one night she was at the beach with the children, and we were husband and wife again. I sat watching the game. Far off, as though from the streets behind the black and white ball park, I could hear the power mowers.

After dinner Terry came to the living room where I was reading on the couch. Upstairs the children were watching television.

'Hank came to the beach.'

'He found you? On a hot Sunday at Plum Island? My God, the man's in love.'

'He says he is.'

'Really.'

'Oh, I know it's just talk, it's just a line—he wants to see me tonight.' She was smoking. 'I wish I hadn't last night. But I did and it doesn't seem really right to say yes and then next morning say no, I mean it's not like I was drunk or something, I knew what I was doing. But I'm scared, Jack.' She sat on the couch; I moved to make room, and she took my hand. 'Look at me. What do you *really* think? Or really feel. You're not scared of this? People screwing other people?'

'No, I'm not scared.'

'Then why am I? When I'm the one who—Jesus.'

'What did you feel at the beach?'

'Guilty. Watching my children and talking to him.'

'Did you tell him you'd meet him?'

She lowered her eyes and said, 'Yes.'

'And now you don't feel like it because it's embarrassing to leave the house when I know where you're going. If I didn't know, you'd have got out with some excuse. Does Hank know that I know?'

'I didn't tell him. It just seemed too much, when we're all together. Won't you feel strange? When you see him tomorrow?'

'I don't think so. What are you going to do tonight?'

'I'm going to think about it.'

She went to the kitchen. I listened to her washing the dishes: she worked very slowly, the sounds of running water and the dull clatter of plate against plate as she put them in the drainer coming farther and farther apart so that I guessed (and rightly) she had done less than half the dishes when I heard her quickly cross the floor and go into the bathroom. She showered fast, she must have been late, then she opened the bathroom door to let the steam out. Late or not, of course she spent a long while now with the tubes and brushes and small bottles of her beauty, which was natural anyway and good, but when people came over or we went out she worked on it. I had always resented that: if a car pulled up in front of the house she fled to the bathroom and gave whoever it was a prettier face than she gave me. But I thought, too, that she gave it to herself. She closed the bathroom closet, ran the lavatory tap a final time, and came out briskly into the bedroom; lying propped on the couch, I looked over the Tolstoy book; she had a towel around her, and I watched her circling the bed, to our closet. She was careful not to look at me. On the way to the mirror she would have to face me or turn her head; so I raised the book and read while she pushed aside hangered dresses, paused, then chose something. I felt her glance as she crossed the room to the full-length mirror. I tried to read, listening to the snapping of the brassiere, the dress slipping over her head and down her body, and the brush strokes on her hair. Then I raised my eyes as she stepped into the living room wearing her yellow dress and small shiny yellow shoes, her hair long and soft, and behind the yellow at her shoulders it was lovely. When I looked at her she opened her purse and dropped in a fresh pack of cigarettes, watching it fall. She had drawn green on her eyelids.

'Well—' she said.

'All right.'

'I'll do the dishes when I get back.'

'No sweat.'

She looked at me, her eyes bright with ambivalence: love or affection or perhaps only nostalgia and, cutting through that tenderness, an edge of hatred. Maybe she too knew the marriage was forever changed and she blamed me; or maybe it wasn't the marriage at all but herself she worried about, and she was going out now into the night, loosed from her moorings, and she saw me as the man with the axe who had cut her adrift onto the moonless bay. My face was hot. She turned abruptly and went upstairs and I listened to her voice with the children. She lingered. Then she came downstairs and called to me from the kitchen: 'The movie should be over around eleven.' I read again. I could have been reading words in Latin. Then the screen opened and she was back in the kitchen, my heart dropping a long way; she went through the bathroom into the bedroom, the car keys jingled as she swept them from the dresser, and my heart rose and she was gone. After a while I was able to read and I turned back the pages I had read without reading; I read for twenty minutes until I was sure Hank was gone too, then I went to the bedroom and phoned Edith.

' "Ivan Ilyitch's life was most simple and most ordinary and therefore most terrible." '

'Who said that?'

She wasn't literary but that didn't matter; I loved her for that too and anyway I didn't know what did matter with a woman except to find one who was clean and peaceful and affectionate and then love her.

'Tolstoy. Our lives aren't so simple and ordinary.'

'Is she gone too?'

'A movie. That's what she tells me so the kids can hear repeated what she told them. A new twist to the old lying collusion of husband and wife against their children. But she also told me the truth.'

'He's going to see some Western. He says they relax him and help him write next day. I hate Westerns.'

'I love them. There's one on the tube tonight and I'll watch it with the kids.'

'We'll have to do something about these cars.'

'Maybe a car pool of sorts.'

'Dear Mother, please buy me a car so I can see my lover while Hank sees his.'

'Is she really that rich?'

'She's that rich. I miss you.'

'Tomorrow. Eleven?'

'I'll go shopping.'

'I'll go to the library.'

'You use that too much. Some day she'll walk over and see if you're there.'

'She's too lazy. Anyway, if things keep on like this maybe I can stop making excuses.'

'Don't count on it.'

'Being a cuckold's all right, but it's boring. Get a sitter and take a taxi.'

'Go watch the movie with your children.'

Terry hadn't put her beauty things away; they were on the lavatory and the toilet tank, and I replaced tops on bottles and put all of it into the cabinet. I went to the foot of the stairs and called.

'What!' When their voices were raised they sounded alike; I decided it was Sean.

'Turn to Channel Seven!'

'What's on!'

'Cowboys, man! Tough hombre cowboys!'

'Cowboys! Can we watch it!'

'Right!'

'All of it!'

'Yeah! All of it!'

'Are you gonna watch it!'

'I am! I'll be up in a while!'

I got a pot out of the dishwater and washed it for popcorn. Once Sean called down that it had started and I said I knew, I knew, I could hear the horses' hooves and I'd be up evermore ricky-tick. There were Cokes hidden in the cupboard so the kids wouldn't drink them all in one day. I poured them over ice and opened a tall bottle of Pickwick ale and got a beer mug and brought everything up on a tray.

'Hey neat-o,' Natasha said.

'Popcorn!'

I pulled the coffee table in front of the couch and put the tray on it.

'Sit between us,' Natasha said.

Sean hugged me when I sat down.

'We got a good Daddy.'

'Now Mom's watching a movie and we're watching a movie,' Natasha said.

'What movie did Momma go to?'

'I believe a Western.'

'You didn't want to go?'

'Nope. I wanted to see this one. He's going to hit that guy soon.'

'Which guy?'

'The fat mean one.'

'How do you know?'

'Because if he doesn't hit him we won't be happy.'

When the movie was over, I tucked them in and kissed them and went downstairs to Tolstoy and the couch; as I read I kept glancing at my watch and at midnight I thought how she never uses the seat belt, no matter how many times and how graphically and ominously I tell her. I kept reading and I remembered though trying not to Leonard in Michigan: he had married young and outgrown his wife and he hated her. When he was drunk, he used to say Nobody hates his wife as much as I hate mine. And one night drinking beer— he was a big weight-lifting man and drank beer like no one I've ever known—he said I've thought of a way a man can kill his wife. You take her for a ride, you see, and you have a crash helmet with you and it's just resting there on the seat between you, she wonders what it's there for, but the dumb bitch won't say anything, she won't say anything about anything and the world can fall down and still she'll just blink her Goddamn dumb eyes and stare and never let you know if there's anything burning behind them, then you get out on some quiet straight country highway and put that son of a bitch on your head and unbuckle her seat belt and hold onto that son of a bitch and floorboard into a telephone pole and throw the crash helmet way the fuck out into the field—

I wished the movie hadn't ended and I was still upstairs watching it with the children; the TV room was a good room to be in, the cleanest in the house because it was nearly bare: a couch, two canvas deck chairs, the TV, and a coffee table. A beach ball and some toy trucks and cars were on the floor. The secret was not having much life in the room. It was living that defeated Terry: the rooms where we slept and ate and the living room and dishes and our clothes. The problem was a simple one which could be solved with money, but I would never make enough so that I could pay someone to do Terry's work. So there was no solution. Two years ago Terry had pneumonia and was in the hospital for a week. Natasha and Sean and I did well. Everyone made his own bed and washed his own plate and glass and silver, and we took turns with the pots; every day I washed clothes, folded them as soon as they were dry, and put them away; twice that week I vacuumed the house. All this took little time and I never felt harried. When Terry came home, I turned over the house to her again, and the children stopped making their beds and washing their dishes, though I'd told her how good they had been. We could do that again now, and I could even have my own laundry bag and put my things in it every night, wash my clothes once a week and wash my own dishes and take turns with the pots, I could work in the house as though I lived with another man. But I wouldn't do it. If Terry had always kept house and was keeping it now, then I could help her without losing and I would do it. But not the way she was now.

In Michigan when I was in graduate school, she found us an old farmhouse in the country for a hundred a month, and for a while she was excited, I'd come home and find the furniture rearranged, and one afternoon she painted the bathroom orange. The landlord had paid for the paint, and for two buckets of yellow for the kitchen; he was an old farmer, he lived down the dirt road from us, he liked Terry, and he told her when she finished the kitchen he'd buy paint for the other rooms. Whatever colors she wanted. For a few days she talked about different colors, asked me what I thought the bedrooms should be, and the halls, and then a week went by and then another and one day when I was running down the road Mr. Kenfield was at his mailbox and he asked me how the painting was coming. I called over my shoulder: 'Fine.' That afternoon we painted the kitchen. I was sullen because I should have been studying, and we painted in near silence, listening to the radio, while Natasha watched and talked. When we were done I said: 'All right, now tell Kenfield you're too busy to paint the other rooms. At least now when he comes for coffee he'll see the yellow walls. And if he pisses he'll see the orange ones. Now I'm going upstairs to do my own work.'

All through graduate school that's what she kept doing: my work. When I brought a book home she read it before I did, and when my friends came over for an afternoon beer and we talked about classes and books and papers, she sounded like a graduate student. Once I daydreamed about her soul: she and Rex and I were sitting at our kitchen table drinking beer, and I watched her talking about *Sons and Lovers* and I remembered her only a year ago when I was a lieutenant junior-grade and she was complaining about the captain's snotty treatment of reserve officers, deriding the supply officer's bureaucratic handling of the simplest matters, and saying she wished there were still battleships so I could be on one and she could go aboard. And in that kitchen in the farmhouse in Michigan I daydreamed that Rex and I were ballplayers and now it was after the game and Terry had watched from behind the dugout and she was telling us she saw early in the game that I couldn't get the curve over, and she didn't think I could go all the way, but in the fifth she saw it happen, she saw me get into the groove, and then she thought with the heat I'd tire, but after we scored those four in the seventh— and he *didn't* tag him, I *know* he didn't—she knew I'd go all the way— And she kept talking, this voice from behind the dugout. And from behind the dugout she came up to my den where I worked and brought a book downstairs and later when I came down at twilight, blinking from an afternoon's reading, I'd find her on the couch, reading.

A couple of years ago in this house in Massachusetts, she put Sean to bed on the same dried sheet he had wet the night before; I noticed it when I went up to kiss the children goodnight. That was two days after I had gone to the basement and found on the stairs a pot and a Dutch oven: the stairway was dimly lit, and at first I thought something was growing in them, some plant of dark and dampness that Terry was growing on the stairs. Then I leaned closer and saw that it had once been food; it was covered with mold now, but in places I could see something under the mold, something we hadn't finished eating. I got the tool or whatever I had gone down for, then I went to the living room; she was sitting on the couch, leaning over the coffee table where the newspaper was spread, and without looking at her—for I couldn't, I looked over her head—I said: 'I found those pots.' She said: 'Oh.' I turned away. I have never heard her sound so guilty. She got up and went down the basement stairs; I heard her coming up fast, she gagged once going through the kitchen, and then she was gone, into the backyard. Soon I heard the hose. I stood in the living room watching a young couple pushing a baby in a stroller; they were across the street, walking slowly on the sidewalk. The girl had short straight brown hair; her face was plain and she appeared, from that distance, to be heavy in the hips and flat-chested. Yet I longed for her. I imagined her to be clean; I pictured their kitchen, clean and orderly before they left for their walk. Then Terry came in, hurrying; from where I stood I could have seen her in the kitchen if I'd turned, but I didn't want to; she went through the kitchen, into the bathroom, and shut the door; then I heard her throwing up. I stood watching the girl and her husband and child move out of my vision. After a while the toilet flushed, the lavatory tap ran, she was brushing her teeth. Then she went outside again.

For two days we didn't mention it. Every time I looked at her— less and less during those two days—I saw the pot and Dutch oven again, as though in her soul.

But when I kissed little Sean and smelled his clean child's flesh and breath, then the other—last night's urine—I went pounding down the stairs and found her smoking a cigarette at the kitchen table, having cleared a space for herself among the dirty dishes; she was reading the *TV Guide* with a look of concentration as though she were reading poetry, and in that instant when I ran into the room and saw her face before she was afraid, before she looked up and saw the rage in mine, I knew what that concentration was: she was pushing those dishes out of her mind, as one sweeps crumbs off a table and out of sight, and I saw her entire life as that concentrated effort not to face the dishes, the urine on the sheets, the pots in the dark down there, on the stairs. I said low, hoarse, so the children wouldn't hear: 'And what *else*. Huh? What *else*.' She didn't know what I was talking about. She was frightened, and I knew I had about three minutes before her fright, as always, turned to rage. 'What *else* do you hide from behind *TV Guides*? Huh? Who in the hell *are* you?'

'What didn't I do?' She was still frightened, caught. She pushed back her chair, started to rise. She gestured at the dishes. 'I'll do these as soon as I finish my—' and we both looked at the ash tray, at the smoldering cigarette she could not have held in her fingers.

'It's not what you didn't do, it's *why*. I can list a dozen whats every day, but I can't name one reason. *Why* do I live in the foulest house I know. Why is it that you say you love me but you give me a shitty house. Why is it that you say you love your children but they go unbathed for days, and right now Sean is lying in last night's piss.'

'I forgot.'

'Goddamnit,' and I was nearly whispering, 'that's your *TV Guide* again, you're hiding, you didn't forget anymore than you forgot those pots—'

'Will you stop talking about those pots!'

'Shhh. I haven't mentioned them since I found them.'

'They've been in your eyes! Your Goddamn nitpicking eyes!'

And she fled from the room. I stood listening: her steps slowed at the top of the stairs, calmly entered Sean's room, and then she was talking, her voice sweet, motherly, loving. Sean jumped to the floor. After a while Terry came down with the dirty sheet; she went through the kitchen without speaking, into the wash room; I heard her taking wet clothes from the washer to the dryer, then putting a new load in the washer. She started both machines. So she had forgotten the clothes in the washer too, was behind on that too; yet neither of those was true. She hadn't forgotten, and she wasn't merely behind. She was . . . what? I didn't know. For a moment I had an impulse to go through the entire house, a marauding soldier after her soul: to turn over the ironing basket and hold before her eyes the shirts I hadn't seen in months; to shine a flashlight under the children's beds, disclosing fluffs of dust, soiled pajamas, apple cores; to lift up the couch cushions and push her face toward the dirt and beach sand, the crayons and pencils and pennies—over every inch of every room, into every cluttered functionless drawer (but no: they functioned as waste baskets, storage bins for things undone). I wanted to do that: take her arm and pull and push her to all these failures which I saw, that night, as the workings of an evasive and disordered soul.

I left the kitchen as she entered it from the wash room. I went on the front porch for a cigarette in the dark. It was fall then, and for a while I was able to forget the house. The air was brisk but still, and I was warm enough in my sweat shirt; I walked down to the end of the block and back, smelling that lovely clean air. Then I went back into the house. As soon as I stepped in, it all struck me: it was there waiting, jesting with me, allowing me the clean walk in the air, the peace, only to slap me when I walked in.

I stayed in the living room with a book. After two pages I laid it aside and looked for one that would serve as well as the autumn night had; I found one, and after two pages I was right, there was neither house nor Terry. The book was *Saturday Night and Sunday Morning,* and I saw myself in the book, a single man drinking gin and loving a married woman. I thought of the sleeping children above me and was ashamed; but I also felt the slow and persuasive undertow of delight.

Then I heard her singing in the kitchen. She was washing the dishes now; beyond her, from the closed wash room, came the rocking of the washer, the hum of the dryer. I didn't want her to sing. She sings alone in the kitchen when she's angry, brooding.

So I knew then I wouldn't be able to keep reading the book; she would do something. I read faster, as though speed would force a stronger concentration, would block her out. I was able to read for nearly an hour. It took her that long to clean the kitchen; the washer and dryer had stopped, but she hadn't removed the dry clothes and put the wet ones in the dryer. So when she came into the living room, a bourbon and water in her hand, all fright and guilt gone now, her face set in that look of hers that makes me know there are times she could kill me, I looked up at her, then stood and looked scornfully not at her face but past her, and said in a low, cold voice that I would go put the clothes in the dryer.

'Wait. I want to talk to you.'

We stood facing each other.

'We can talk while the clothes are drying.'

'No. Because I'm not ready to fold the others. And don't look at me like that, I'll fold them, Goddamnit.'

I sat down, got out of the position of being squared off, got out of range.

'I'm tired of being judged. Who do you think you are anyway? Who are you to judge me? I *did* forget Sean had wet last night. If you got them up one morning out of every thousand, if *you* loved them as much as you say you do—oh, that was shitty, accusing me of not loving my children, it's the way you always fight, like a catty, bitchy woman—lying inn*uen*dos— if *you* ever got them up you'd know he hadn't wet for four or five days before that, so I wasn't used to—'

'Three days. He's been telling me every morning.'

'All right: three. Anyway, I forgot.' She had finished her cigarette; she found another on the bookshelf. 'And I *did* forget those pots. I cooked in them the night you had the party.'

'What night I had the party?'

'Whatever Goddamn night it was. When you were—' she mocked a child's whine '—so depressed—you and your fucking self-indulgent bad moods—'

'What *night* are you talking about?'

'When you called up your *friends* to have this impromptu God-damn party.'

'They're your friends too.'

'Oh sure: me and the boys. They bring their wives over because they have to; I get to talk to the wives. It's *your* party, with *your* friends, in *my* Goddamn house I'm supposed to keep clean as Howard *John*son's.'

'You know my friends like you. We were discussing the pots. The famous pots on the stairs.'

'You supercilious shit.' I smiled at her. 'I cooked in them that night, and you were in your funky mood, and you had to call Hank and Roger and Jim and Matt, I didn't even have time to clean the Goddamn kitchen, and I put those pots on the stairs, I was going to wash them when everybody went home but they stayed half the Goddamn night—'

'I recall you dancing.'

'So I forgot them that night, I probably got drunk, I don't know, and the next day I wasn't thinking about dirty *pots*. I just don't go around thinking about pots! And I forgot them until you found them. And that's the absolute God's truth!'

She went to the kitchen and came back with a fresh drink and stood looking at me.

'I hate to say this, baby,' I said. 'But you're full of shit. I can believe you forgot them that night, what with drinking and dancing. Although I don't see why you couldn't have washed them while these quote friends of mine unquote wandered in—other women do that, you know—I realize you probably had to put your face on and so forth before they came, but after they came I think you could have got someone to talk to you in the kitchen for ten minutes while you washed a Dutch oven and a pot—'

'Ten minutes!'

'Fifteen, then.'

'A lot you know. Would my husband have sat with me? Hell no, he's busy flirting—'

'Oh, stop that crap. Now: I can even believe that you forgot them next morning. But I cannot and will not cater to your lie by trying to believe that you forgot them for the weeks they've been down there—'

'It hasn't been weeks.'

Now her voice didn't have that shrill edge; it was quieter, sullen, and cunning.

'While you were describing your ordeal of merging the problem of two dirty pots with the problem of enjoying a party, I was scratching around through my file of memories—I have this penchant for nostalgic memories, you know—and what I come up with is this: the party was on Friday, the twenty-first of September; today is the twentieth of October; those pots were there about a month. Are you going to stand there drinking my booze and tell me that you did not miss those pots for one month? Or, for one month, descend the basement stairs?'

Then she was throwing things: first the glass, exploding on the wall behind me; I got up from the chair and ducked the copper ash tray, but she got my shoulder with her lighter. I started toward the kitchen, where the car key hung on a nail; she got in front of me and choked me with both hands. 'You crazy bitch—' I shoved hard and she fell back against the table, bumping her hip. She came after me but I was gone, slamming the door, leaping from the top step and running across the lawn to the car. I heard the screen door opening then I was in the car, locking all four doors and jabbing the key twice then into the slot and as I turned it and the car started she grabbed the door handle; I accelerated and was gone.

I went to Plum Island and got out and walked on the beach. The moon was out and on the water, and a cold wind blew out to sea. I walked until I was too cold and Terry was gone, my head clear, I was only shivering and walking. Sometimes I stopped and faced the water, taking deep breaths, the wind pushing at my back. Then I drove to a bar where fishermen and men who worked with their hands sat drinking beer with their big wives. I sat at the bar, turning the stool so my back was to the color television, and after two glasses of ale I thought surely she must hate me, and I felt good, sitting there in her hatred. I knew what she felt when she came at me with her bright, tearful eyes and shrill voice and reaching, choking hands: she wanted my death. And sitting in the bar, watching the couples, I liked that.

I remembered the night I had called my friends to come over and drink; I had been sitting on the lawn toward evening, drinking beer and watching the children play; then they came to me and sat on the grass at my feet and I stroked their heads like dogs, and talked to them, and when Terry came out I was telling them a story, making it up as I went along, and I put them in the story: When Natasha and Sean Were Cowboys, it was called; they were comic and heroic, mostly heroic, they endured blizzards, they raised a baby cougar, they captured an outlaw. While I told the story, Terry barbecued pork chops. I felt serene and loving but somehow sad. And it was that sad love that made me, when the children were in bed, call Hank and Matt and Roger and Jim.

Then sitting at that bar, watching the couples who looked past and over me at the movie or variety show or whatever, I remembered clearly the lawn, the children, the story, and my mood, and I remembered eating dinner on the lawn too: barbecued pork chops, baked beans, green salad, garlic bread—I sat in the bar seeing my paper plate in the sunset evening on the lawn, back in September. The baked beans. I saw my fork going into the pile of beans on my plate; and I remembered later, in the kitchen, Sean and I standing over the Pyrex dish and finishing the last of the beans. She had cooked on the grill and in a Pyrex dish.

She had lied. Though at first I thought she had only been mistaken. Because I hate lies so, and I didn't want to believe she would lie. But finally I told myself no: no, she lies. For the story was too good: my mood, my party, had caused her to forget her work. When confronted with the mold and stench of those pots, the urine on the sheets, she reached back for the one night she could use as an excuse.

So she avoided work and she lied. Then what does she want? I thought. What on earth does she want? And right away I knew: to be beautiful, charming, intelligent, seductive, a good cook, a good drinker, a good fuck. In short, to be loved by men and admired by women. A passive life. A receptive life.

I remember once the landlord's daughter came by, a girl of sixteen; she wanted to go into the attic, she thought she left her bicycle pump there. It was a Saturday afternoon; I answered the door and when she told me what she wanted, I thought: *A bicycle pump. My pitiful wife is to be done in by a bicycle pump.* Because the house looked as though it were lived in, not by a family, but a platoon of soldiers holing up before moving on. We had had a party the night before. She had at least moved the party mess to the kitchen, where it still was, along with the breakfast and lunch dishes; on the table, the countertop, in the sink; the kitchen floor was sticky with spilled booze; every bed was unmade; and so on. I let the girl in, and called Terry to show her to the attic; then I went out and got Sean and we rode our bicycles along the Merrimack. When we got back, Terry was standing at the sink, washing dishes.

That night *Uncle Vanya* was on NET. By then our house was in reasonable order, and Terry sat drinking beer and watching the play. Laurence Olivier played Doctor Astrov, and when he said: 'She is beautiful, there's no denying that, but . . . You know she does nothing but eat, sleep, walk about, fascinate us all by her beauty—nothing more . . . And an idle life cannot be pure . . .' I wanted to glance at Terry but did not. She sat and watched and when it was over she said, 'Jesus,' and weaved upstairs to bed. Next afternoon we were supposed to go hear Cannonball Adderley at Lennie's; I had put the money aside on payday; we were going with Hank and Edith, but all morning and through lunch she said she wasn't going, her life had reached a turning point, the landlord's daughter (*oh her face!* she said; *she was so hurt, and so—scornful!*) and *Uncle Vanya* were too much, she would work, she would work, she would start right now by paying for being a slob, she would not go hear Cannonball Adderley. I told her she was being foolish, that if she were serious her house would need a long, thorough cleaning, and that she might as well wait for Monday morning, the traditional day for taking on a load of shit. But she wouldn't go. So I went, and told Hank and Edith that Terry was turning over leaves. I didn't have to say more; they like mysteries. Cannonball was playing at four. I got home about eight. The children were in bed, the kitchen was clean, and in the living room Terry was asleep in the warm hum of her portable hair dryer. The house was neither dirtier nor cleaner than when I left. I never asked how she spent the afternoon. I guessed she did normal surface cleaning, and spent a lot of time with the children; it's what she does when she feels guilty. For three days after that she made all the beds as soon as we got up in the morning; on the fourth day, without a word about *Uncle Vanya* or girls looking for bicycle pumps, or Cannonball Adderley, her slow momentum stopped, like a bicyclist going up a steep hill: she got off and walked the bike. Everything went back to below normal.

In that bar on the night she gripped my throat, really gripped it— and for how long would she have squeezed if I hadn't been able to push her away? she had right away shut off my windpipe—in that bar, I saw something: I saw her sitting with the *TV Guide* among those dishes, with that look of concentration which was real, yes, but it wasn't concentrating *on* something, it was concentrating away from her work. She was saying no. And I thought: Why, that's her word: No. It is what she said to the life that waited for her each morning, perched on the foot of the bed. She simply refused to live it, by avoiding work, by lying about it, and by—yes: I believed it: violence. It wasn't me she hated, me she wanted to kill: it was the questions I raised. Yet I couldn't really separate my questions from me any more than I could separate Terry from her house. She is what she does, I tell her; and I suppose, for her, I am what I ask. And that is why, I thought, our quarrels usually ended violently: because she could not or would not answer my questions about pots on the stairs and Sean lying in last night's piss. So she hit me.

And now tonight she was out with Hank and I remembered the day I found the pots and went up to the living room and told her and she went downstairs; I remembered how I stood at the window and watched the couple pushing their baby in a stroller; the girl was, as I have said, rather plain, and her breasts were a little too small, and her hips a little too wide, but I stood watching her, and that is what I wanted and what I have refused all the years to admit I wanted: a calm, peaceful life with that plain, clean girl pushing her stroller in the sunlight of that afternoon.

§3     SHE came home long after midnight, an hour and twenty minutes into a new Monday, coming through the back door into the kitchen, where I sat drinking bourbon, having given up on Tolstoy, sitting and sipping now. She stood just inside the door, looking at me, shaking her head: 'Not this way, Jack. Not after ten—' Then her eyes filled, her lips and cheeks began to contort, she bit off her voice and went to the refrigerator for ice. I stood, to go to her; but then I didn't move. I stood near the wall and watched her make the drink; her back was turned, her head lowered, the hair falling on both sides of her face, and I saw us as in a movie and all I had to do now was cross the room and take her shoulders and turn her and look into her eyes, then hold and kiss her. *We can try again*, I would say. And: *Yes, darling*, she would say: *Oh yes yes*. I stood watching her. When she turned, her eyes were dry, her cheeks firm.

'I've been drinking alone in DiBurro's, for the first time in my life, alone in a bar—'

'What happened?'

'Never mind what happened. I've been thinking about love, and I want to tell you this, I want to tell you these things in my heart, but I don't want to see your face. Your cold, guilty face.' She sat at the table, facing the back door; I leaned against the wall, waiting. 'All right then: I'll move.' She turned her chair so she was profiled to me. 'Don't worry, you'll get rid of me some day, but not like this, not this sordid, drunken adultery, do you know—no, you wouldn't because you never look at me—do you know that I drink more than any woman we know? I'm the only one who gets drunk as the men at parties. I'm the only one who starts drinking before her husband comes home. So you'll get rid of me anyway: I'll become a statistic. Because, you see, I don't keep a Goddamn Howard Johnson's for you, because I read a lot and, you know, think a lot, and I read someplace that booze and suicide claim many of us, us housewives; did you know that? No other group in the country goes so often to the bottle and the sleeping pill. I guess that's how they do it, with pills. Although as a child I knew a woman who played bridge with my mother, she shot herself one afternoon, a tiny hole in the temple, they said—from a tiny pistol, Daddy said, a woman's gun—she had been in and out of hospitals like others were in and out of supermarkets—maybe there's not much difference, they're both either a bother or terminal—and she was convinced she had cancer. That's what the ladies said, my mother and her friends, but they weren't known for truth, on summer afternoons they had chocolate Oreos and Cokes and talked of little things, said trump and no-trump and I pass; I used to walk through and see their souls rising with the cigarette smoke above their heads. Oh yes, they would rather believe relentless old cancer was eating the bones or liver or lungs of their dead friend than to believe one of the zombies in their midst had chosen one sunny afternoon to rise from the dead. She's the only suicide I've known. And I've only known one alcoholic, unless I'm one, which I'm not. I drink a lot at parties and on nights like this one when my husband sends me off to fuck his friend. I don't drink at lunch or early afternoon, but at ten in the morning a real lush will talk to you smelling of booze, a nice, pleasant enough smell but awfully spooky when the sun's still low and the dew hasn't burned off the grass, like in high school Sue's mother was an alcoholic, she was rich and lovely so maybe it was all right, she didn't really need to function much anyway. She always smelled of booze, she was usually cheerful and friendly, and you never saw her glass until five o'clock, at the cocktail hour. So much for statistics.'

She went to the sink and poured another bourbon.

'Don't you want to stop that?'

She turned with the ice tray in her hands.

'Give me a reason, Jack.'

I looked at her for a moment, then I looked around the room and down into my glass. She poured the drink and sat at the table and I watched the side of her face.

'A man must have done those statistics,' she said. 'They sound like a fraud. Because he was treating housewife like a profession, like lawyer or doctor or something, and that's wrong, he's including too many of us; if he had done the same with men, just called them all husbands, you can bet they'd have the highest rate. Most of them I know are pretty much drunks anyway, and they commit suicide in all sorts of cowardly ways; sometimes in the bank I wait in line and watch the walking suicides there, the men on my side of the counter and on the other, those lowered eyes and turned-down lips and fidgety glances around like God might catch them dying without a fight. So they should classify us if they must classify us by our husbands' jobs: how many pharmacists' wives are too drunk to cook at night? How many teachers' wives slit their fucking throats? But that wouldn't be accurate either. We are an elusive sex, hard to pin down. Though everyone tries to. I know: I have red hair. She has that red-headed temper, Daddy used to say. I was thinking about him tonight. Once when I was ten he took me fishing. We stood barefoot on the sand and cast out into the surf for flounder. The fishing rod was very long; I had to hold it with two hands and I shuffled forward with my side to the sea, and the rod was behind me almost dragging in the sand, then I arced it high over my head and the line went out, not as far as his but better than I had done before, and he said it: 'That's better.' I reeled in praying I'd hook one, please dear God for one sweet fish. Wasn't that absurd? To think the luck of catching a fish would make me somehow more lovable? Because then it'd follow that to be unlucky was to be unlovable, wouldn't it? And I must have believed that, as a child. And while I was drinking alone tonight I thought maybe I still believe that. But of course luck isn't an element in my life now. I don't fish or play cards; but there's always skill. So should I expect my cooking and screwing to make me more lovable? Maybe. I suppose a man can't be expected to love a woman who fails in the

kitchen and the bed. I'll admit that—even though I believe conversation and companionship are more important—but I'll admit that
first a man has to be well fed and fucked. 'Only God, my dear,
could love you for yourself alone and not your yellow hair.' What
if I cooked badly? Or were paralyzed and couldn't screw? Because
maybe then you do hate me for my house, because it's dirty sometimes—'

'I don't hate you.' She looked at me: only for a moment, then she
turned away and finished her drink and rose for another. 'Terry—'

'How would you know if you hate me? You don't even know
me. You say, 'You are what you do.' But do you really believe that?
Does that mean I'm a cook, an errand runner, a fucker, a bed maker,
and on and on—a Goddamn *cleaning* woman, for Christ sake? If
you—*you*, you bastard—' looking at me, then looking away '—lost
all discipline, just folded up and turned drunk and was fired, *I'd*
love you, and I'd get a job and support us too. Maybe no one else
would love you. You'd be a different man, to them: your friends
and your students. But not to me. I'd love you. I'd love you if you
went about at night poisoning dogs. So what is it that I love? If
action doesn't matter. I love you—' looking at me, then away '—I
love Jack Linhart. And I say you're more than what you do. But if
you love me for what I do instead of for what I am—there *is* a difference, I *know* there is—then what are you loving when I screw
Hank? Because if you love me for what I do then you can't want me
to be unfaithful because if I screw somebody else it's because I love
him, so either you don't love me and so you don't care or you don't
know me and you just love someone who looks like me, and what
you like to do is add to my tricks. Screw Hank. Shake hands. Sit,
roll over, play dead, fetch—loving me like a dog. Because I'm not
like that, I simply love a dog, I had dogs, four of them, they all dis-
appeared or died or got killed, like everything else around here, like
me, and I just *loved* them: fed them and petted them and demanded
no tricks. No fucking tricks! But not you.' She stood up and looked
at me. 'Am I right? You don't love me, you love the tricks? Is that
true? My stupid spaghetti sauce, the martini waiting in the freezer
when you come home in the afternoons, the way I for Christ's
sweet sake look and walk and screw?'

'I love Edith,' I said, and looked her full in the face; probably I
didn't breathe. Her face jerked back, as if threatened by a blow;
then she was shaking her head, slowly at first then faster back and
forth, and I said: 'Terry. Terry, yes: I love her. I don't love you. I

haven't for a long time. I don't know why. Maybe no one ever knows why. I'm sorry, Terry, but I can't help it, I—'

'Nooooo,' she wailed, and she was across the room, dropping her glass, tears now, shaking her head just below my face, pounding my chest, not rage but like a foiled child: she could have been striking a table or wall. 'No, *Jack*. No, *Jack*—' Then she shoved me hard against the wall and I bounced off and pushed her with both hands: she fell loudly on her back, her head thumped the floor, and I crouched with clenched fists, looking down at her frightened face and its sudden pain. She rolled on one side and slowly got up.

'Come on,' I said. 'Come take it.'

She looked at my face and fists, then shook her head.

'No. No, you're right: I've hit you too much. You're right to push me down. I've hit you too much.'

She went to the sink and stood with her back to me, bent over the counter with her head on her arms, one fist in a light rhythmic beat; after a while she turned. Tears were on her cheeks and she sniffed once and then again.

'All right. I won't cry and I won't hit you. Edith. So Edith then. All right. Jesus.' She looked around for her glass. I moved to pick it up from the floor, but she said, 'Oh fuck you,' and I straightened again. She took a glass from the cupboard and poured a long drink; the ice tray was empty. She went to the refrigerator and put the glass on top of it and opened the freezer compartment, then stood holding the door and looking in at the trays and vapor and frozen juice cans, and I thought then she would cry; but she didn't, and after a while she banged out an ice tray and went to the sink and ran water on the back of the tray and pulled the lever but the ice didn't come out; then she squeezed the dividers with her hands, then jerked back, dropping the tray and shaking a hand: 'I hate these Goddamn cutting ice trays.' She ran hot water again and worked the lever and got some cubes. Then she stood leaning against the stove, facing me across the table.

'That fucking bitch whore Edith. My fucking friend Edith. So up Terry. Alone then. I should have known. I did know. I knew all the time. I just wouldn't let myself know that I knew. How long have you been screwing her?'

'May. Late May.'

'Yes. I thought so. I thought so tonight going to meet Hank and I thought so while we high school screwed in the car, I saw you, the way you look at her like you haven't looked at me in years, and

I saw you screwing her and when Hank finished I told him I wanted to be alone, just to take me back to DiBurro's where my car was. Did you love me until you fell in love with Edith?'

'No.' I shook my head. 'No. I guess that's why I lo—'

'Don't say it! I don't have to keep hearing that. I—' She lowered her head, the hair covering her eyes, then she went to her purse on the table and got a cigarette and lit it at the stove, holding her hair back behind her neck. When she turned to face me she looked down at the gold wedding ring on her finger, then she twisted it as though to pull it off, but she didn't; she just kept turning it on her finger and looking at it.

'We must have had a lot of people fooled. A lot of people will be surprised. My boyfriend.' She let her ring hand fall. 'I'm thirty years old, I've lost my figure—'

'No, you haven't.'

'Don't, Jack. I've lost my figure, I'm not young anymore, I don't even want to be young anymore, I've become just about what I'll become—' I could not look at her: I went to the refrigerator needing motion more than I needed ale, and got a bottle and opened it and went to the door and stood half-turned, so my back wasn't to her but my face wasn't either. 'But there was a time when I wanted to be young again, I never told you that, I didn't see any reason to load you down with it. I remember once nursing Sean when he woke in the night in Ann Arbor, I had the radio on in the kitchen turned down low and listening to music and watching Sean, and of course I loved him but I was almost halfway through my twenties and I'd been married all that time. Then *La Mer* came on the radio and all at once I was back five years, the year before I met you, the summer I was nineteen and all of us used to go to Carolyn Shea's house because it was the biggest and her parents were the best, her mother and father would come and talk to us in the den where the record player was, she was just a little patronizing to the girls but not to the boys, only because she was a woman; but he wasn't patronizing to anyone at all. The boys would come over: Raymond Harper and Tommy Zuern and Warren Huebler and Joe Fleming, and sometimes they'd bring cherrystones, or steamers, and Mr. Shea would help them open the cherrystones and if they brought steamers Mrs. Shea would steam them and we'd sit in the kitchen with beer or wine. We were there all the time, all that summer, and no one was in love with anyone, we all danced and went to movies and the beach, and all that summer we played *La Mer*. When it came on the radio that night in Ann Arbor I thought of Raymond getting knocked off a destroyer at night and they never found him, and Tommy got fat and serious, and Joe became an undertaker like his father, and Warren just went away; and Leslie had an abortion, then married someone else and went to live in Nebraska, and Carolyn married a rich jerk from Harvard Law, and Jo Ann married a peddler and turned dumb to survive, and then there was me nursing my baby in Ann Arbor, Michigan, and I started to cry, loud and shaking, and I thought you'd hear and think Sean had died and I clamped my teeth shut but I couldn't stop crying because I knew my life was gone away because you didn't have a rubber with you because we'd never made love before—and isn't that tender and sweet to think of now? —and I was foolish enough to believe you when you said you wouldn't come inside me, then foolish enough not to care when I knew you were about to and I went to bed that night with Natasha alive in me and next morning when I woke I knew it. Then you got rubbers but every time I knew it didn't matter; I gave up hope, but I thought if I was lucky anyway, I'd start dating others. I would make love with you but I would date others. I was twenty years old. So now you say you don't love me. You love Edith.' Her lower lip trembled, then she spun around, her back to me, and slapped the counter with both hands. 'I won't cry. You bastard, you won't make me cry. I've given you my *liiife*.' She wiped her eyes once, quickly, with the back of a hand and faced me again. 'Oh, how I *hate* your Goddamn little girl students you bring in here to baby-sit, those naïve, helpless little shits, what I'd *give* for their chance, to be young and able to finish college and *do* something, I could be in New *York* now, I could be *any*where but *no*. I had to get *mar*-ried. I should have aborted—' Her voice lowered to almost a whisper, and she stopped glaring at me and looked somewhere to my side, her eyes fixed on nothing, just staring: 'I thought of it. I didn't get the name of an abortionist but I did get the name of a girl who'd had one, just by manipulating a conversation I got that done, but I didn't go on. Not because I was scared either. What I was scared of was being knocked up and getting married to my boyfriend. That's what you were: my boyfriend. But no, not Terry, she wanted to do the right thing. So I did. And now Natasha's here and so of course I'm glad I didn't kill her. After you see a child and give it a name you can never think about abortion. But I've wasted my life. I knew it all the time but I didn't let myself, I was going to make the best of it, I was going to keep on being a girl in love. All right, then. You're having an affair with Edith and you love her and you don't love me. All right. I won't cry and I won't hit you. When are you leaving?'

'I don't know.'

'You might as well go today.'

'I guess so.'

'Is Edith leaving?'

'We've never talked about it.'

'Oh, you must have.'

'No.'

'So you might be like the coyote.'

It was a joke we'd had from the Roadrunner cartoons; one of us trying something fearful and new was like the coyote: poised in midair a thousand feet above a canyon and as long as he doesn't look down he won't fall.

'It doesn't matter,' I said. 'I wouldn't take her from Hank anyway, if he wants her.'

'So it's not her: it's me. Well Jesus. I've been telling you and telling you you don't love me. But I never really meant it. I never believed it at all. Was it the house?'

'I don't know.'

'No. I guess you can't know, anymore than I can know why I still love you. Jack?' Her lip trembled. 'Don't you love me even a little?'

I looked above her, over the pots on the stove, at the wall. Then I closed my eyes and shook my head and said: 'No, Terry.' Then without looking at her I left. I went to the bedroom and undressed in the dark and got into bed. I heard her in the kitchen, weeping softly.

Sometimes I slept and all night she did not come to bed and all night I woke and listened to her. For a while she stayed in the kitchen: she stopped crying and I went to sleep listening to her silence, and when I woke I knew she was still there, sitting at the table under the light. I had not been heartbroken since I was very young; but I could remember well enough what it was like and I wished Terry were leaving me, I wished with all my heart that she had come to me one afternoon and looked at me with pity but resolve and said: *I'm sorry but I must go*— I wish I were now lying in bed grieving for my wife who had stopped loving me. I rolled one way and then another and then lay on my back and breathed shallow and slow as though sleeping, but I couldn't; I felt her sitting in the kitchen and I felt her thinking of me with Edith and me divorced laughing on a sunny sidewalk with some friend, and I felt her heart's grieving, and then I was nearly crying too. I sat up, slowly shaking my head, then lit a cigarette and lay on my back, listening to her silence, then my legs tightened, ready to go to her, but I drew on the cigarette and shook my head once viciously on the pillow and pushed my legs down against the mattress. Then I heard her taking pots from the stove: footsteps from the stove to the sink, and the sound of the heavy iron skillet lowered into the dry sink, footsteps again and this time the higher ringing sound of the steel pot and then higher again of the aluminum one. She began scraping one of them with a knife or fork or spoon. She knocked the pot against the inside of the plastic garbage can and started scraping another. Then she washed and dried them and hung them on the pegboard. She ran water into the sink and I lay staring into the night as she washed the dishes. She washed them quickly, then she was moving about and I guessed she was circling the table, wiping it clean, and after that the stove. Still she was moving with quick steps, into the laundry room and out again, to the sink, and she lowered a bucket into it and turned on the water; I swung my feet to the floor and sat on the edge of the bed. When she started mopping the floor I went to the kitchen. She knew I was there at the doorway but she didn't look up: she was bent over the stroking sponge mop, her head down, toward me; water had splashed on the front of her yellow dress; she was mopping fast, pushing ahead of her a tiny surf of dirty water and soap. Finally she had to stand straight and look at me. Her forehead was dripping, her hair was stringy with sweat, and I could not imagine her with Hank a few hours earlier.

'Come to bed.'

'No. I want to clean my house. I've been a pig and I've beaten you and thrown things at you. I know it's too late for you but maybe not for me, maybe I can at least be good for my babies. Or maybe you'll miss them and want to come back and the house will be clean. Couldn't you just stay and keep screwing Edith? Couldn't you be happy then?'

'You don't want that.'

'No, I guess not.' Mopping again, bent over. 'I don't know. Maybe I could change. Go to bed, love; I want to clean my house.'

I slept lightly. Sometimes I heard Terry moving about the house, and I felt the night leave and the day grow lighter and warmer; at one warm and light time I heard a vacuum cleaner beneath my dreams. When I heard the children's voices I woke up; but I would not open my eyes. I lay on my side and listened to their voices. After a while I heard Terry upstairs, in Sean's room above me. She was walking from one spot to another; then she pushed furniture across the floor. I opened my eyes and looked into the living room: Natasha was standing in the doorway.

'You should see the house.'

'What's she doing upstairs?'

'She just fed us and cleaned up our mess and now she's doing the upstairs.'

Sean called from the kitchen: 'Is that Daddy you're talking to?'

I winked at Natasha.

'Is that true you don't love Mom?' she said.

'Who told you that? The morning paper?'

'I heard Mom last night.'

'Oh? Who was she talking to?'

Sean came in, carrying a full glass of orange juice; he held it out in front of him, his forearm extended, and watched it while he stiffly walked to the bed.

'Thanks, chief,' I said, and kissed him.

'I couldn't hear you,' Natasha said. 'Just Mom.'

'Are you getting divorced?' Sean said.

'Wow. You really know how to wake a fellow up.'

Upstairs the vacuum cleaner went on. I imagined what Terry had got from under the bed.

'Natasha said you were leaving.'

'That's an idea. Where should I go? Join the Mounties?'

'I want to live with you,' Sean said.

'I'm not going to choose,' Natasha said.

'Ah me. You shouldn't listen to drunk grown-ups fighting, sweetheart. It's always exaggerated.'

'Mom said you were leaving and you love Edith and you screwed her.'

'Do you know what that means?'

'Yes.'

'What?' Sean said. 'What what means?'

'Nothing,' I said, looking at him and feeling Natasha's eyes on me. 'Just grown-up foolishness.' I looked at Natasha. 'Let's get on our bikes.'

'You haven't eaten yet.'

'Let's go to the river,' Sean said.

'We'll stop someplace where I can eat and you two can have something to drink.'

I told them to get the bikes out while I dressed. When they were gone, I called Edith to tell her I couldn't meet her. Hank answered. 'I can't run today,' I said. 'I'm sick. The flu. Tell Edith I have the flu and maybe she'll feel guilty for spreading it to her friends.'

White clouds were piled in the sky, and from the southwest gray was coming. I led Natasha and Sean in single file down our street, to the river. From our left the air was turning cooler and the gray was coming. We stopped at a small grocery store and got a quart of apple cider and stood on the sidewalk, drinking from the bottle and looking across the blacktop at the dark river.

'Is it true about you and Edith?' There was in her eyes a will to know, a look of deep interest; nothing more.

'Is what true?' Sean said. He was down there, below our voices and souls, looking at the river.

'It is and it isn't,' I said to Natasha's eyes. 'I don't know if I have the wisdom to explain it to a little girl I love.'

She took a quarter from her pocket and gave it to Sean.

'Go buy us something to eat.'

He hurried into the store.

'Where'd you get that?'

'My allowance.'

'I'll explain as well as I can,' I said. I watched her eyes. 'I don't want to abort it.' They hadn't changed.

'What's that mean?'

'To kill something before it's fully developed. Like a party you're planning. Or a baby inside the mother.'

'Oh.'

Now I remembered Terry lowering her voice: *I should have aborted;* even in her raging grief the old instinct of an animal protecting her young was there. Then I looked at the river and the lush woods on the other side, turning bright green as the gray and black moved faster over us; at the horizon the last puffs of white and strips of blue were like daylight under a tent wall; I turned from Natasha because there were tears in my eyes, not for her because she was strong and young and there was hope, but for Terry and her trembling lip: *Jack? Don't you love me even a little?* I am afraid of water; but looking out at the river I wanted suddenly to be in its flow, turning over once, twice, with the current; going down with slow groping arms, and hands opening and shutting on cool muddy death, my hair standing out from my head as I went bubbling down to the bottom. I shuddered, as much with remorse as fear. Then my wish was over. I stood alive again and breathed the rain-scented air and I knew that I would grow old with Terry.

'Mother and I have made mistakes,' I said. She was standing at my side, almost touching; I kept my eyes on the woods across the river. Sea gulls crossed my vision. 'You must trust us to make things better for everyone. Your mother and I love each other. She's a good and wonderful woman, and don't worry about anything you heard last night, people are all sorts of things, and one mistake is only a small part of a person, Mother's very good, and Edith is very good, and—'

'And so are you,' she said, and slipped her hand into mine and I couldn't go on.

The sky was completely gray now and it watched us ride home; we put our bikes in the garage and crossed the lawn and as we climbed the back steps it began to rain. We stood in the darkened kitchen and watched it coming down hard and loud. Sean was touching my leg. I tousled his hair, then turned on the light. The room changed: when it was dark and we had looked out at a day as dark as our kitchen, I had felt we were still out there in the rain, the three of us, somewhere by the river and trees; I could live in that peace, from one fresh rain-filled moment to the next, forever. Now with the light we were home again; our bodies were lightly touching but the flow, the unity, was gone. We were three people in a troubled house. I touched them and went to the bedroom. Terry was putting my clothes in a suitcase. She looked clean and very tired; she had showered and changed clothes. She tried to smile, failed, tried again, and made it.

'Was it awful?' she said.

'Was what awful? Why are you doing that?'

'I thought that's where you went. To tell the kids.'

I pushed the suitcase to make room, and lay on the bed; I would not look at her.

'Unpack it,' I said.

'Why? Couldn't you tell them?'

'I don't want to.'

'I'll call them in and we'll both tell them.'

'I mean I don't want to leave.'

She stepped closer to the bed and I was afraid she would touch me.

'You really don't?'

'No.'

'Is it the kids? I mean I know it's the kids but is it just the kids? You could see them, you know. Whenever you wanted. And I'd never move away, I'd live here as long as you teach here—so if it's just telling them, we can do it and get it over with, these things are always hard, but we can do it—'

'It's not that.' I shut my eyes. 'Unpack the suitcase.'

Across the bed I felt her pain and hope. I kept my eyes shut and listened to her moving from the bed to the closet and hanging up my clothes. Then she came around to my side of the bed and sat on the edge and put a hand on my cheek.

'Hey,' she said softly. 'Look at me.'

I did.

'It'll be all right,' she said. 'You'll see. It'll be all right again.'

She slept the rest of the afternoon, then woke to cook dinner; during dinner she and the children talked, and sometimes I talked with the children, but mostly I listened to their voices and the rain outside the window. After cleaning the kitchen Terry went back to bed and slept late next morning; then she called Edith and asked her to go to lunch.

'Do you have to?' I said.

She stood in the kitchen, in a short skirt and a bright blouse and a raincoat, looking pretty the way women do when they meet each other for lunch.

'I've loved her,' she said. 'I want to keep loving her.'

The rain had stopped for a while, but now it was coming down again. They were a long time at lunch; the children were bored, so I let them watch a movie on television. It was an old movie about British soldiers in India; I explained to the children that the British had no business being there, then we were all free to enjoy watching the British soldiers doing their work. They were all crack shots and awfully brave. The movie hadn't ended when Terry came upstairs and, smiling happily, said: 'Don't you want to come down?'

'Just for a minute. I want to see the rest of this.'

I followed her downstairs and put on some water for one cup of tea. Her face was loving and forgiving and I could not bear to look at her, I could not bear the images of her in warm collusion with Edith; for I could see it all: we would gather again in living rooms, the four of us, as though nothing had happened. And perhaps indeed nothing had.

'She wants you to go see her tonight.' Her cheeks were flushed, her eyes bright, and she smelled of bourbon. 'She's going to tell Hank, she's probably told him by now, she said he won't mind—'

'I know.'

Bubbles were forming beneath the water in the pot. I held the cup with the tea bag and waited.

'I told her about Hank and me, right away, as soon as I'd told her I knew about you two, and it's all right, I told her it was like her with you, because she wasn't trying to steal you or anything, it was to save herself, she said, and—'

'I don't want to hear it.'

'You don't?'

'No. I don't know why. I just don't.'

The water was boiling, and I poured it into the cup.

'I'm sorry,' I said. 'I'm sure it was a fine afternoon with Edith.'

'It was.' I looked at her. She was watching me with pity. 'It was wonderful.'

I went upstairs. Going up, I could hear the rifles cracking. That night I went to see Edith and Hank. They were drinking coffee at the kitchen table; the dishes were still there from dinner, and the kitchen smelled of broiled fish. From outside the screen door I said hello and walked in.

'Have some coffee,' Hank said.

I shook my head and sat at the table.

'A drink?' he said.

'Aye. Bourbon.'

Edith got up to pour it.

'I think I'll take in a movie,' Hank said.

Edith was holding the bottle and watching me, and it was her face that told me how close I was to crying. I shook my head: 'There's no need—'

But he was up and starting for the back door, squeezing my shoulder as he passed. I followed him out.

'Hank—'

He turned at his car.

'Listen, I ought to dedicate my novel to you.' He smiled and took my hand. 'You helped get it done. It's so much easier to live with a woman who feels loved.'

We stood gripping hands.

'Jack? You okay, Jack?'

'I'm okay. I'll be laughing soon. I'm working on the philosophy of laughter. It is based on the belief that if you're drowning in shit, buoyancy is the only answer.'

When I got back to the kitchen, Edith was waiting with the drink. I took it from her and put it on the table and held her.

'Hank said he'd guessed long ago,' she said. 'He said he was happy for us and now he's sad for us. Which means he was happy you were taking care of me and now he's sorry you can't.'

I reached down for the drink and, still holding her, drank it fast over her shoulder and then quietly we went to the guest room. In the dark she folded back the spread and sheet; still silent and standing near each other we slowly undressed, folding clothes over the backs of chairs, and I felt my life was out of my hands, that I must now play at a ritual of mortality and goodbye, the goodbye not only to Edith but to love itself, for I would never again lie naked with a woman I loved, and in bed then I held her tightly and in the hard grip of her arms I began to shudder and almost wept but didn't, then I said: 'I can't make love, I'm just too sad, I—' She nodded against my cheek and for a long while we quietly held each other and then I got up and dressed and left her naked under the sheet and went home.

Like a cat with corpses, Terry brings me gifts I don't want. When I come home at night she hands me a drink; she cooks better than any woman I know, and she watches me eat as though I were unwrapping a present that she spent three months finding. She never fails to ask about my day, and in bed she responds to my hesitant, ambivalent touch with a passion I can never match. These are the virtues she has always had and her failures, like my own, have not changed. Last summer it took the house about five weeks to beat her: she fought hard but without resilience; she lost a series of skirmishes, attacks from under beds, from closets, the stove, the vegetable bin, the laundry basket. Finally she had lost everything and since then she has waked each day in her old fashion which will be hers forever: she wakes passively, without a plan; she waits to see what the day will bring, and so it brings her its worst: puts and clothes and floors wait to be cleaned. We are your day, they tell her. She pushes them aside and waits for something better. We don't fight about that anymore, because I don't fight; there is no reason to. Except about Edith, she is more jealous than ever; perhaps she is too wise to push me about Edith; but often after parties she accuses me of flirting. I probably do, but it is meaningless, it is a jest. She isn't violent anymore. She approaches me with troubled eyes and says maybe she's wrong but it seemed to her that I was a long time in the kitchen with— I assure her that she's wrong, she apologizes, and we go to bed. I make love to her with a detachment that becomes lust.

Now that it is winter the children and I have put away our bicycles, oiled and standing side by side in the cellar, the three of them waiting, as Sean says, for spring and summer. We go sledding. The college has a hill where students learn to ski and on weekends it is ours; Natasha and Sean always beg Terry to come with us and she always says no, she has work to do, she will go another time. I know what it costs her to say this, I know how she wants to be with us, all of us going shrilly down the hill, and then at the top a thermos of chocolate for the children and a swallow of brandy for mama and papa. But she knows that with the children I'm happy, and she always says she will go another time. We sled and shout for a couple of hours until we're wet and cold, and when we come home with red cheeks Terry gives us hot chocolate.

Last week Hank sold his novel, and Saturday night he and Edith gave a party to celebrate. At noon that day Hank and I ran five miles; the sky was blue then; later in the afternoon clouds came and by night snow was falling. When I went up to his office he had finished writing (he has started another novel) and his girl was there; she is nineteen, a student, and she has long blonde hair and long suede boots and the office smelled of her cigarette smoke. Hank has not started smoking again. He is very discreet about his girl and I think only Terry and I know; we don't talk about it, Terry and I, because she can't. I know it bothers her that she can't, I know she wishes she were different, but she isn't. Edith knows too, about Hank and his girl; they don't lie to each other anymore.

'It's not love,' she said that night at the party. We had gone to the front porch to breathe and watch the snow. 'It's marriage. We have a good home for Sharon. We respect each other. There's affection. That's what I wish you could have: it's enough. It's sad, watching you two. She loves you and you never touch her, you don't look at her when you talk. Last summer, after we stopped seeing each other, I went to the zoo that week, I took Sharon to the zoo; and we went to see the gorilla: he was alone in his cage, and there were women with their children watching him. They're herbivores—did you know that? They're gentle herbivores. I don't like zoos anyway and I shouldn't have gone but it was such an awful week, finding out how to live this time, I'd been through that in May and then there was you and then in July there wasn't, so I took Sharon to the zoo. And I looked in the gorilla's eyes and he looked so human—you know?—as if he *knew* everything, how awfully and hopelessly and forever trapped he was. It's not like watching a flamingo. He was standing there looking at us looking at him, all the young mothers in their pants and skirts the colors of sherbet and the jabbering children. Then he reached down like this and shit in his hand. He was watching us. He held up the handful of shit—' and she held her hand up, shoulder-high, palm toward me '—and then he brought it to his mouth and licked it. His eyes were darting from side to side, watching us. They were merry and mischievous, his eyes. Then he licked it again. Around me the mothers were gasping and some of the children were laughing; then they all hurried away. Murmuring. Distracting their children. But I stayed, and he looked at me like he was smiling and then he showed me his shit again and then he licked it and then he showed it to me again; he almost looked inquisitive; but by then I was squeezing Sharon's hand and looking in his eyes and I was crying, standing there weeping on a sunny afternoon in front of a gorilla, and he watched me for a while, curious at first, and then he lowered his hand with the shit and we just stood looking at each other, he was looking into my eyes, and he knew that I knew and I knew that he knew, and if he could have cried he would have too. Then I left. And after a few weeks when I was able to see someone besides myself I'd see you and I'd think of that trapped gorilla, standing in his cage and licking his own shit. And I wanted to cry for you too—not just me, because I love you and can't touch you, can't be alone with you, but I wanted to cry for you. And I did. And I still do. Or at least I feel like it, I cry down in my soul. Oh Jack—are you trying at all?'

'There's nothing to try with.'

I could not look at her eyes, for I wanted to hold her and there was no use in that now. I moved to the window and looked in; from the couch Terry looked up and smiled; she held the smile when

Edith moved into her vision and stood beside me. I turned from the window. Around the streetlight the falling snow was lovely. Terry had stopped watching us after the smile; she was talking ardently with Hank and Roger, and I thought poised like that—a little high on bourbon, talking, being listened to, being talked to—she was probably happy. I raised my glass to the snow and the night.

'Here's to the soul of Jack Linhart: it has grown chicken wings and flaps near the ground.' I drank. 'I shall grow old and meek and faithful beside her, and when the long winter comes—' I drank '—and her hair is white as snow I shall lay my bent old fingers on her powdered cheek and—'

'I love you.'

'Do you still?'

'Always.'

'And live with Hank.'

'He's my husband and the father of my child.'

'And he's got a Goddamn— All right: I'm sorry. It's bitterness, that's all; it's—'

'I don't care if he has a girl.'

'You really don't?'

'Some women take up pottery, some do knitting.'

'Oh.'

'Yes.'

'I guess I didn't want to know that.'

'I'm sorry.'

'Jesus. Oh Jesus Christ, I really didn't want to know that. Course there's no reason for you not to have someone, when I can't, when I—Jesus—'

I went inside and got drunk and lost track of Terry until two in the morning, when she brought my coat. I told her I was too drunk to drive. In the car I smelled her perfume, and I thought how sad that is, the scent of perfume on a rejected woman.

'Edith has a lover,' I said.

'I know. She told me a month ago.'

'Do we know him?'

'Do you want to?'

'No.'

'We don't anyway.'

'Why didn't you tell me?'

'I didn't want to talk about it. I think it's sad.'

'It makes her happy.'

'I don't believe it.'

'Oh, you can't tell.'

'Please don't,' she said. She was leaning forward, looking into the snow in the headlights. 'I know you don't love me. Maybe someday you will again. I know you will. You'll see, Jack: you will. But please don't talk like that, okay? Please, because—' Her voice faltered, and she was quiet.

While she took the sitter home I sat in the dark living room, drinking an ale and looking out the window. In the falling snow I saw a lover for Terry. I went to bed before she got home and next morning I woke first. The sky had cleared and the snow was hard and bright under the sun. While I drank tomato juice in the kitchen Natasha and Sean came downstairs.

'Get dressed,' I said. 'We'll go buy a paper.'

'We should go sledding,' Sean said.

'All right.'

'Before breakfast?' Natasha said.

'Why not?'

'We've never gone first thing in the morning,' Sean said. 'It'll be neat.'

'Okay,' Natasha said. 'Is Mom awake?'

'No.'

'We'll write her a note.'

'Okay. You write it. And be quiet going upstairs.'

'We will,' Sean said, and he was gone up the stairs.

'What should I write?'

'That we're going sledding at nine and we'll be back about eleven, hungry as hell.'

'I'll just say hungry.'

I got my coat and filled its pockets with oranges, then went outside and shoveled the driveway while they dressed warmly for the cold morning.

# Over the Hill

§1    HER hand was tiny. He held it gently, protectively, resting in her lap, the brocaded silk of her kimono against the back of his hand, the smooth flesh gentle and tender against his palm. He looked at her face, which seemed no larger than a child's and she smiled.

'You buy me another drink?' she said.

'Sure.'

He motioned to the bartender, who filled the girl's shot glass with what was supposedly whiskey, though Gale knew it was not and didn't care, then mixed bourbon and water for Gale, using the fifth of Old Crow that three hours earlier he had brought into the bar.

'I'll be right back,' he said to the girl.

She nodded and he released her hand and slid from the stool.

'You stay here,' he said.

'Sure I stay.'

He walked unsteadily past booths where Japanese girls drank with sailors. In the smelly, closet-sized restroom he closed the door and urinated, reading the names of sailors and ships written on the walls, some of them followed by obscenities scrawled by a different, later hand. The ceiling was bare. He stepped onto the toilet and reaching up, his coat tightening at the armpits and bottom rib, he printed with a ballpoint pen, stopping often to shake ink down to the point again: *Gale Castete, Pvt. USMC, Marine Detachment, USS Vanguard Dec 1961.* He stood on the toilet with one hand against the door in front of him, reading his name. Then he thought of her face tilted back, the roots of her hair brown near the forehead when it was time for the Clairol again, the rest of it spreading pale blonde around her head, the eyes shut, the mouth half open, teeth visible, and the one who saw this now was not him—furiously he reached up to write an obscenity behind his name, then stopped; for reading it again, he felt a gentle stir of immortality, faint as a girl's whispering breath into his ear. He stepped down, was suddenly nauseated, and left the restroom, going outside into the alley behind the bar, where he leaned against the wall and loosened his tie and collar and raised his face to the cold air. Two Japanese girls entered the alley from a door to his left and walked past him as if he were not there, arms folded and hands in their kimono sleeves, their lowered heads jabbering strangely, like sea gulls.

He took out his billfold, which bulged with wide folded yen and tried unsuccessfully to count it in the dark. He thought there should be around thirty-six thousand, for the night before—at sea —he had received the letter, and that morning when they tied up in Yokosuka he had drawn one hundred and fifty dollars, which was what he had saved since the cruise began in August because she wanted a Japanese stereo (and china and glassware and silk and wool and cashmere sweaters and a transistor radio) and in two more paydays she would have had at least the stereo. That evening he had left the ship with his money and two immediate goals: to get falling, screaming drunk and to get laid, two things he had not done on the entire cruise because he had had reason not to; or so he thought. But first he called home—Louisiana—to hear from her what his mother had already told him in the letter, and her vague answers cost him thirty dollars. Then he bought the Old Crow and went into the bar and the prettiest hostess came and stood beside him, her face level with his chest though he sat on a barstool, and she placed a hand on his thigh and said *Can I sit down?* and he said *Yes, would you like a drink?* and she said *Yes, sank you* and sat down and signaled the bartender and said *My name Betty-san* and he said *What is your Japanese name?* She told him but he could not repeat it, so she laughed and said *You call me Betty-san;* he said *okay, I am Gale. Gale-san? Is girl's name. No,* he said, *it's a man's.*

Now he buttoned his collar and slipped his tie knot into place and went inside.

'You gone long time,' she said. 'I sink you go back ship.'

'No. S'koshi sick. Maybe I won't go back ship.'

'You better go. They put you in monkey house.'

'Maybe so.'

He raised his glass to the bartender and nodded at Betty, then looked at the cuff of his sleeve, at the red hashmark which branded him as a man with four years' service and no rank—three years in the Army and eighteen months in the Marines—although eight months earlier he had been a private first class, nearly certain that he would soon be a lance corporal, then walking back to the ship one night in Alameda, two sailors called him a jarhead and he fought them both and the next day he was reduced to private. He was twenty-four years old.

'I sink you have sta'side wife,' Betty said.

'How come?'

'You all time quiet. All time sink sink sink.'

She mimicked his brooding, then giggled and shyly covered her face with both hands.

'My wife is butterfly girl,' he said.

'Dat's true?'

He nodded.

'While you in Japan she butterfly girl?'

'Yes.'

'How you know?'

'My mama-san write me a letter.'

'Dat's too bad.'

'Maybe I take you home tonight, okay?'

'We'll see.'

'When?'

'Bar close soon.'

'You're very pretty.'

'You really sink so?'

'Yes.'

She brought her hands to her face, moved the fingertips up to her eyes.

'You like Japanese girl?'

'Yes,' he said, 'Very much.'


§2    **N**ow he could not sleep and he wished they had not gone to bed so soon, for at least as they walked rapidly over strange, winding, suddenly quiet streets he had thought of nothing but Betty and his passion, stifled for four and a half months, but now he lay smoking, vaguely conscious of her foot touching his calf, knowing the Corporal of the

Guard had already recorded his absence, and he felt helpless before the capricious forces which governed his life.

Her name was Dana. He had married her in June, two months before the cruise, and their transition from courtship to marriage involved merely the assumption of financial responsibility and an adjustment to conflicting habits of eating, sleeping, and using the bathroom, for they had been making love since their third date, when he had discovered that he not only was not her first, but probably was not even her fourth or fifth. In itself, her lack of innocence did not disturb him. His moral standards were a combination of Calvinism (greatly dulled since leaving home four and a half years earlier), the pragmatic workings of the service, and the ability to think rarely in terms of good and evil. Also, he had no illusions about girls and so on that third date he was not shocked. But afterward he was disturbed. Though he was often tormented by visions of her past, he never asked her about it and he had no idea of how many years or boys, then men, it entailed; but he felt that for the last two or three or even four years (she was nineteen) Dana had somehow cheated him, as if his possession of her was retroactive. He also feared comparison. But most disturbing of all was her casual worldliness: giving herself that first time as easily as, years before, high school girls had given a kiss, and her apparent assumption that he did not expect a lengthy seduction any more than he expected to find that she was a virgin. It was an infectious quality, sweeping him up, making him feel older and smarter, as if he had reached the end of a prolonged childhood. But at the same time he sensed his destruction and, for moments, he looked fearfully into her eyes.

They were blue. When she was angry they became suddenly hard, harder than any Gale had ever seen, and looking at them he always yielded, afraid that if he did not she would scream at him the terrible silent things he saw there. His memories of the last few days before the cruise—the drive in his old Plymouth from California to Louisiana, the lack of privacy in his parents' home—were filled with images of those eyes as they reacted to the heat and dust or a flintless cigarette lighter or his inability to afford a movie or an evening of drinking beer.

He took her home because in Alameda she had lived with her sister and brother-in-law (she had no parents: she told him they were killed in a car accident when she was fifteen, but for some reason he did not believe her) and she did not like her sister; she wanted to live alone in their apartment, but he refused, saying it was a waste of money when she could live with her sister or his parents without paying rent. They talked for days, often quarreling, and finally, reluctantly, she decided to go to Louisiana, saying even *that* would be better than her sister's. So he took her home, emerging from his car on a July afternoon, hot and tired but boyishly apprehensive, and taking her hand he led her up the steps and onto the front porch where nearly five years before, his father—a carpenter—had squinted down at him standing in the yard and said: *So you joined the Army. Well, maybe they can make something out of you. I shore couldn't do no good.*

§3      STRANGE fish and octopus and squid were displayed uncovered in front of markets, their odors pervading the street. The morning was cold, damp, and gray: so much like a winter day in Louisiana that Gale walked silently with Betty, thinking of rice fields and swamps and ducks in a gray sky, and of the vanished faces and impersonal bunks which, during his service years, had been his surroundings but not his home.

They walked in the street, dodging through a succession of squat children with coats buttoned to their throats and women in kimonos, stooped with the weight of babies on their backs, and young men in business suits who glanced at Gale and Betty, and young girls who looked like bar hostesses and, like Betty, wore sweaters and skirts; men on bicycles, their patient faces incongruous with their fast-pumping legs, rode heedlessly through all of them, and small taxis sounded vain horns and braked and swerved and shifted gears until they had moved through the passive faces and were gone. Bars with American names were on both sides of the street. Betty entered one of the markets and, after pausing to look at the fish outside, Gale followed her and looked curiously at rows of canned goods with Japanese labels, then stepped into the street again. Above the market a window slid open and a woman in a kimono looked down at the street, then slowly laid her bedding on the market roof and, painfully, Gale felt the serenity of the room behind her. Betty came out of the market, carrying a paper bag.

'Now I make you sukiyaki,' she said.

'Good. I need some shaving gear first.'

'Okay. We go Japanese store.'

'Where is it?'

'Not far. You sink somebody see you?'

'Naw. Everybody's on the ship now. They'll be out this afternoon.'

'What they do when you go back? Put you in monkey house?'

'Right.'

'When you go back?'

'Next week. Before she goes to sea.'

'Maybe you better go now.'

'They'd lock me up anyhow. One day over the hill or six, it doesn't matter.'

'Here's store.'

'You buy 'em. They wouldn't understand me.'

'What you want?'

'Shaving cream, razor, and razor blades.'

He gave her a thousand yen.

'Dat's too much.'

'Keep the rest.'

'Sank you. You nice man.'

She went into the drugstore. He waited, then took her bags when she came out and, walking back to her house, treating her with deference and marveling at her femininity and apparent purity and honesty, he remembered how it was with Dana at first, how he had gone to the ship each morning feeling useful and involved with the world and he had had visions of himself as a salty, leather-faced, graying sergeant-major.

§4 —*and she was gone for a week before we could even find her and even when we got out there she told us she wasn't coming with us, she was going to stay with him and it took your daddy about a hour to talk her into coming with us and you know how mad he gets, I don't see how he didn't whip her good right there, that's what I felt like doing, and it's a good thing that boy wasn't there or I know your daddy would killed him. I don't know how long it was going on before, she used to go out at night in your car, she'd tell us she was going to a show and I guess we should have said no or followed her or something but you just don't know at the time, then Sunday she didn't come home and her suitcase was gone so I guess she packed it while I was taking a nap and stuck it in the car. I hate to be writing this but I don't know what else a mothers supposed to do when her boys wife is running around like that. We'll keep her here til you tell us what your going to do, she don't have any money and daddy has the car keys. Tell us what your going to do, I hope its divorse because she's no good for you. I hate to say it but I could tell soon as I seen her, theres something about a girl of her kind and you just married too fast. Its no good around here, she stays in your room most of the time and just goes to the kitchen when she feels like it at all hours and gets something to eat by herself and I don't think we said three words since we got her back—*

He returned the letter to his pocket, lighted a cigarette, poured another glass of dark, burning rum that a British sailor had left with Betty months before, and looked at his watch. It was seven o'clock; Betty had been gone an hour, promising to wake him when she came home from the bar. During the afternoon they had eaten sukiyaki, Betty kneeling on the opposite side of the low table, cooking and serving as he ate, shaking her head each time he asked her to eat instead of cook, assuring him that in Japan the woman ate last; he ate, sitting cross-legged on the floor until his legs cramped, then he straightened them and leaned back on one arm, the other hand proudly and adeptly manipulating a pair of chopsticks or lifting a tumbler of hot *sake* to his lips. After eating she turned on the television set and they sat on the floor and watched it for the rest of the afternoon. She reacted like a child: laughing, frowning, watching intently. He understood nothing and merely held her hand and smoked until near evening, when they watched an American Western with Japanese dialogue and he smiled.

Now he rose, brought the rum and his glass to the bedroom, undressed, went back to the living room for an ash tray and cigarettes, then lay in bed and pulled the blankets up to his throat. He lay in the dark, his hands on his belly, knowing that he could not take her back and could not divorce her; then he started drinking rum again, with the final knowledge that he did not want to live.

§5     **H**E stood in the Detachment office, his legs spread, his hands behind his back, and stared at the white bulkhead behind the Marine captain. That afternoon, as his defense counsel told the court why he had gone over the hill, he had felt like crying and now, faced with compassion, he felt it again. But he would not. He had waited two weeks at sea for his court-martial and every night, sober and womanless and without mail, he had lain in bed with clenched jaws and finally slept without crying. Now he shut his eyes, then opened them again to the bulkhead and the voice.

'If you had told me about it, I would've got you off the ship. Emergency leave. I'd have flown you back. Why didn't you tell us?'

'I don't know, sir.'

'All right, it's done. Now I want you to know what's going to happen. They gave you three months confinement today. We don't keep people in the ship's brig over thirty days, so you'll be sent to Yokosuka when we get back there and you'll serve the rest of your sentence in the Yokosuka brig. So we'll have to transfer you to the Marine Barracks at Yokosuka. When you get out of the brig, you'll report there for duty. Do you understand all that?'

'No, sir.'

'What don't you understand?'

'When will I get back to the States?'

'You'll finish your overseas tour with the Barracks at Yokosuka. You'll be there about a year.'

'A year, sir?'

'Yes. I'm sorry. But by the time you get out of the brig, the ship will be back in the States.'

'Yes, sir.'

'One other thing. You've worked in this brig. You know my policies and you know the duties of the turnkeys and prisoner chasers. While you're down there, I expect you to be a number one prisoner. Don't give your fellow Marines a hard time.'

'Yes, sir.'

'All right. If you need any help with your problem, let me know.'

'Yes, sir.'

He waited, blinking at the bulkhead.

'That's all,' the captain said.

He clicked his heels together, pivoted around, and strode out. A chaser with a nightstick was waiting for him outside the door. Gale stopped.

'Son of a bitch,' he whispered. 'They're sending me to Yokosuka.'

'Go to your wall locker and get your toilet articles and cigarettes and stationery,' the chaser said.

Gale marched to his bunk, the chaser behind him, and squatted, opening the small bulkhead locker near the head of his bunk, which was the lower one, so that his hands were concealed by the two bunks above his and he was able to slide one razor blade from the case and hide it in his palm. He packed his shaving kit with one hand and brought the other to his waist and tucked the razor blade under his belt.

He rose and the chaser marched him to the brig on the third deck, where Fisher, the turnkey, took his shaving kit and stationery and cigarettes from him and put them in a locker.

'It's letter-writing time now,' Fisher said. 'You can sit on the deck and write a letter.'

'Sir, Prisoner Castete would like to smoke.'

'Only after meals. You missed the smoke break.'

'Sir, Prisoner Castete will write a letter.'

Fisher gave him his stationery and pen and he sat on the deck beside two sailors who glanced at him, then continued their writing.

He did not write. He sat for half an hour thinking of her scornful, angry, blue eyes looking at him or staring at the living room wall in Louisiana as she spoke loudly into the telephone:

*What do you expect me to do when you're off on that damn boat? I bet you're not just sitting around over there in Japan.*

*No! I haven't done a damn thing. Goddammit, Dana, I love you. Do you love me?*

*I don't know.*

*Do you love him?*

*I don't know.*

*What are you going to do?*

*What do you mean, what am I going to do?*

*Well, you have to do something!*

*It looks like I'm going to sit right here in this house.*

*That's not what—oh you Goddamn bitch, you dirty Goddamn bitch, how could you do it to me when I love you and I never even looked at these gooks, you're killing me, Dana, sonofabitch you're killing me—*

*Son. Son!*

*Mama?*

*She was going to hang up on you and you calling all the way from Japan and spending all that money—*

*Were you standing right there?*

*Yes, and I couldn't stand it, the way she was talking to you—*

*Why were you standing there?*

*Well, why shouldn't I be there when the phone rings in my own house and my boy's—*

*Never mind. Where's Dana?*

*In the bedroom, I guess. I don't know.*

*Let me talk to her.*

*She won't come.*

*You didn't ask her.*

*Gale, you're wasting time and money.*

*Mama, would you please call her to the damn phone?*

*All right, wait a minute.*

*What do you want?*

*Dana, we got to talk.*

*How can we talk when your mother's standing right here and you're across the ocean spending a fortune?*

*If I write you a letter, will you answer it?*

*Yes.*

*What?*

*Yes!*

*I got to know everything, all about it. Did you think you loved him?*

*I don't know.*

*Is he still hanging around?*

*No.*

*Dana, I love you. Have you ever run around on me before this?*

*No.*

*Why did you do it?*

*I told you I don't know! Why don't you leave me alone!*

*I'll write to you.*

*All right.*

*Bye. Answer my letter. I love you.*

*Bye.*

The letter-writing period ended and he handed the blank paper and pen to Fisher, who started to say something but did not.

Gale did not start crying until after he was put into a cell and the door was locked behind him and he had unfolded his rubber mattress and was holding one end of it under his chin and with both hands was working it into a mattress cover and he thought of Dana, then of himself, preparing his bed in a cell thousands of miles away, then he started, the tears flowing soundlessly down his cheeks until he was blinded and could not see his hands or even the mattress and it seemed that he would never get the cover on it and he desperately wanted someone to do it for him and lay the mattress on the deck and turn back the blanket and speak his name. He dropped the mattress, threw the cover against the bulkhead, unfolded the blanket, and lay down and covered himself, then gingerly took the razor blade from under his belt, touching it to his left wrist, for a moment just touching, then pressing, then he slashed, knowing in that instant of cutting that he did not want to; that if he had, he would have cut an artery instead of the veins where now the blood was warm and fast, going down his forearm, and when it reached the inside of his elbow he said:

'Fisher.'

But there was no answer, so he threw off the blanket and stood up, this time yelling it:

'Fisher!'

Fisher came to the door and looked through the bars and Gale showed him the wrist; he said sonofabitch and was gone, coming back with the keys and opening the door, pulling Gale out into the passageway and grabbing the wrist and tying a handkerchief around it, muttering.

'You crazy bastard. What are you? Crazy?'

Then he ran to the phone and dialed the dispensary, watching Gale, and when he hung up he said:

'Lie on your back. I oughta treat you for shock.'

Gale lay on the deck and Fisher turned a waste basket on its side and rolled it under his legs, then threw a blanket over him.

'Son of a bitch!' he said. 'They'll hang me. How'd you get that Goddamn razor?'

§6 THE doctor was tall, with short gray hair and a thin gray moustache. He was a commander, so at least there was that much, at least they didn't send a lieutenant. The doctor filled his cup at the percolator, then faced Gale and looked at him, then came closer until Gale could smell the coffee.

'You didn't do a very good job, did you, son?'

'No, sir.'

'Do you ever do a good job at anything?'

'No, sir.'

The doctor's eyes softened and he raised his cup to his lips, watching Gale over its rim, then he lowered the cup and swallowed and wiped his mouth with the back of his hand.

'You go on and sleep now,' he said, 'without any more silly ideas. I'll see you tomorrow and we'll talk about it.'

'Yes, sir.'

Gale stepped into the passageway where the chaser was waiting and they marched down the long portside passageway, empty and darkened save for small red lights, Gale staring ahead, conscious of the bandage on his wrist as though it were an emblem of his uncertainty and his inability to change his life. He knew only that he faced a year of waiting for letters that would rarely come, three months of that in the brig where he would lie awake and wonder who shared her bed and, once released from the brig, he would have to return to Betty or find another girl so he would not have to think of Dana every night (although, resolving to do this, he already knew it would be in vain); and that, when he finally returned to the States, his life would be little more than a series of efforts to avoid being deceived and finally, perhaps years later, she would—with one last pitiless glare—leave him forever. All this stretched before him, as immutable as the long passageway where he marched now, the chaser in step behind him, yet he not only accepted it, but chose it. He figured that it was at least better than nothing.

# The Doctor

§1        I N late March, the snow began to melt. First it ran off the slopes and roads, and the brooks started flowing. Finally there were only low, shaded patches in the woods. In April, there were four days of warm sun, and on the first day Art Castagnetto told Maxine she could put away his pajamas until next year. That night he slept in a T-shirt, and next morning, when he noticed the pots on the radiators were dry, he left them empty.

Maxine didn't believe in the first day, or the second, either. But on the third afternoon, wearing shorts and a sweat shirt, she got the charcoal grill from the garage, put it in the backyard, and broiled steaks. She even told Art to get some tonic and limes for the gin. It was a Saturday afternoon; they sat outside in canvas lawn chairs and told Tina, their four-year-old girl, that it was all right to watch the charcoal but she mustn't touch it, because it was burning even if it didn't look like it. When the steaks were ready, the sun was behind the woods in back of the house; Maxine brought sweaters to Art and the four children so they could eat outside.

Monday it snowed. The snow was damp at first, melting on the dead grass, but the flakes got heavier and fell as slowly as tiny leaves and covered the ground. In another two days the snow melted, and each gray, cool day was warmer than the one before. Saturday afternoon the sky started clearing; there was a sunset, and before going to bed Art went outside and looked up at the stars. In the morning, he woke to a bedroom of sunlight. He left Maxine sleeping, put on a T-shirt, trunks, and running shoes, and carrying his sweat suit he went downstairs, tiptoeing because the children slept so lightly on weekends. He dropped his sweat suit into the basket for dirty clothes; he was finished with it until next fall.

He did side-straddle hops on the front lawn and then ran on the shoulder of the road, which for the first half mile was bordered by woods, so that he breathed the scent of pines and, he believed, the sunlight in the air. Then he passed the Whitfords' house. He had never seen the man and woman but had read their name on the mailbox and connected it with the children who usually played in the road in front of the small graying house set back in the trees. Its dirt yard was just large enough to contain it and a rusting Ford and an elm tree with a tire-and-rope swing hanging from one of its branches. The house now was still and dark, as though asleep. He went around the bend and, looking ahead, saw three of the Whitford boys standing by the brook.

It was a shallow brook, which had its prettiest days in winter when it was frozen; in the first weeks of spring, it ran clearly, but after that it became stagnant and around July it dried. This brook was a landmark he used when he directed friends to his house. 'You get to a brook with a stone bridge,' he'd say. The bridge wasn't really stone; its guard walls were made of rectangular concrete slabs, stacked about three feet high, but he liked stone fences and stone bridges and he called it one. On a slope above the brook, there was a red house. A young childless couple lived there, and now the man, who sold life insurance in Boston, was driving off with a boat and trailer hitched to his car. His wife waved goodbye from the driveway, and the Whitford boys stopped throwing rocks into the brook long enough to wave too. They heard Art's feet on the blacktop and turned to watch him. When he reached the bridge, one of them said, 'Hi, Doctor,' and Art smiled and said 'Hello' to them as he passed. Crossing the bridge, he looked down at the brook. It was moving, slow and shallow, into the dark shade of the woods.

About a mile past the brook, there were several houses, with short stretches of woods between them. At the first house, a family was sitting at a picnic table in the side yard, reading the Sunday paper. They did not hear him, and he felt like a spy as he passed. The next family, about a hundred yards up the road, was working. Two little girls were picking up trash, and the man and woman were digging a flower bed. The parents turned and waved, and the man called, 'It's a good day for it!' At the next house, a young couple were washing their Volkswagen, the girl using the hose, the man scrubbing away the dirt of winter. They looked up and waved. By now Art's T-shirt was damp and cool, and he had his second wind.

All up the road it was like that: people cleaning their lawns, washing cars, some just sitting under the bright sky; one large bald man lifted a beer can and grinned. In front of one house, two teenage boys were throwing a Frisbee; farther up the road, a man was gently pitching a softball to his small son, who wore a baseball cap and choked up high on the bat. A boy and girl passed Art in a polished green M.G., the top down, the girl's unscarfed hair blowing across her cheek as she leaned over and quickly kissed the boy's ear. All the lawn people waved at Art, though none of them knew him; they only knew he was the obstetrician who lived in the big house in the woods. When he turned and jogged back down the road, they waved or spoke again; this time they were not as spontaneous but more casual, more familiar. He rounded a curve a quarter of a mile from the brook; the woman was back in her house and the Whitford boys were gone too. On this length of road he was alone, and ahead of him squirrels and chipmunks fled into the woods.

Then something was wrong—he felt it before he knew it. When the two boys ran up from the brook into his vision, he started sprinting and had a grateful instant when he felt the strength left in his legs, though still he didn't know if there was any reason for strength and speed. He pounded over the blacktop as the boys scrambled up the lawn, toward the red house, and as he reached the bridge he shouted.

They didn't stop until he shouted again, and now they turned, their faces pale and open-mouthed, and pointed at the brook and then ran back toward it. Art pivoted off the road, leaning backward as he descended the short rocky bank, around the end of the bridge, seeing first the white rectangle of concrete lying in the slow water. And again he felt before he knew: he was in the water to his knees, bent over the slab and getting his fingers into the sand beneath it before he looked down at the face and shoulders and chest. Then he saw the arms, too, thrashing under water as though digging out of caved-in snow. The boy's pale hands did not quite reach the surface.

In perhaps five seconds, Art realized he could not lift the slab. Then he was running up the lawn to the red house, up the steps and shoving open the side door and yelling as he bumped into the kitchen table, pointing one hand at the phone on the wall and the other at the woman in a bright yellow halter as she backed away, her arms raised before her face.

'Fire Department! A boy's drowning!' Pointing behind him now, toward the brook.

She was fast; her face changed fears and she moved toward the phone, and that was enough. He was outside again, sprinting out of a stumble as he left the steps, darting between the two boys, who stood mute at the brook's edge. He refused to believe it was this simple and this impossible. He thrust his hands under the slab, lifting with legs and arms, and now he heard one of the boys moaning behind him, 'It fell on Terry, it fell on Terry.' Squatting in the water, he held a hand over the Whitford boy's mouth and pinched his nostrils together; then he groaned, for now his own hand was killing the child. He took his hand away. The boy's arms had stopped moving—they seemed to be resting at his sides—and Art reached down and felt the right one and then jerked his own hand out of the water. The small arm was hard and tight and quivering. Art touched the left one, running his hand the length of it, and felt the boy's fingers against the slab, pushing.

The sky changed, was shattered by a smoke-gray sound of winter nights—the fire horn—and in the quiet that followed he heard a woman's voice, speaking to children. He turned and looked at her standing beside him in the water, and he suddenly wanted to be held, his breast against hers, but her eyes shrieked at him to do something, and he bent over and tried again to lift the slab. Then she was beside him, and they kept trying until ten minutes later, when four volunteer firemen descended out of the dying groan of the siren and splashed into the brook.

No one knew why the slab had fallen. Throughout the afternoon, whenever Art tried to understand it, he felt his brain go taut and he tried to stop but couldn't. After three drinks, he thought of the slab as he always thought of cancer: that it had the volition of a killer. And he spoke of it like that until Maxine said, 'There was nothing you could do. It took five men and a woman to lift it.'

They were sitting in the backyard, their lawn chairs touching, and Maxine was holding his hand. The children were playing in front of the house, because Maxine had told them what happened, told them Daddy had been through the worst day of his life, and they must leave him alone for a while. She kept his glass filled with gin and tonic and once, when Tina started screaming in the front yard, he jumped out of the chair, but she grabbed his wrist and held it tightly and said, 'It's nothing, I'll take care of it.' She went around the house, and soon Tina stopped crying, and Maxine came back and said she'd fallen down in the driveway and skinned her elbow. Art was trembling.

'Shouldn't you get some sedatives?' she said.

He shook his head, then started to cry.

Monday morning an answer—or at least a possibility—was waiting for him, as though it had actually chosen to enter his mind now, with the buzzing of the alarm clock. He got up quickly and stood in a shaft of sunlight on the floor. Maxine had rolled away from the clock and was still asleep.

He put on trousers and moccasins and went downstairs and then outside and down the road toward the brook. He wanted to run but he kept walking. Before reaching the Whitfords' house, he crossed to the opposite side of the road. Back in the trees, their house was shadowed and quiet. He walked all the way to the bridge before he stopped and looked up at the red house. Then he saw it, and he didn't know (and would never know) whether he had seen it yesterday, too, as he ran to the door or if he just thought he had seen it. But it was there: a bright green garden hose, coiled in the sunlight beside the house.

He walked home. He went to the side yard where his own hose had lain all winter, screwed to the faucet. He stood looking at it, and then he went inside and quietly climbed the stairs, into the sounds of breathing, and got his pocketknife. Now he moved faster, down the stairs and outside, and he picked up the nozzle end of the hose and cut it off. Farther down, he cut the hose again. He put his knife away and then stuck one end of the short piece of hose into his mouth, pressed his nostrils between two fingers, and breathed.

He looked up through a bare maple tree at the sky. Then he walked around the house to the Buick and opened the trunk. His fingers were trembling as he lowered the piece of hose and placed it beside his first-aid kit, in front of a bucket of sand and a small snow shovel he had carried all through the winter.

# In My Life

I had my hair in curlers all afternoon the day they electrocuted Sonny Broussard. Or the day before, I guess, because they did it at midnight. That seems in a way a strange time to do it, but when you think about it, it starts to make sense. Better for it to happen at night. At least I think I wouldn't want it first thing in the morning, staying awake all night, then dawn, then sunrise through the cell window and it waiting for me; I think I'd rather wait all day and see the sun set and the dark come and know now in the night I was going. But maybe that's only because I work nights and don't like mornings. His real name was Willard, he was big, and sometimes I still remember his weight on top of me and his smell of booze and nigger.

'I bet you liked it,' Charlie said once. 'I bet you twitched a little.'

'Shit. I was dry as a cracker. I just lay there and watched him with my legs like this and I was saying to myself *Dear Jesus* because I thought when he finished he'd cut my throat and that's why I wouldn't even shut my eyes.'

'Didn't he say nothing, all that time?'

'*There*. He said *There* when he finished. He said it twice. When he was leaving he stumbled, he was still pulling up his pants, and he knocked over the lamp—there used to be one over there on the dresser, a little lamp I had—and it broke and he started running. That's when I stopped being so scared and I wanted to kill him and I called the sheriff.'

Charlie is married. It seems after you get to be twenty-five there's nothing around but married men. I was married when I was eighteen, we had to, but I miscarried, and inside of two years I couldn't stand the sight of him. His name was Brumby, and I came to hate that name, and I would pronounce it hating. I'd say, 'Okay,

*Brum*by.' One morning I woke up and he was gone. I went in the kitchen and there was a note on the table, with the salt shaker resting on it. I was grinning when I picked it up. It said: *I'm sorry, I'll send money. Brumby*. I laughed, I was so glad he finally took it on himself to leave. But while I was laughing there was a little frost in my insides, listening to the quiet in the house. Then I turned on the radio and put water on for coffee. While it was dripping I took a shower, humming. I went naked to the kitchen, it was summer and already the morning getting hot; a mama blue jay was making a racket in the fig tree. I got a cup of coffee and a cigarette and turned up the radio so I could hear it in the bathroom and went back and made up my face. The radio was playing hillbilly. I took a long time with my face, I felt good and free, and I prayed: *Thank you sweet Jesus, don't let him change his mind*. He left me the car. That afternoon I went to town and bought a yellow dress at Penney's; when I got home I put it on and drove up the little white shell road through the pines to the highway. The Bons Temps was a mile down the highway and I went there and asked them if they needed a cocktail waitress and Mr. Breaux hired me because I'm pretty. Brumby sent me a money order for fifty dollars and asked if I was going to divorce him, and when I got around to it, I did.

The only time I ever missed him was around dusk and I knew it wasn't really him I missed. The sun would go down and I'd have the lights but it wasn't the same. But I was lucky: I'd be fixing supper about that time and getting dressed and made up for work. I'm glad I don't work in the day, especially in winter when it gets dark early. If I worked in the daytime I'd leave a light on when I left in the morning so it'd be there to come home to. We have Blue Law in our parish, so sometimes on Sunday afternoons I go see my sister and her husband in Opelousas or go to a movie and I always turn some lights on first, the overhead light in the kitchen and the floor lamp in the living room. On a good sunny day I can't even tell they're on, the sun comes in so bright in those rooms.

They took a long time getting around to killing Sonny, almost sixteen months after he walked in the front door (I keep them locked now and I have a dog that barks at niggers walking past on the road and a pistol that I at least know how it works) and did what he pleased and stumbled out drunk. So I had a lot of time to get over him; or it. Everybody at the Bons Temps was nice to me while it was still in the papers. Then I had my period. Then Earl came along: he was married, he was a postman, and on Friday and Saturday nights he played electric guitar in the hillbilly band at the Bons Temps. I'd say Earl saved me in a way. I still felt different, like I had sores or something, and I thought Sonny Broussard being a nigger would keep a man away; but then one Saturday night Earl came home for a cup of coffee with me and everything was all right. I woke up wondering if he still felt the same in the morning. He couldn't get out on week nights, so I didn't see him till Friday and as soon as he grinned I knew it was okay. So it was every Friday and Saturday nights for a couple of months, and I'd watch him get up and dress fast in the cold. In the morning I'd wake up late and lie there smoking and looking out at the frost on the grass that was left, and the brown earth, and beyond that the pines in the sun. Or some mornings it was doing that slow cold rain and I didn't want to get up and light the heaters, it was so cold, and I'd stay in bed a long time till I felt like the quiet was going to explode; then I'd get up and soon the bacon was sizzling and smelling. Then his wife found out and she even wrote me a letter calling me a hateful woman for carrying on with her man; the letter came to the Bons Temps and I read it thinking, *Her man? Why it wasn't even him, it was just a couple of times a week, about four hours all told.* But that was the end of it with Earl; his wife was waiting up for him. But I was all right then, Earl had taken care of me.

There was Vern between Earl and Charlie, while Sonny Broussard was waiting, and most of the time I didn't think about him; but sometimes I did and I wished it had come out at the trial that he had done other things too, robbery or maybe an old knifing, but he hadn't. It was just that one thing with me and I had called the sheriff, I had wanted him dead when he knocked over the lamp and ran; I wanted him dead when the sheriff and a deputy came, then went up the shell road way back up in the pines where some nigger shacks were; I wanted him dead when they caught him that same afternoon in Port Arthur, Texas; and I wanted him dead when I saw him in the courthouse. But when they said they would do it I felt funny, sort of like surprised, and scared too. Then, like I say, there was Earl and he didn't mind; and the trucker Vern that came home on a Friday night and stayed with me all day till time for work Saturday, then he was on the road again; I haven't seen him since but some day I hope to. Charlie is good to me, though. He's a big rough man and it doesn't matter if his wife waits up for him or not, he'll tell her it's none of her business where he's been. Once he stayed until the sun was coming up, and there were shadows from the pines.

They killed Sonny Broussard on a Thursday in March. In late afternoon I took my curlers out real slow, then the sun was going and I turned on the lights and put the rice on and played the radio; while I was brushing my hair I tried to picture him in the prison, they probably had every corner lighted up, and I wondered was he eating supper. I don't care about niggers one way or the other. I hated his smell and his black and his booze breath and him in me, I hated his panting and grunting over my face, and his big hands pressing mine back on the pillow. I'd never go with one on purpose. His lawyer wasn't much older than me, already getting sloppy fat and with a crewcut. He asked if I put up a fight; I said not much, I was scared he'd kill me. That was all he asked me about that. He mostly tried to show Sonny Broussard had a clean record and that night he was dead drunk.

Brushing my hair at the bathroom mirror I thought myself pretty and I wondered how long I'd be pretty, so many days and nights go by, and I forget where they go, and I wonder if it's like that to get old, if the time will come when I dye it black over the gray and if I won't be able to remember that Vern's last name was Mackey and that I knew him between Earl and Charlie in the winter of nineteen fifty-six. Then I thought about Sonny Broussard standing there when I woke up with my heart pounding and he dropped his pants and pulled back the sheet and spread my legs like parting canes in a canebrake and I was so dry but still he done it fast, maybe a couple of minutes like Charlie is first time around, then him saying *There. There.*

I thought maybe I could tell Charlie. But for a long time he wasn't at the Bons Temps that night; even for a Thursday there wasn't much of a crowd, not even enough people to change the air, so at eleven o'clock I could still smell the dance wax. I kept looking at the door and the clock. About eleven o'clock I got nervous and it got worse, I always had a cigarette going in my ash tray at the bar. Then about eleven thirty-five I was serving a table of four, my tray was wet and the quarters and nickels sticking, but still this fellow was prying up every one of them until his pressing on the tray made it hard to hold. When he had the last nickel, Charlie behind me said: 'Jill.'

I spun around and almost grabbed him. He was bigger in his mackinaw, a big broad face with thick reddish hair.

'I thought you wouldn't come.'

'Hell yeah,' he said. He was grinning.

Then for a while I talked to Charlie at the bar and waited table; I was still nervous but happy too because he'd be with me that night. I looked at the clock at five minutes to twelve while I was waiting for Curtis to mix a Vodka Collins and open three beers. Then I brought them to the table. The juke box had stopped so I took my quarter tip and punched three Hank Williams songs. It said one minute, and Hank was singing. I looked at the maybe twenty faces scattered about at the tables, there were some men together but mostly couples, older than me, and I watched their cigarettes and their hands and faces. I thought *Sweet Jesus*. I thought *I have felt his body and now they are going to burn it.* Then I thought *No.* Then I said it out loud, 'No,' and it was midnight.

We got home at one-fifteen and went into the kitchen that was lighted up. This time I didn't put on coffee, I said I'd drink with him a little, and I took from the cupboard the bourbon he kept there for his time with me. He was being careful, he wasn't sure how to treat me, he hadn't known tonight was the night until I went fast from the dance floor and stood beside him sitting so big on the bar stool and I put my face on his arm and said, 'He's dead, Charlie.' So now he made us some drinks, we had one in the kitchen, the next one in bed, naked under the covers, but I still wasn't sure I wanted to do anything. We were on our sides, looking at one another, propped on our elbows so we could drink.

'It was just a couple of minutes,' I said. 'That he was in me.'

'Yes.'

He was watching me, and I thought for a second how good it was that he was relaxed, not like Earl, he never hurried to leave.

'If they shot him that morning,' I said. 'Or if you'd known me then and you'd dragged him out of his shack and beat him up.'

'I would've.'

'Do you want another drink?'

'Nope.'

'Could we just lay here a while?'

'Sure.'

He put our glasses on the bedside table and lay on his back with one arm out for me and I got my head on it and lay half on my side so all of me was snug against him.

'Can you wait a while?' I said.

'There's other nights coming.'

'I've had eleven,' I said. 'I don't count him.'

'You're off to a good start.'

'One knocked me up and he was a slob,' I said.

Pretty soon I fell asleep. A long time later he woke me up and I said yes I wanted to. Over his shoulder there was pale light at the window.

# If They Knew Yvonne

*to Andre and Jeb*

§1  I grew up in Louisiana, and for twelve years I went to a boys' school taught by Christian Brothers, a Catholic religious order. In the eighth grade our teacher was Brother Thomas. I still have a picture he gave to each boy in the class at the end of that year; it's a picture of Thomas Aquinas, two angels, and a woman. In the left foreground Aquinas is seated, leaning back against one angel whose hands grip his shoulders; he looks very much like a tired boxer between rounds, and his upturned face looks imploringly at the angel. The second angel is kneeling at his feet and, with both hands, is tightening a sash around Aquinas's waist. In the left background of the picture, the woman is escaping up a flight of stone stairs; her face is turned backward for a final look before she bolts from the room. According to Brother Thomas, some of Aquinas's family were against his becoming a priest, so they sent a woman to his room. He drove her out, then angels descended, encircled his waist with a cord, and squeezed all concupiscence from his body so he would never be tempted again. On the back of the picture, under the title *Angelic Warfare*, is a prayer for purity.

Brother Thomas was the first teacher who named for us the sins included in the Sixth and Ninth Commandments which, in the Catholic recording of the Decalogue, forbid adultery and coveting your neighbor's wife. In an introductory way, he simply listed the various sins. Then he focused on what apparently was the most significant: he called it self-abuse and, quickly sweeping our faces, he saw that we understood. It was a mortal sin, he said, because first of all it wasted the precious seed which God had given us for marriage.

Also, sexual pleasure was reserved for married people alone, to have children by performing the marriage act. Self-abuse was not even a natural act; it was unnatural, and if a boy did it he was no better than a monkey. It was a desecration of our bodies, which were temples of the Holy Ghost, a mortal sin that resulted in the loss of sanctifying grace and therefore could send us to hell. He walked a few paces from his desk, his legs hidden by the long black robe, then he went back and stood behind the desk again and pulled down on his white collar: the front of it hung straight down from his throat like two white and faceless playing cards.

'Avoid being alone,' he said. 'When you go home from school, don't just sit around the house—go out and play ball, or cut the grass, or wash your dad's car. Do *any*thing, but use up your energy. And pray to the Blessed Mother: take your rosary to bed at night and say it while you're going to sleep. If you fall asleep before you finish, the Blessed Mother won't mind—that's what she *wants* you to do.'

Then he urged us to receive the Holy Eucharist often. He told us of the benefits gained through the Eucharist: sanctifying grace, which helped us fight temptation; release from the temporal punishment of purgatory; and therefore, until we committed another mortal or venial sin, a guarantee of immediate entrance into heaven. He hoped and prayed, he said, that he would die with the Holy Eucharist on his tongue.

He had been talking with the excited voice yet wandering eyes of a man repeating by rote what he truly believes. But now his eyes focused on something out the window, as though a new truth had actually appeared to him on the dusty school ground of that hot spring day. One hand rose to scratch his jaw.

'In a way,' he said softly, 'you'd actually be doing someone a favor if you killed him when he had just received the Eucharist.'

I made it until midsummer, about two weeks short of my fourteenth birthday. I actually believed I would make it forever. Then one hot summer night when my parents were out playing bridge, Janet was on a date, and I was alone in the house, looking at *Holiday* magazine—girls in advertisements drinking rum or lighting cigarettes, girls in bulky sweaters at ski resorts, girls at beaches, girls on horseback—I went to the bathroom, telling myself I was only going to piss, lingering there, thinking it was pain I felt but then I knew it wasn't, that for the first wakeful time in my life it was about to happen, then it did, and I stood weak and trembling and, shutting my eyes, saw the faces of the Virgin Mary and Christ and Brother Thomas, then above them, descending to join them, the awful diaphanous bulk of God.

That was a Tuesday. I set the alarm clock and woke next morning at six-thirty, feeling that everyone on earth and in heaven had watched my sin, and had been watching me as I slept. I dressed quickly and crept past Janet's bedroom; she slept on her side, one sun-dark arm on top of the sheet; then past the closed door of my parents' room and out of the house. Riding my bicycle down the driveway I thought of being struck by a car, so I rode on the sidewalk to church and I got there in time for confession before Mass. When I got home Janet was sitting on the front steps, drinking orange juice. I rode across the lawn and stopped in front of her and looked at her smooth brown legs.

'Where'd you go?'

'To Mass.'

'Special day today?'

'I woke up,' I said. 'So I went.'

A fly buzzed at my ear and I remembered Brother Thomas quoting some saint who had said if you couldn't stand an insect buzzing at your ear while you were trying to sleep, how could you stand the eternal punishment of hell?

'You set the alarm,' she said. 'I heard it.'

Then Mother called us in to breakfast. She asked where I had been, then said: 'Well, that's nice. Maybe you'll be a priest.'

'Ha,' Daddy said.

'Don't worry, Daddy,' Janet said. 'We don't hate Episcopalians anymore.'

I got through two more days, until Friday, then Saturday afternoon I had to go to confession again. Through the veil over the latticed window Father Broussard told me to pray often to the Virgin Mary, to avoid those people and places and things that were occasions of sin, to go to confession and receive Communion at least once a week. The tone of his whispering voice was kind, and the confessional itself was constructed to offer some comfort, for it enclosed me with my secret, and its interior was dark as my soul was, and Christ crucified stared back at me, inches from my face. Father Broussard told me to say ten Our Fathers and ten Hail Marys for my penance. I said them kneeling in a pew at the rear, then I went outside and walked around the church to the cemetery. In hot sun I moved among old graves and took out my rosary and began to pray.

Sunday we went to eleven o'clock Mass. Janet and I received Communion, but Mother had eaten toast and coffee, breaking her fast, so she didn't receive. Most Sundays she broke her fast because we went to late Mass, and in those days you had to fast from midnight until you received Communion; around ten in the morning she would feel faint and have to eat something. After Mass, Janet started the car and lit a cigarette and waited for our line in the parking lot to move. I envied her nerve. She was only sixteen, but when she started smoking my parents couldn't stop her.

'I just can't keep the fast,' Mother said. 'I must need vitamins.'

She was sitting in the front seat, opening and closing her black fan.

'Maybe you do,' Janet said.

'Maybe so. If you have to smoke, I wish you'd do it at home.'

Janet smiled and drove in first gear out of the parking lot. Her window was down and on the way home I watched her dark hair blowing in the breeze.

That was how my fourteenth summer passed: baseball in the mornings, and friends and movies and some days of peace, of hope —then back to the confessional where the smell of sweat hung in the air like spewed-out sin. Once I saw the student body president walking down the main street; he recognized my face and told me hello, and I blushed not with timidity but shame, for he walked with a confident stride, he was strong and good while I was weak. A high school girl down the street gave me a ride one day, less than an hour after I had done it, and I sat against the door at my side and could not look at her; I answered her in a low voice and said nothing on my own and I knew she thought I was shy, but that was better than the truth, for I believed if she knew what sat next to her she would recoil in disgust. When fall came I was glad, for I hoped the school days would break the pattern of my sins. But I was also afraid the Brothers could see the summer in my eyes; then it wasn't just summer, but fall and winter too, for the pattern wasn't broken and I could not stop.

In the confessional the hardest priest was an old Dutchman who scolded and talked about manliness and will power and once told me to stick my finger in the flame of a candle, then imagine the eternal fire of hell. I didn't do it. Father Broussard was firm, sometimes impatient, but easy compared to the Dutchman. The easiest was a young Italian, Father Grassi, who said very little: I doubt if he ever spoke to me for over thirty seconds, and he gave such light penances—three or four Hail Marys—that I began to think he couldn't understand English well enough to know what I told him.

Then it was fall again, I was fifteen, and Janet was a freshman at the college in town. She was dating Bob Mitchell, a Yankee from Michigan. He was an airman from the SAC Base, so she had to argue with Mother for the first week or so. He was a high school graduate, intelligent, and he planned to go to the University of Michigan when he got out. That's what she told Mother, who believed a man in uniform was less trustworthy than a local civilian. One weekend in October Mother and Daddy went to Baton Rouge to see L.S.U. play Ole Miss. It was a night game and they were going to spend Saturday night with friends in Baton Rouge. They left after lunch Saturday and as soon as they drove off, Janet called Bob and broke their date, then went to bed. She had the flu, she said, but she hadn't told them because Mother would have felt it was her duty to stay home.

'Would you bring me a beer?' she said. 'I'll just lie in bed and drink beer and you won't have to bother with me at all.'

I sat in the living room and listened to Bill Stern broadcast Notre Dame and S.M.U. I kept checking on Janet to see if she wanted another beer; she'd smile at me over her book—*The Idiot*—then shake her beer can and say yes. When the game was over I told her I was going to confession and she gave me some money for cigarettes. I had enough to be ashamed of without people thinking I smoked too. When I got home I told her I had forgotten.

'Would you see if Daddy left any?'

I went into their room. On the wall above the double bed was a small black crucifix with a silver Christ (Daddy called it a graven image, but he smiled when he said it); stuck behind the crucifix was a blade from a palm frond, dried brown and crisp since Palm Sunday. I opened the top drawer of Daddy's bureau and took out the carton of Luckies. Then something else red-and-white caught my eye: the corner of a small box under his rolled-up socks. For a moment I didn't take it out. I stood looking at that corner of cardboard, knowing immediately what it was and also knowing that I wasn't learning anything new, that I had known for some indefinite and secret time, maybe a few months or a year or even two years. I stood there in the history of my knowledge, then I put down the cigarette carton and took the box of condoms from the drawer. I had slid the cover off the box and was looking at the vertically arranged rolled condoms when I heard the bedsprings, but it was too late, her bare feet were already crossing the floor, and all I could do was raise my eyes to her as she said: 'Can't you find—' then stopped.

At first she blushed, but only for a second or two. She came into the room, gently took the box from me, put the cover on, and looked at it for a moment. Then she put it in the drawer, covered it with socks, got a pack of cigarettes, and started back to her room.

'Why don't you bring me a beer,' she said over her shoulder. 'And we'll have a little talk.'

When I brought the beer she was propped up in bed, and *The Idiot* was closed on the bedside table.

'Are you really surprised?' she said.

I shook my head.

'Does it bother you?'

'Yes.'

'You're probably scrupulous. You confess enough for Eichmann, you know.'

I blushed and looked away.

'Do you know that some people—theologians—believe a mortal sin is as rare as a capital crime? That most things we do aren't really that evil?'

'They must not be Catholics.'

'Some of them are. Listen: Mother's only mistake is she thinks it's a sin, so she doesn't receive Communion. And I guess that's why she doesn't get a diaphragm—that would be too committed.'

This sort of talk scared me, and I was relieved when she stopped. She told me not to worry about Mother and especially not to blame Daddy, not to think of him as a Protestant who had led Mother away from the Church. She said the Church was wrong. Several times she used the word love, and that night in bed I thought: love? love? For all I could think of was semen and I remembered long ago a condom lying in the dust of a country road; a line of black ants was crawling into it. I got out of bed, turned on a lamp, and read the *Angelic Warfare* prayer, which ends like this: *O God, Who has vouchsafed to defend with the blessed cord of St. Thomas those who are engaged in the terrible conflict of chastity! grant to us Thy suppliants, by his help, happily to overcome in this warfare the terrible enemy of our body and souls, that, being*

*crowned with the lily of perpetual purity, we may deserve to re-*
*ceive from Thee, amongst the chaste bands of the angels, the palm*
*of bliss. . . .*

Janet didn't do so well in the war. That January she and Bob
Mitchell drove to Port Arthur, Texas, and got married by a justice
of the peace. Then they went to Father Broussard for a Catholic
marriage, but when he found out Janet was pregnant he refused.
He said he didn't think this marriage would last, and he would not
make it permanent in the eyes of God. My parents and I knew
nothing of this until a couple of weeks later, when Bob was dis-
charged from the Air Force. One night they told us, and two days
later Janet was gone, up to Michigan; she wrote that although Bob
wasn't a Catholic, he had agreed to try again, and this time a priest
had married them. Seven months after the Texas wedding she had
twin sons and Mother went up there on the bus and stayed two
weeks and sent us postcards from Ann Arbor.

You get over your sister's troubles, even images of her getting
pregnant in a parked car, just as after a while you stop worrying
about whether or not your mother is living in sin. I had my own
troubles and one summer afternoon when I was sixteen, alone in
the house, having done it again after receiving Communion that
very morning, I lay across my bed, crying and striking my head
with my fist. It was a weekday, so the priests weren't hearing con-
fessions until next morning before Mass. I could have gone to the
rectory and confessed to a priest in his office, but I could not do
that, I had to have the veiled window between our faces. Finally
I got up and went to the phone in the hall. I dialed the rectory and
when Father Broussard answered I told him I couldn't get to
church but I had to confess and I wanted to do it right now, on the
phone. I barely heard the suspicious turn in his voice when he told
me to come to the rectory.

'I can't,' I said.

'What about tomorrow? Could you come tomorrow before
Mass, or during the day?'

'I can't, Father. I can't wait that long.'

'Who is this?'

For a moment we were both quiet. Then I said: 'That's all right.'

It was an expression we boys used, and it usually meant none of
your business. I had said it in a near-whisper, not sure if I could
speak another word without crying.

'All right,' he said, 'let me hear your confession.'

I kneeled on the floor, my eyes closed, the telephone cord stretched tautly to its full length:

'Bless me Father, for I have sinned; my last confession was yesterday—' now I was crying silent tears, those I hadn't spent on the bed; I could still talk but my voice was in shards '—my sins are: I committed self-abuse one time—' the word *time* trailing off, whispered into the phone and the empty hall which grew emptier still, for Father Broussard said nothing and I kneeled with eyes shut tight and the receiver hurting my hot ear until finally he said:

'All right, but I can't give you absolution over the phone. Will you come to the rectory at about three?'

'Yes, Father.'

'And ask for Father Broussard.'

'Yes, Father, thank you, Father—' still holding the receiver after he hung up, my eyes shut on black and red shame; then I stood weakly and returned to the bed—I would not go to the rectory— and lay there feeling I was the only person alive on this humid summer day. I could not stop crying, and I began striking my head again. I spoke aloud to God, begging him to forgive me, then kill me and spare me the further price of being a boy. Then something occurred to me: an image tossed up for my consideration, looked at, repudiated—all in an instant while my fist was poised. I saw myself sitting on the bed, trousers dropped to the floor, my sharp-edged hunting knife in my right hand, then with one quick determined slash cutting off that autonomous penis and casting it on the floor to shrivel and die. But before my fist struck again I threw that image away. No voices told me why. I had no warning vision of pain, of bleeding to death, of being an impotent freak. I simply knew; it is there between your legs and you do not cut it off.

§2 YVONNE Millet finally put it to good use. We were both nineteen, both virgins; we started dating the summer after our freshman year at the college in town. She was slender, with black hair cut short in what they called an Italian Boy. She was a Catholic, and had been taught by nuns for twelve years, but she wasn't bothered as much as I was. In the parked car we soaked our clothes with sweat, and sometimes I went home with spotted trousers which I rolled into a bundle and dropped in the basket for dry cleaning. I confessed this and petting too, and tried on our dates to keep dry, so that many nights I crawled aching and nauseated into my bed at home. I lay very still in my pain, feeling quasi-victorious: I believed Yvonne and I were committing mortal sins by merely touching each other, but at least for another night we had resisted the graver sin of orgasm. On other nights she took me with her hand or we rubbed against each other in a clothed pantomine of lovemaking until we came. This happened often enough so that for the first time in nearly seven years I stopped masturbating. And Saturday after Saturday I went proudly to confession and told of my sins with Yvonne. I confessed to Father Grassi, who still didn't talk much, but one Saturday afternoon he said: 'How old are you, my friend?'

'Nineteen, Father.'

'Yes. And the young girl?'

I told him she was nineteen. Now I was worried: I had avoided confessing to Father Broussard or the Dutchman because I was afraid one of them would ask about the frequency of our sins, then tell me either to be pure or break up with her and, if I did neither of these, I could not be absolved again. I had thought Father Grassi would not ask questions.

'Do you love her?'

'Yes, Father.'

'At your age I think it is very hard to know if you really love someone. So I recommend that you and your girl think about getting married in two or three years' time and then, my friend, until you are ready for a short engagement and then marriage, I think each of you should go out with other people. Mostly with each other, of course, but with other people too. That may not help you to stay pure, but at least it will help you know if you love each other.'

'Yes, Father.'

'Because this other thing that's going on now, that's not love, you see. So you should test it in other ways.'

I told him I understood and I would talk to my girl about it. I never did, though. Once in a while Yvonne confessed but I have no idea what she told the priest, for she did not see things the way I saw them. One night, when I tried to stop us short, she pulled my hand back to its proper place and held it there until she was ready for it to leave. Then she reached to the dashboard for a cigarette, tapped it, and paused as though remembering to offer me one.

'Don't you want me to do it for you?' she said.

'No, I'm all right.'

She smoked for a while, her head on my shoulder.

'Do you really think it's a worse sin when it happens to you?' she said.

'Yes.'

'Why?'

I told her what the Brothers had taught me.

'You believe that?' she said. 'That God gave you this seed just to have babies with, and if you waste it He'll send you to hell?'

'I guess so.'

'You have wet dreams, don't you?'

'That's different. There's no will involved.'

'What about me? It just happened to me, and I didn't use up any eggs or anything, so where's my sin?'

'I don't know. Maybe sins are different for girls.'

'Then it wouldn't be a sin for me to masturbate either. Right? I don't, but isn't that true?'

'I never thought of that.'

'Well, don't. You think too much already.'

'Maybe you don't think enough.'

'You're right: I don't.'

'I'll tell you why it's a sin,' I said. 'Because it's reserved for married people.'

'Climax?'

'Yes.'

'But you're supposed to be married to touch each other too,' she said. 'So why draw the line at climax? I mean, why get all worked up and then stop and think that's good?'

'You're right. We shouldn't do any of it.'

'Oh, I'm not sure it's as bad as all that.'

'You're not? You don't think it's a sin, what we do?'

'Maybe a little, but it's not as bad as a lot of other things.'

'It's a mortal sin.'

'I don't think so. I believe it's a sin to talk about a girl, but I don't think what you do with her is so bad.'

'All right: if that's what you think, why don't we just go all the way?'

She sat up to throw her cigarette out the window, then she nestled her face on my chest.

'Because I'm scared,' she said.

'Of getting pregnant?'

'I don't think so. I'm just scared of not being a virgin, that's all.'

Then she finished our argument, won it, soaked her small handkerchief in my casuistry. Next morning at breakfast I was tired.

'You're going to ruin your health,' Mother said. 'It was after one when you got home.'

I flexed my bicep and said I was fine. But now Daddy was watching me from his end of the table.

'I don't care about your health,' he said. 'I just hope you know more than Janet did.'

'*Honey*,' Mother said.

'She got it reversed. She started babies before she was married, then quit.'

That was true. Her twin boys were four now, and there were no other children. Bob had finished his undergraduate work and was going to start work on a Ph.D. in political science. Early in the summer Mother had gone up there and stayed two weeks. When she got back and talked about her visit she looked nervous, as though she were telling a lie, and a couple of times I walked into the kitchen where Mother and Daddy were talking and they stopped until I had got what I wanted and left.

'I won't get pregnant,' I said.

'Neither will Yvonne,' Daddy said. 'As long as you keep your pants on.'

Then finally one night in early fall we drove away from her house, where we had parked for some time, and I knew she would not stop me, because by leaving her house she was risking questions from her parents, and by accepting that she was accepting the other risk too. I drove out to a country road, over a vibrating wooden bridge, the bayou beneath us dark as earth on that moonless night, on through black trees until I found a dirt road into the woods, keeping my hand on her small breast as I turned and cut off the ignition and headlights. In a moment she was naked on the car seat, then I was out of my clothes, even the socks, and seeing her trusting face and shockingly white body I almost dressed and took her home but then she said: Love me, Harry, love me—

The Brothers hadn't prepared me for this. If my first time had been with a whore, their training probably would have worked, for that was the sort of lust they focused on. But they were no match for Yvonne, and next morning I woke happier than I had ever been. At school that day we drank coffee and held hands and whispered. That night on the way to her house I stopped at a service station and bought a package of condoms from a machine in the men's room. That was the only time I felt guilty. But I was at least perceptive enough to know why: condoms, like masturbation and whores, were something the Brothers knew about. I left that piss-smelling room, walked into the clear autumn night, and drove to Yvonne's, where they had never been.

For the rest of the fall and a few weeks of winter, we were hot and happy lovers. I marveled at my own joy, my lack of remorse. Once, after a few weeks, I asked her if she ever felt bad. It was late at night and we were sitting at a bar, eating oysters on the half-shell. For a moment she didn't know what I meant, then she smiled.

'I feel wonderful,' she said.

She dipped her last oyster in the sauce, and leaned over the tray to eat it.

'Do we have enough money for more?' she said.

'Sure.'

They were ninety cents a dozen. We watched the Negro open them, and I felt fine, eating oysters and drinking beer at one in the morning, having made love an hour ago to this pretty girl beside me. I looked at her hair and wondered if she ought to let it grow.

'Sometimes I worry though,' she said.

'Getting pregnant?'

'Nope, I never said you had to use those things. I worry about you.'

'Why me?'

'Because you used to think about sins so much, and now you don't.'

'That's because I love you.'

She licked the red sauce from her fingers, then took my hand, squeezed it, and drank some beer.

'I'm afraid someday you'll start feeling bad again, then you'll hate me.'

She was right to look for defeat in that direction, to expect me to move along clichéd routes. But, as it turned out, it wasn't guilt that finally soured us. After a couple of months I simply began noticing things.

I saw that she didn't really like football. She only enjoyed the games because they gave her a chance to dress up, and there was a band, and a crowd of students, and it was fun to keep a flask hidden while you poured bourbon into a paper cup. She cheered with the rest of us, but she wasn't cheering for the same thing. She cheered because we were there, and a young man had run very fast with a football. Once we stood up to watch an end chasing a long pass: when he dived for it, caught it, and skidded on the ground, she turned happily to me and brushed her candied apple against my sleeve. Watch out, I said. She spit on her handkerchief and rubbed the sticky wool. She loved sweets, always asked me to buy her Mounds or Hersheys at the movies, and once in a while she'd get a pimple which she tried to conceal with powder. I felt loose flesh at her waist when we danced, and walking beside her on the campus one afternoon I looked down and saw her belly pushing against her tight skirt; I lightly backhanded it and told her to suck her gut in. She stood at attention, saluted, then gave me the finger. I'm about to start my period, she said. Except for the soft flesh at her waist she was rather thin, and when she lay on her back her naked breasts spread and flattened, as though they were melting.

Around the end of November her parents spent a weekend with relatives in Houston, leaving Yvonne to take care of her sister and brother, who were fourteen and eleven. They left Saturday morning, and that night Yvonne cooked for me. She was dressed up, black cocktail dress, even heels, and she was disappointed when she saw I hadn't worn a coat. But she didn't say anything. She had already fed her brother and sister, and they were in the den at the back of the house, watching television. Yvonne had a good fire in the living room fireplace, and on the coffee table she had bourbon, a pitcher of water, a bucket of ice, and a sugar bowl.

'Like they do in Faulkner,' she said, and we sat on the couch and drank a couple of toddies before dinner. Then she left me for a while and I looked into the fire, hungry and horny, and wondered what time the brother and sister would go to bed and if Yvonne would do it while they were sleeping. She came back to the living room, smiled, blushed, and said: 'If you're brave enough, I am. Want to try it?'

We ate by candlelight: oyster cocktails, then a roast with rice and thick dark gravy, garlic-tinged. We had lemon ice-box pie and went back to the fireplace with second cups of coffee.

'I love to cook,' she said from the record player. She put on about five albums, and I saw that we were supposed to sit at the fire and talk for the rest of the evening. The first album was Jackie Gleason, *Music, Martinis, and Memories*, and she sat beside me, took my hand and sipped her coffee. She rested her head on the back of the couch, but I didn't like to handle a coffee cup leaning back that way, so I withdrew my hand from hers and hunched forward over the coffee table.

'I think I started cooking when I was seven,' she said to my back. 'No, let's see, I was eight—' I looked down at her crossed legs, the black dress just covering her knees, then looked at the fire. 'When we lived in Baton Rouge. I had a children's cookbook and I made something called Chili Concoction. Everybody was nice about it, and Daddy ate two helpings for supper and told me to save the rest for breakfast and he'd eat it with eggs. He did, too. Then I made something called a strawberry minute pie, and I think it was pretty good. I'll make it for you some time.'

'Okay.'

I was still hunched over drinking coffee, so I wasn't looking at her. I finished the coffee and she asked if I wanted more, and that irritated me, so I didn't know whether to say yes or no. I said I guess so. Then watching her leave with my cup, I disliked myself and her too. For if I wasn't worthy of the evening, then wasn't she stupid and annoyingly vulnerable to give it to me? The next album was Sinatra; I finished my coffee, then leaned back so our shoulders touched, our hands together in her lap, and we listened. Once she took a drag from my cigarette and I said keep it, and lit another. The third album was Brubeck. She put some more ice in the bucket, I made toddies, and she asked if I understood *The Bear*. I shrugged and said probably not. She had finished it the day before, and she started talking about it.

'Hey,' I said. 'When are they going to sleep?'

She was surprised, and again I disliked myself and her too. Then she was hurt, and she looked at her lap and said she didn't know, but she couldn't make love anyway, not here in the house, even if they were sleeping.

'We can leave for a while,' I said. 'We won't go far.'

She kept looking at her lap, at our clasped hands.

'They'll be all right,' I said.

Then she looked into my eyes and I looked away and she said: 'Okay, I'll tell them.'

When she came back with a coat over her arm I was waiting at the door, my jacket zipped, the car key in my hand.

We broke up in January, about a week after New Year's. I don't recall whether we fought, or kissed goodbye, or sat in a car staring mutely out the windows. But I do remember when the end started; or, rather, when Yvonne decided to recognize it.

On New Year's Eve a friend of ours gave a party. His parents were out of town, so everyone got drunk. It was an opportunity you felt obliged not to pass up. Two or three girls got sick and had to have their faces washed and be walked outside in the cold air. When Yvonne got drunk it was a pleasant drunk, and I took her upstairs. I think no one noticed: it was past midnight, and people were hard to account for. We lay on the bed in the master bedroom, Yvonne with her skirt pulled up, her pants off, while I performed in shirt, sweater, and socks. She was quiet as we stood in the dark room, taking our pants off, and she didn't answer my whispered Happy New Year as we began to make love, for the first time, on a bed. Then, moving beneath me, she said in a voice so incongruous with her body that I almost softened but quickly got it back, shutting my ears to what I had heard: This is all we ever do, Harry—this is all we ever do.

The other thing I remember about that night is a time around three in the morning. A girl was cooking hamburgers, I was standing in the kitchen doorway talking to some boys, and Yvonne was sitting alone at the kitchen table. There were other people talking in the kitchen, but she wasn't listening; she moved only to tap ashes and draw on her cigarette, then exhaled into the space that held her gaze. She looked older than twenty, quite lonely and sad, and I pitied her. But there was something else: I knew she would never make love to me again. Maybe that is why, as a last form of possession, I told. It could not have been more than an hour later, I was drunker, and in the bathroom I one-upped three friends who were bragging about feeling tits of drunken girls. I told them I had taken Yvonne upstairs and screwed her. To add history to it, I even told them what she had said.

§3      WAITING in line for my first confession in five months I felt some guilt but I wasn't at all afraid. I only had to confess sexual intercourse, and there was nothing shameful about that, nothing unnatural. It was a man's sin. Father Broussard warned me never to see this girl again (that's what he called her: this girl), for a man is weak and he needs much grace to turn away from a girl who will give him her body. He said I must understand it was a serious sin because sexual intercourse was given by God to married couples for the procreation of children and we had stolen it and used it wrongfully, for physical pleasure, which was its secondary purpose. I knew that in some way I had sinned, but Father Broussard's definition of that sin fell short and did not sound at all like what I had done with Yvonne. So when I left the confessional I still felt unforgiven.

The campus was not a very large one, but it was large enough so you could avoid seeing someone. I stopped going to the student center for coffee, and we had no classes together; we only saw each other once in a while, usually from a distance, walking between buildings. We exchanged waves and the sort of smile you cut into your face at times like that. The town was small too, so occasionally I saw her driving around, looking for a parking place or something. Then after a while I wanted to see her, and I started going to the student center again, but she didn't drink coffee there anymore. In a week or so I realized that I didn't really want to see her: I wanted her to be happy, and if I saw her there was nothing I could say to help that.

Soon I was back to the old private vice, though now it didn't seem a vice but an indulgence, not as serious as smoking or even drinking, closer to eating an ice cream sundae before bed every night. That was how I felt about it, like I had eaten two scoops of ice cream with thick hot fudge on it, and after a couple of bites it wasn't good anymore but I finished it anyway, thinking of calories. It was a boring little performance and it didn't seem worth thinking about, one way or the other. But I told it in the confessional, so I could still receive the Eucharist. Then one day in spring I told the number of my sins as though I were telling the date of my birth, my height, and weight, and Father Broussard said quickly and sternly: 'Are you sorry for these sins?'

'Yes, Father,' I said, but then I knew it was a lie. He was asking me if I had a firm resolve to avoid this sin in the future when I said: 'No, Father.'

'No what? You can't avoid it?'

'I mean no, Father, I'm not really sorry. I don't even think it's a sin.'

'Oh, I see. You don't have the discipline to stop, so you've decided it's not a sin. Just like that, you've countermanded God's law. Do you want absolution?'

'Yes, Father. I want to receive Communion.'

'You can't. You're living in mortal sin, and I cannot absolve you while you keep this attitude. I want you to think very seriously—'

But I wasn't listening. I was looking at the crucifix and waiting for his voice to stop so I could leave politely and try to figure out what to do next. Then he stopped talking, and I said: 'Yes, Father.'

'*What?*' he said. '*What?*'

I went quickly through the curtains, out of the confessional, out of the church.

On Sundays I went to Mass but did not receive the Eucharist. I thought I could but I was afraid that as soon as the Host touched my tongue I would suddenly realize I had been wrong, and then I'd be receiving Christ with mortal sin on my soul. Mother didn't receive either. I prayed for her and hoped she'd soon have peace, even if it meant early menopause. By now I agreed with Janet, and I wished she'd write Mother a letter and convince her that she wasn't evil. I thought Mother was probably praying for Janet, who had gone five years without bearing a child.

It was June, school was out, and I did not see Yvonne at all. I was working with a surveying crew, running a hundred-foot chain through my fingers, cutting trails with a machete, eating big lunches from paper bags, and waiting for something to happen. There were two alternatives, and I wasn't phony enough for the first or brave enough for the second: I could start confessing again, the way I used to, or I could ignore the confessional and simply receive Communion. But nothing happened and each Sunday I stayed with Mother in the pew while the others went up to the altar rail.

Then Janet came home. She wrote that Bob had left her, had moved in with his girlfriend—a graduate student—and she and the boys were coming home on the bus. That was the news waiting for me when I got home from work, Mother handing me the letter as I came through the front door, both of them watching me as I read it. Then Daddy cursed, Mother started crying again, and I took a beer out to the front porch. After a while Daddy came out too and we sat without talking and drank beer until Mother called us to supper. Daddy said, 'That son of a bitch,' and we went inside.

By the time Janet and the boys rode the bus home from Ann Arbor, Mother was worried about something else: the Church, because now Janet was twenty-three years old and getting a divorce and if she ever married again she was out of the Church. Unless Bob died, and Daddy said he didn't care what the Church thought about divorce, but it seemed a good enough reason for him to go up to Ann Arbor, Michigan, and shoot Bob Mitchell between the eyes. So while Janet and Paul and Lee were riding south on the Greyhound, Mother was going to daily Mass and praying for some answer to Janet's future.

But Janet had already taken care of that too. When she got off the bus I knew she'd be getting married again some day: she had gained about ten pounds, probably from all that cheap food while Bob went to school, but she had always been on the lean side anyway and now she looked better than I remembered. Her hair was long, about halfway down her back. The boys were five years old now, and I was glad she hadn't had any more, because they seemed to be good little boys and not enough to scare off a man. We took them home—it was a Friday night—and Daddy gave Janet a tall drink of bourbon and everybody talked as though nothing had happened. Then we ate shrimp *étouffée* and after supper, when the boys were in bed and the rest of us were in the living room, Janet said by God it was the best meal she had had in five years, and next time she was going to marry a man who liked Louisiana cooking. When she saw the quick look in Mother's eyes, she said: 'We didn't get married in the Church, Mama. I just told you we did so you wouldn't worry.'

'You *didn't?*'

'Bob was so mad at Father Broussard he wouldn't try again. He's not a Catholic, you know.'

'There's more wrong with him than that,' Daddy said.

'So I can still get married in the Church,' Janet said. 'To somebody else.'

'But Janet—'

'Wait,' Daddy said. 'Wait. You've been praying for days so Janet could stop living with that son of a bitch and still save her soul. Now you got it—right?'

'But—'

'Right?'

'Well,' Mother said, 'I guess so.'

They went to bed about an hour past their usual time, but Janet and I stayed up drinking gin and tonic in the kitchen, with the door closed so we wouldn't keep anybody awake. At first she just talked about how glad she was to be home, even if the first sign of it was the Negroes going to the back of the bus. She loved this hot old sticky night, she said, and the June bugs thumping against the screen and she had forgotten how cigarettes get soft down here in the humid air. Finally she talked about Bob; she didn't think he had ever loved her, he had started playing around their first year up there, and it had gone on for five years more or less; near the end she had even done it too, had a boyfriend, but it didn't help her survive at all, it only made things worse, and now at least she felt clean and tough and she thought that was the first step toward hope.

The stupid thing was she still loved the philandering son of a bitch. That was the only time she cried, when she said that, but she didn't even cry long enough for me to get up and go to her side of the table and hold her: when I was half out of my chair she was already waving me back in it, shaking her head and wiping her eyes, and the tears that had filled them for a moment were gone. Then she cheered up and asked if I'd drive her around tomorrow, down the main street and everything, and I said sure and asked her if she was still a Catholic.

'Don't tell Mother this,' she said. 'She's confused enough already. I went to Communion every Sunday, except when I was having that stupid affair, and I only felt sinful then because he loved me and I was using him. But before that and after that, I received.'

'You can't,' I said. 'Not while you're married out of the Church.'

'Maybe I'm wrong, but I don't think the Church is so smart about sex. Bob wouldn't get the marriage blessed, so a priest would have told me to leave him. I loved him, though, and for a long time I thought he loved me, needed me—so I stayed with him and tried to keep peace and bring up my sons. And the Eucharist is the sacrament of love and I needed it very badly those five years and nobody can keep me away.'

I got up and took our glasses and made drinks. When I turned from the sink she was watching me.

'Do you still go to confession so much?' she said.

I sat down, avoiding her eyes, then I thought, what the hell, if you can't tell Janet you can't tell anybody. So looking at the screen door and the bugs thumping from the dark outside, I told her how it was in high school and about Yvonne, though I didn't tell her name, and my aborted confession to Father Broussard. She was kind to me, busying herself with cigarettes and her drink while I talked. Then she said: 'You're right, Harry. You're absolutely right.'

'You really think so?'

'I know this much: too many of those celibates teach sex the way it is for them. They make it introverted, so you come out of their schools believing sex is something between you and yourself, or between you and God. Instead of between you and other people. Like my affair. It wasn't wrong because I was married. Hell, Bob didn't care, in fact he was glad because it gave him more freedom. It was wrong because I hurt the guy.' A Yankee word on her tongue, *guy*, and she said it with that accent from up there among snow and lakes. 'If Bob had stayed home and taken a *Playboy* to the bathroom once in a while I might still have a husband. So if that's a sin, I don't understand sin.'

'Well,' I said. Then looking at her, I grinned and it kept spreading and turned into a laugh. 'You're something, all right,' I said. 'Old Janet, you're something.'

But I still wasn't the renegade Janet was, I wanted absolution from a priest, and next morning while Mother and Daddy were happily teasing us about our hangovers, I decided to get it done. That afternoon I called Father Grassi, then told Janet where I was going, and that I would drive her around town when I got back. Father Grassi answered the door at the rectory; he was wearing a white shirt with his black trousers, a small man with a ruddy face and dark whiskers. I asked if I could speak to him in his office.

'I think so,' he said. 'Do you come from the Pope?'

'No, Father. I just want to confess.'

'So it's you who will be the saint today, not me. Yes, come in.'

He led me to his office, put his stole around his neck, and sat in the swivel chair behind his desk; I kneeled beside him on the carpet, and he shielded his face with his hand, as though we were in the confessional and he could not see me. I whispered, 'Bless me Father, for I have sinned,' my hands clasped at my waist, my head bowed. 'My last confession was six weeks ago, but I was refused absolution. By Father Broussard.'

'Is that so? You don't look like a very bad young man to me. Are you some kind of criminal?'

'I confessed masturbation, Father.'

'Yes? Then what?'

'I told him I didn't think it was a sin.'

'I see. Well, poor Father Broussard: I'd be confused too, if you confessed something as a sin and then said you didn't think it was a sin. You should take better care of your priests, my friend.'

I opened my eyes: his hand was still in place on his cheek, and he was looking straight ahead, over his desk at the bookshelf against the wall.

'I guess so,' I said. 'And now I'm bothering you.'

'Oh no: you're no trouble. The only disappointment is you weren't sent by the Pope. But since that's the way it is, then we may just as well talk about sins. We had in the seminary a book of moral theology and in that book, my friend, it was written that masturbation was worse than rape, because at least rape was the carrying out of a natural instinct. What about that?'

'Do you believe that, Father?'

'Do you?'

'No, Father.'

'Neither do I. I burned the book when I left the seminary, but not only for that reason. The book also said, among other things, let the buyer beware. So you tell me about sin and we'll educate each other.'

'I went to the Brothers' school.'

'Ah, yes. Nice fellows, those Brothers.'

'Yes, Father. But I think they concentrated too much on the body. One's own body, I mean. And back then I believed it all, and one day I even wanted to mutilate myself. Then last fall I had a girl.'

'What does that mean, you had a girl? You mean you were lovers?'

'Yes, Father. But I shouldn't have had a girl, because I believed my semen was the most important part of sex, so the first time I made love with her I was waiting for it, like my soul was listening for it—you see? Because I wouldn't know how I felt about her until I knew how I felt about ejaculating with her.'

'And how did you feel? Did you want to mutilate yourself with a can opener, or maybe something worse?'

'I was happy, Father.'

'Yes.'

'So after that we were lovers. Or she was, but I wasn't. I was just happy because I could ejaculate without hating myself, so I was still masturbating, you see, but with her—does that make sense?'

'Oh yes, my friend. I've known that since I left the seminary. Always there is too much talk of self-abuse. You see, even the term is a bad one. Have you finished your confession?'

'I want to confess about the girl again, because when I confessed it before it wasn't right. I made love to her without loving her and the last time I made love to her I told some boys about it.'

'Yes. Anything else?'

'No, Father.'

'Good. There is a line in St. John that I like very much. It is Christ praying to the Father and He says: 'I do not pray that You take them out of the world, but that You keep them from evil.' Do you understand that?'

'I think so, Father.'

'Then for your penance, say alleluia three times.'

Next afternoon Janet and I took her boys crabbing. We had an ice chest of beer and we set it under the small pavilion at the center of the wharf, then I put out six crab lines, tying them to the guard rail. I remembered the summer before she got married Janet and I had gone crabbing, then cooked them for the family: we had a large pot of water on the stove and when the water was boiling I held the gunny sack of live crabs over it and they came falling out, splashing into the water; they worked their claws, moved sluggishly, then died. And Janet had said: *I keep waiting for them to scream.*

It was a hot day, up in the nineties. Someone was water-skiing on the lake, which was saltwater and connected by canal to the Gulf, but we had the wharf to ourselves, and we drank beer in the shade while Paul and Lee did the crabbing. They lost the first couple, so I left the pavilion and squatted at the next line. The boys flanked me, lying on their bellies and looking down where the line went into the dark water; they had their shirts off, and their hot tan shoulders and arms brushed my legs. I gently pulled the line up until we saw a crab just below the surface, swimming and nibbling at the chunk of ham.

'Okay, Lee. Put the net down in the water, then bring it up under him so you don't knock him away.'

He lowered the pole and scooped the net slowly under the crab.

'I got him!'

'That's it. You just have to go slow, that's all.'

He stood and lifted the net and laid it on the wharf.

'Look how big,' Paul said.

'He's a good one,' I said. 'Put him in the sack.'

But they crouched over the net, watching the crab push his claws through.

'Poor little crab,' Lee said. 'You're going to die.'

'Does it hurt 'em, Harry?' Paul said.

'I don't know.'

'It'd hurt me,' he said.

'I guess it does, for a second or two.'

'How long's a second?' Lee said.

I pinched his arm.

'About like that.'

'That's not too long,' he said.

'No. Put him in the sack now, and catch some more.'

I went back to my beer on the bench. Paul was still crouching over the crab, poking a finger at its back. Then Lee held open the gunny sack and Paul turned the net over and shook it and the crab fell in.

'Goodbye, big crab,' he said.

'Goodbye, poor crab,' Lee said.

They went to another line. For a couple of hours, talking to Janet, I watched them and listened to their bare feet on the wharf and their voices as they told each crab goodbye. Sometimes one of them would stop and look across the water and pull at his pecker, and I remembered that day hot as this one when I was sixteen and I wanted to cut mine off. I reached deep under the ice and got a cold beer for Janet and I thought of Yvonne sitting at that kitchen table at three in the morning, tired, her lipstick worn off, her eyes fixed on a space between the people in the room. Then I looked at the boys lying on their bellies and reaching down for another crab, and I hoped they would grow well, those strong little bodies, those kind hearts.

# Going Under

*to Holly*

**M**IRANDA is wearing purple and waiting in the open doorway, behind her are the yellow walls of the living room and the orange couch where they have loved, her hair is nearly black, it is very long, and her body is long and slender. She is twenty-one years old; the day she was born Peter was fifteen. In her purple sweater and pants she is lovely, and he presses his face into her shoulder, her hair, he is squeezing her and her heels lift from the floor, then he kisses her and breathes from deep in her throat the scorched smell of dope. He looks at her green eyes: they are glazed and she is smiling, but it is a smile someone hung there; Miranda is someplace else. But now her eyes are making some appeal, then they move away from Peter's and when they return they are simply green again, bright again, and she nestles into his chest and murmurs, 'Only one little pipe,' and he holds her ever more tightly, crushing against her the loneliness he always feels when she lowers between them the glass wall of her smoking; the muscles of his arms and chest are taut with squeezing her, he is working isometrics against his heart, and it begins to give, it is subdued, it won't scream at her. It knows the heavy price of pushing Miranda further away.

He holds and kisses her again, and they move through the living room—her black and white photographs are on the walls; soon she will start working with color—and into the kitchen where she makes him a martini. She is not really a drinker, she has never drunk a whole martini, but he has taught her to make them and she likes to and when it is ready she tastes it, then hands it to him, and he sits at the table and watches her strong fingers peeling boiled shrimp. Her face is straining against the dope, she is trying to listen to him as he props his feet on a chair and sips the martini and unwinds. He tells her about his afternoon and the traffic driving home from Boston and she listens with exaggerated concentration; her responding smiles come a moment late and are held a moment too long.

By candlelight they eat shrimp cocktail while the sole broils, her kitchen is light blue, and from the walls hang red and orange pots and mugs; Dylan songs come from the record player in her bedroom, they eat fish and drink Chablis, she has only a couple of glasses because she is already high, he helps her with the dishes, and they linger still in the kitchen. He finishes the wine, the candles burn and drip and in their light her face overwhelms him, his blood is quick, she sees this and her smile vanishes, her face ages with passion, they rise and she leans over and blows out the candles, and they walk down the hall toward the music in the dark.

In the morning he wakes first; early sunlight comes through the window and he goes to it and looks out at the bright snow on the hemlock branches that nearly touch the frosted pane. He gets back in bed. After a while Miranda begins to wake; he feels her watching him, and he turns his head. She is staring at him, the way his children used to stare from their baby beds; he would pass the bedroom door and see Kathi lying on her back, plump fingers rubbing the satin border of her blanket, her eyes staring wide and blank as though her mind were still asleep. Miranda is the only adult he's ever seen wake that way. He is about to speak to her but she closes her eyes and is asleep. When she wakes again he brings her grapefruit juice and they lie warmly and drink.

'Let's eat lobsters tonight,' he says. 'I'll cook them.'

She looks away. Her eyes do not leave his but she looks away. It's a talent she has.

'I won't be able to,' she says.

'Oh. Well, maybe tomorrow night.'

'I don't think I'll be able to then either.'

'I thought we had plans for tonight. A movie.'

'Did we?'

'I guess we didn't.'

This is the way they end up talking. Miranda has a fiancé; Peter doesn't know why. That is, he doesn't know why, having a fiancé, she began making love with him; or, making love with him, still has a fiancé. Now he knows, and she knows he does, that her fiancé is making some demand; perhaps he called yesterday and asked her to come to Connecticut today. Probably he did, and probably that pressure is why she smoked last night. But Peter can only work with probabilities, with guesses, for the centrifugal force of their evasion takes them further and further from the center of themselves. He lies quietly, feeling the weekend stretching out before him and now in the room demons are about and he turns to Miranda, his touch is gentle and she believes it is gentle, for that is what she needs now; she wants forgiveness and she believes he is giving it to her, but he is not. Not now. He has done that long ago, forgiven her in advance for every betrayal he had already decided to take. It is not forgiveness now, it is not even tenderness, his gentle fingers are wily, they don't show how desperate he is, they stroke away her fear, they draw love to her warm surfaces, joyfully she takes him and he has what he wants: the demons are gone. Yet there is more: demons gone are demons forgotten, and now he is free to watch her face and love her, and she is free too, she feels absolved, her eyes are uncluttered, they are passionate and profound, and she says: 'I love you, Peter, I love you—'

That moment carries him through the rest of the day; or it helps him do what he must do to get through a winter Saturday. He is a disk jockey and five afternoons a week his voice leaves him and goes into ears he will never know. When he was younger he was an actor. Then he had a son and named him David, and then a daughter and they named her Kathi, and he went into radio. For a while he hated his life, and at night he drank. Then after a couple of months he started feeling good. He started feeling very good. His work was not exciting, but he liked making money and bringing it home to Norma and David and Kathi. He liked having money to go see plays, and he liked not having to worry about being in one. He put on weight and made friends who came over on Saturday nights. This happy adjustment to the possibility of peace coincided with his admission that he had no more talent than thousands of others, and he would have spent his life trying to do TV commercials while he looked for work on the stage. For a long time he enjoyed those pleasures that money and family love can bring. But now his family is in Colorado and Norma is married to an affluent man and, though he sends money for the children, they don't need it.

They left last summer and on that morning he woke with a heart heavy and dead, as if waking for the funeral of his dearest friend, and he drank juice and took bacon from the refrigerator and laid three strips in a skillet, but he was trembling and his stomach fluttering and he put the slices back in the package, shoving them curved and folded under the cellophane. He would have had a drink but he didn't want their memory through the years to smell and taste again booze on their father's morning lips. Then he was faint with fear and he breathed deeply several times and got into the shower, his heart no longer grieving as if for another's death: it was his own execution he cleansed himself for, scrubbing under the hot spray, trying to feel and see nothing but his hand and the bar of soap and his lathered and dripping flesh, but he saw himself driving there and he saw them coming out of the house with love and goodbye in their faces and he raged aloud *No No No*, eyes closed and fists swinging at air and spray and then he slipped: his feet gone and arms reaching, one against the flat wet wall, the other toward the handle of the glass door, clutching at it and missing as his head struck the back of the tub and he lay gazing up at the spray that now hit his belly and groin; then he closed his eyes and waited to be knocked out. After a while he opened his eyes and touched his head. A swelling; no blood. He stood up: he was able to. He would be able to shave now, to put on clothes, to drive there, to do it all. Before leaving the bathroom he looked once at the tub where he wanted to lie bleeding while the water struck him hot, then warm, and finally cold while he slept.

The day was blue and warm, the breeze from the east: a beach day. They were waiting on the front steps of the house he had left: plump, red-haired Kathi, her eyes excited and green and troubled with love, eight years old yet Peter knew that as well as her fatherless Colorado mornings and nights and the shyness of stepfather suppers she saw every moment of his waking and preparing which now he mustered himself to conceal. His son was ten, his light brown hair over his ears and down close to his shoulders, near blond from their days at the sea, bony once but now muscles too, his shoulders broad and sloping, and his hand in Peter's was loving, but Peter could feel in it too his separate peace and he knew that because Kathi was a girl he would live in a different way in her memory than in his son's. When Peter left home, David would not help Kathi and Norma help him load the car, and when Peter went inside and kissed him, holding his turning face, he would not leave the house, so Peter went out with Kathi and Norma and kissed them both and started the car; then David came running, it was dusk and in that light he ran gray and without features, then he stooped and picked up something from the dark lawn, he was close to the window now, arm lifting as he ran, his face clear now, crying, shouting *You bum You bum You bum* and throwing something that missed as Peter fled. When they saw each other two days later the boy had accepted Peter's betrayal; he moved back into Peter's love, accepted that too, but his acceptance had about it an aura of manly decision, and Peter could feel his eyes and his touch saying: *You have chosen to go. All right. Then I must grow without you and since there's nothing I can do but accept it, I might as well do better than that: I choose it.* So on the front steps as the three of them sat, the car in the driveway to their right packed for the trip west, David's blue eyes were pained for his father and for himself, yet that pain was muted by his resolve to endure. Holding him, Peter tried very hard to be grateful for that resolve.

Then Norma came out and when she saw them she turned her head and stood wiping her eyes, then faced them and pressed Peter's hand and started for the car. He rose and pulled Kathi and David up with him. They followed Norma to the car. She turned and, looking at some point on his neck or chest, she reached for him, hugged him very hard, patted his back, whispered, 'Take care,' and had turned and was gone even as he whispered the 'You too' she never heard. She circled the car and got in and he couldn't see her face till he crouched between David and Kathi, only a glance at her profile, her fingers brushing quickly at her eyes, then he was looking into their faces, and then long hugs and many kisses, tight squeezes till they all gasped, and saying again and again, 'At Christmas you'll fly out,' then he asked who had first turn in the front seat, it was Kathi, and he picked her up and put her on the seat and buckled her in and while he was doing that David got into the back and buckled his belt. Norma had mercifully started the engine and he leaned in and kissed David and then stepped back smiling, waving, calling out to their mournful and smiling faces to have a good trip, to write him about the trip, to paint pictures of the trip, to send him pictures of the trip, giving them that final image as they drove away, their arms waving out the windows: their father standing erect and smiling in the morning sun, wishing them well.

Then he drove home through tears and again tried to prepare a meal and again could not eat; then he lay on his bed and submitted with curiosity and hope to the rape of grief. He lay there for an hour while the faces of David and Kathi assaulted him. Then he gave up: he could neither die of a broken heart nor go crazy. He got up from the bed, smoothed the wrinkles he had made, took off his clothes, laid them neatly on the bed, put on jockstrap and gym shorts, his heart still heavy as he tied his white leather running shoes, but his blood quickening with challenge and hope; he tied a red handkerchief around his forehead to keep sweat out of his eyes and went outside, and he ran.

It is what he is doing now, wearing a nylon running suit, a windbreaker, mittens, and a ski cap. He is now two miles from home on a road going east from his apartment. He lives in a small town, so already he is out in the country; he runs past farmhouses, country homes, service stations. There are not many cars and most of the time he has the privacy of his own sounds—his steady breathing, his feet on the wet plowed and sanded blacktop—and, more than that, the absolute privacy of his body staking its claim on a country road past white hills and dark green trees, gray barns, and naked elms and maples and oaks waiting for spring: his body insisting upon itself, pumping blood and pounding up hills. Running is the only act in his life that gives him what he pays for. It is as simple as that.

Two and a half miles from his house, at the top of a hill, he looks across the sparkling white meadows, shadowed by trees and barns, and sees the Merrimack and chunks of ice flowing to the sea. Then he turns and starts back. Sweat has turned to ice on his handlebar moustache, he is running against a cold wind that has now frozen a drop of sweat on his freeze-burning cheek, he can see the droplet of ice at the bottom of his vision, one nostril is frozen partly shut, the temperature is around nineteen but the wind hits him with a chill below zero, his jockstrap is frozen hard as a shield at his crotch, and its edges chafe his legs. He approaches a man walking, a man over sixty, beneath his clothing he is wiry, he is walking briskly on the side of the road in boots and corduroys and sweaters and mackinaw, his face is red in the cold, and somehow Peter knows he is not walking to someplace, he is walking to walk, and when Peter is close enough they smile at each other and the man says, 'I wish I could do that,' and Peter says, 'You don't need to.' The man's eyes are good ones, and Peter waves and runs on, feeling light-hearted at the sight of the old man with a smile and a fast walk and bright eyes; and against and through the cold wind he runs happily home with aching lungs.

Dusk comes to his rooms before it comes to the sky. He turns on the lights and goes outside and stands on the shoveled and icy sidewalk and watches it come. He is drinking a hot toddy. On the common across the street, where stoned kids sprawl in the warm seasons, pines and bare maples and elms cast their final shadows on the snow. Beyond the common is a white church whose lighted steeple rises above the trees, above everything in the town, and stands against the darkening sky. There is a wide strip of light to the west, but all color has gone with the sun and as he sips and shivers and watches, the light fades and dusk is here, the worst time for the lonely, when sounds are louder and silence has a shape Peter can feel as he walks through it, and when death on a cold wind touches the windows. Then dusk is gone too, night has come dark and cold, Peter looks up at the stars and tries to recall this morning with Miranda, but the memory is cerebral and nothing against the dark. He goes inside and, like his children, he is wary of turning corners and opening closet doors, and he wants to tell his children they are right, that long ago when he told them it was only their imagination he was right too but not right enough, for what they saw yet couldn't see frightened them, and it was real.

He makes another drink and turns the records over, he is listening to Brubeck and Mulligan, and he sits on the bed, looking at the yellow phone on the bedside table. His body is vibrant from his run, he feels strong and able, and he'd better be, for now the demons are here, they are moving in the room, they are waiting. They won't come and get him. Always they watch and keep their distance; when he feels strong they watch quietly, like prone dogs; when he weakens they grow restive, and he can almost hear them. He has learned the rules: they are powerless to close that final distance, they cannot seize him unless he opens his own gates. He picks up the phone and dials the area code of loss, then the numbers of where they live. Norma answers.

'Are you all right?' she says.

'Yes,' and he tightens his closed eyes and pictures her in the house in Colorado. She has not changed with the times: her brown hair is cut short, she uses lipstick, she smokes Luckies. She is wearing slacks and a tight sweater, showing the good curves of her body that finally he could no longer touch. He has not seen the house; probably he never will. The children have written to him that it is new and big and has large windows and from the kitchen window they look at mountains. Kathi painted a picture of the house and sent it to him; it seems to be a ranch house. She drew her own face grinning out her bedroom window. Beyond the house a smiling sun shone over the mountains, and a grinning dog stood on the green lawn.

He asks for the children and she says she'll get them, she leaves the phone and he listens to her calling them, he strains to hear every sound in the house, and now he is listening for smells and colors too, for warmth and light, he is listening for joy and sorrow and everything he doesn't know, and now Kathi is on one phone and David on another, and Peter's voice is warm and cheerful: 'I liked your letters and your pictures. How are you?'

'Fine.' 'Fine; how are you?'

'Good. What were you doing?'

'When?'

'Just now. When I called.'

'Watching TV.' 'Cartoons,' Kathi says. 'It's snowing.'

'Is it a good snow?'

'Yeah!' David says. 'We didn't go to school.' 'So we get three days off,' Kathi says. ' 'Cept tomorrow we're supposed to have skiing lessons. But maybe we won't.'

'Skiing lessons? Both of you?'

'Yeah,' David says. 'We're in the same group too.' 'It's hard to walk on them.'

'Do you like it?'

'It's neat!' David says.

'Do you like it, Kathi?'

'Maybe so. I'll see.'

'Good. You learn to ski, and then it'll be spring and then in summer we'll go to the beach every sunny day, I'm getting bunk beds to go in my living room—'

'Bunk beds?' David says. 'Neat!'

'I want the top,' Kathi says.

'We'll work it out, and I'm going to try to work mornings from six to ten instead of afternoons so we'll have the rest of the day for the beach, I'm pretty sure I can swing it, and we'll get brown as old wet driftwood—' then they are all talking about summer coming, and flying to Boston, they are talking about the beach, David wants boiled lobsters at the cheap screened picnic table restaurant near the sea, Kathi hates school, she wants summer, David doesn't mind school, he says Kathi won't make friends, that's why she doesn't like it, and when she assents with her silence (Peter can feel that silence: it is hot-faced while a chill creeps like fog over her heart) his own heart breaks, his arms yearn to hold her, to protect her, to do anything that will take her happily through her days, realizing at once that this is true and not true, for he will do anything for Kathi except submit to the death of living with and trying once more after the long killing pain to love her mother, and all he can say is, 'Try, Kathi; I was shy too; you have to try, no one will come to you, people aren't like that, they go their own ways, you give it a try, you hear.' Knowing he is saying nothing, and now they are all saying I love you, they are all smacking kisses into the three phones, his closed eyes see Kathi and David, then they start over again I love you I love you I love you and kisses and kisses over the wires, through his clear night and their late afternoon snow, and when he hangs up he does not cradle the receiver, demons move in from the walls, he reaches over and depresses the button and then he calls Jo. As always her voice is guarded, as though she were a fugitive. He asks her to dinner. Her voice doesn't change, but she accepts. Then he takes off the records, turns on the radio so he will not come home to silence, leaves on the lights, and flees his apartment.

Some people divorce because they hope for resurrection and afterwards you can see in them a new energy, a new strength. But Peter believes Jo did it with her last effort, like a suicide stepping onto the chair and ducking her head into the noose.

'It's been so long since I've had a good meal,' she says.

'What do you eat?'

'Frozen things. Things in cans. Pizza. It's rotten to do it to the girls. Sometimes I feel guilty and I cook something and eat it with them.'

They have brandy and they have pulled their chairs near the fireplace, where two logs are burning. In the restaurant she smoked a lot and talked a lot, and she ate a large meal, oysters on the half-shell, broiled scallops, and Peter, his back tingling like a nervous gunfighter's (for the demons followed him into his car, and in the chatter behind him they stalked among tables), savored his shrimp broiled on a stick with tomato and bacon and resting on a nest of spinach, he sipped Chablis, putting a stake on the good meal, the bottle of wine, and Jo was good to be with, better than eating alone;

but she has not laughed since dinner, her smile is forced, and in her voice and dark eyes her ache is bitter, it is defiant, and he feels they are not at a hearth but are huddled at a campfire in a dangerous forest.

He met her in the early fall, before Miranda. She is one of his listeners, one of the women he talks to on weekday afternoons, the only one he really knows. In the fall the station had a contest with one hundred winners: the wives who wrote the best letters telling why they should leave their husbands at home and go to a New England Patriot football game. *All my life I've been watching men,* she wrote. *When I was a very little girl I watched boys throwing rocks and beating each other up and racing across the schoolyard after school. When I was a teen-ager I watched them playing football and basketball, and at home they played street hockey and when the ponds froze they played ice hockey across the street from my window. I watched them drive off in cars, I watched them hitchhike to Florida, I watched them go into the service and I watched them come home strutting and winking about their adventures. I always believed when I got married it would be my turn. My husband would watch me. He doesn't. He watches football on television. If I'm going to spend my life watching men who aren't watching me, then at least once it should be fun, and I should be able to dress up and go out to do it. Maybe my husband will see me on television and then he can watch me watching.*

Peter sat with her at the game, she told him about her letter, she was pleased that he remembered it. During the game he watched her. She was excited, she was having fun, but there was a desperate quality about her fun, as though she had just been released from prison. It was the same that night, after the studio party where they drank enough to impassion their intent: in the motel she made love with a fury, but he knew it was forced, that her tightening arms, her bucking hips were turned against the fetters which clanked at her heart. The affair was short because that clanking never went away. It was in her voice: when she was pretending—and nearly always she pretended—her voice was low and flat, as if she had just waked from a deep sleep; but most of the time her voice was high and brittle with cheer, her laughter was forced and shrill, and he could hear in it the borders of hysteria. Like most unfaithful wives she was remorseless: she felt she deserved a lover. Yet it did her no good. Her heart was surrounded by obdurate concentric circles of disappointment and bitterness; she could not break through, so

Peter couldn't either, and finally they broke it off and both pretended that aversion to the deceptions and stolen time of adultery was the reason.

'You always liked to eat,' Peter says.

'I know.'

'What else don't you like anymore?'

'It's not that I don't like things.'

'You can't, is that it?'

'Yes. Sometimes I take pills.'

'To cheer you up?'

'They're not *that* good. He keeps calling, he doesn't want me to go through with the divorce, he wants me to take him back. Sometimes I think I ought to. It's not worth it.'

'What's not worth it?'

She shrugs. Peter is angry, he wants to tell her that for years he hasn't thought about sin, hasn't believed in sin, hasn't used the word sin, but now he is thinking depression is a sin, perhaps the only one that many people can commit. But he takes their glasses to the kitchen for more brandy. Her house is clean; he knows that unhappy women often lapse into disorder and dirt, and walking back to the living room he feels affection for Jo, he thinks of her dusting furniture as his voice comes over the radio. He sits beside her and tells her funny stories, he clowns for her, and it is like the stage again, he is not Peter Jackman, he is a changing face, a cracking voice, he is a field of laughter, and she laughs and sometimes succeeds in really laughing, and when she does this she reaches across the short distance between their chairs and grips his arm or hand, and he regrets but cannot ignore the current in her fingers and without a word he accepts. Still he rises, hoping to leave, but when they kiss her tongue is a desperate cry on his, so he follows her creeping up the stairs past her daughters' rooms and into her bed where with a heart like packed snow he makes love and then lies stroking her face as though with a cool cloth against fever. When she is sleepy he gets up and dresses in the moonlight and she says very quietly: 'Peter? Will you come back sometime?'

He tells her he will, and he goes out into the night.

'I want you to care,' he says.

'I can't,' Miranda says.

She is sitting on the orange couch; at another time he would be sitting beside her, but his (and her) Saturday night has riven them, though he is the only one who knows it; or he believes he is the only one who knows it. So he faces her from a basket chair across the narrow room. She is sipping tea, and she is tired. She is smoking Marlboros, one after the other. Like many girls her age, she smokes almost continually. A part of Peter admires this; he sees it as insouciance toward death. Another part of him sees it as insouciance toward life.

'What does that mean, you can't? Do you mean you can't feel anything because you just aren't able to, or do you mean you can't because you're not supposed to?'

'I'm not supposed to.'

'But did you feel anything when I told you?'

'Yes.'

'Did you like it?'

'No.'

'Then you're not free. And I'm not either. But I already know that. It's you that has to know it. We both made love with other people last night. We're supposed to care. If we can't, then we're trapped in something else.'

'I'm tired,' she says.

She puts out her cigarette and lights another. In the past few minutes he has built a cage around her and behind it her face is confused and frightened. He knows she would like to put on music and smoke dope and quietly merge with the beats and rhythms from her record player. It is late Sunday night, Miranda has an hour ago returned from Connecticut and submitted to his pleas on the phone—he had been phoning every half hour since six o'clock —and has let him come over for a drink. He is drinking bourbon, though he knows he shouldn't, for it will oil his tongue and he will talk and one of his rules with Miranda, one of the rules which allows him to keep her, is not to talk too much of how he feels, for if she knows how much he loves her (she knows), how much he needs her (she knows), she will bolt under the pressure. She doesn't actually bolt: she doesn't send him away, she doesn't walk out on him. She simply goes away inside herself, while she turns to him a smile, gives to him a hand; and that makes him more lonely than any escape by any woman he's ever known. So daily with her he lives with songs he will never sing and screams he will never scream. But tonight he is drinking, and in a fearful moment of release he decides to go to the kitchen and pour himself another, knowing as he watches it pour that he too will be pouring soon, and within his relief there is a core of anger, the contradictions tangled like barbed wire in him again, for what he feels is love and he wants to tell it to Miranda, yet at the same time he is angry because she has managed them so that he can't tell her, and now, going back to the living room with his bourbon, he wants with all his heart to carry her away and make her his wife, yet he also would like to grab her by the shoulders and shake her till she cries.

At the door to the living room he stops. He looks at her quiet and lovely profile: she sips the tea, wipes her lips with the back of her cigarette hand, the lips shaping a kiss as they press themselves dry, then she draws on the cigarette, exhales, and begins again with the tea. She knows now that he is at the door but she doesn't know he is stopping to watch her, and in that moment, when she is drying tea from her lips, he is struck with a purifying love which he knows, if he could sustain it, would save him. He sees a sad young girl who is trying to live as well as she can; who does not hurt him out of spite or malice but only so she can survive; who gives him as much of herself as she is able to and only balks when he demands more; and who has gotten him through many nights. He could not help falling in love with her; what he could have helped was what happened afterward, and he had chosen to make love with a woman who wore an engagement ring; and standing in the doorway he is about to simply say I love you, and kiss her goodnight, and then go home and let her sleep. But now, though she doesn't look at him, she is aware that he is watching her and looking at her profile he knows this and the distance of the moment is broken and he makes a final choice: he crosses the room and settles into the chair.

'Talk to me,' he says.

Her eyes raise to his, then she looks down at her hands with the cigarette and tea, and then she sips and smokes.

'You have to tell me what's happening in you. Do you think it's me you love, is that it? Are you waiting to be sure? Talk to me, Miranda. Why are you making love with me? You can tell me that, can't you? Don't you know it's painful for me when you go off for a weekend and we pretend you didn't? If we could at least talk about it maybe it wouldn't be so bad. If you'd say anything at all about what you feel, even if you'd say you loved him and you were just doing some humbug with me, even that, even if I had that definition of what I am, but you won't even say that much, you just sit there and look at your hands. And there's death in you. With your dope and your silence and your two lovers. You erase yourself.

Well, you're not going to erase me too. And that's what happens when I'm lonely and I end up with Jo. And I'm not going to do that anymore. I've *been* there. Jesus, I've *been* there, Miranda—'

Sitting in the basket chair he is subtly overwhelmed, memory launches a sneak attack, his blood remembers making love with a landlocked heart, and he sits there with the ghosts of love past: the affairs with melancholy wives when he was a husband, and with each new one he believed he was in love, yet always the day came for goodbye and usually it came some time after both hearts had turned away or back onto themselves. No matter, all were goodbyes from the instant of their first hello, all were liaisons whose passions were fed by the empty cupboards of the lovers' homes; and all the time to make these couplings profound instead of privative he tried as best he could to believe he was in love, his love for Norma long dead, killed by their mutual adulteries, symptoms of a more complex distance which he has never truly understood; and with each new woman he said to himself, *She must be the last, she will be the last, she is the last,* because there was death in that repetition of lovers, each goodbye was a little death, and the affairs themselves were too because they were shallow and ephemeral and so he felt shallow and ephemeral too, his soul untapped on his march to death, a stranger between the thighs of a stranger— 'Miranda.' He stands up. He wants to cross the room and take the cup and cigarette from her hands, but he doesn't dare, for he is afraid that his eyes and the touch of his hands cannot reach her. So he stands at his chair and uses his voice. 'Miranda: will you live with me?' She looks up at him and in her eyes there is a flicker of assent, he sees it, grabs it, holds on for his very life while she looks down again into her empty tea cup, her cigarette is finished too, she reaches for the pack, picks it up, changes her mind, puts it down, then changes her mind again and takes a cigarette. 'I love you, Miranda. I can't keep sharing you. I want you to come live with me. Now; tonight.' He looks around the room to see what he can pack in their cars: the photographs from the walls, the table lamps, the coffee table, cushions; from the bedroom the record player and records; he has a vision of the two of them carrying things downstairs, with each load their hearts are lighter, they ascend the stairs together for another load, their impulsiveness gives them easy laughter— 'We can pack some things tonight. Tomorrow morning I'll get a truck and move the rest while you're at work. When you come home it'll be all done. This week I'll build you a darkroom,

there's room in the kitchen, it's too big anyway. We'll do it. Won't
we? I know I shouldn't sound like something wounded you have to
bring in off the street. But I don't have time anymore to be smart—
will you live with me?'
  'I can't.'
  'Why? You want to. I can feel it. It's not him stopping you. If
you really loved him you wouldn't want me at all. So why can't
you?'
  'I'm too young.'
  'You're not too young. You have two lovers.'
  'I wish I didn't have any.'
  'You mean you wish nobody asked you questions.'
  'Yes. That's what I wish.'
  'You can't do that, Miranda. You can't make love and not have
questions. Goddamnit, Miranda—' But there is nothing to say. He
has said it all, and between him and Miranda his guts hang in the air.
He is adrift in those desperate spaces of vulnerability where she will
never follow, there is no way for him to get back, and he yields to
his old stubborn muscle, the heart, and he follows it across the
room, watching himself fall to his knees and take the cigarette from
her hand and put it out, then hold both her hands and look into her
green, brimming eyes and say: 'Miranda, I can't do it anymore. I
can't pretend I love you less, I'm not strong enough to keep pretending I'm strong, I can't keep standing around waiting and staying alive on the little you give, because you're all I've got—don't
you know that? surely you *know* that—I don't have my kids, I
don't have work, I have a job—Miranda: listen. I'm not as crazy
as I sound. Desperate, yes. I mean I know I spend twenty-three
hours every day getting in shape for that one hour when I might
go under. Is that what scares you?' The tears are going down her
cheeks now, and she is slowly shaking her head. 'It has to be that or
nothing, Miranda. I can't go back to the other. Come with me, Miranda. You love me. We'll make it. Come now, baby, come now—'
Her tears are faster, they flow over her lips and drop to her lap, but
still she is shaking her head even as her hand takes the back of his
neck and pulls him forward; her other hand goes around his back,
his face is in her breasts, and he feels against his forehead the beating
of her heart. He tries to stand but her arms hold tightly. His hands
on her knees, he pushes himself up, he stands, and her arms fall
away. She rises with him. Fiercely she hugs him again, and now
there is a turnabout that mollifies his anguish, her silence and her

tears on his cheek pull him out of himself, he is holding her, through her soft hair he is stroking her neck, his lips turn to her ear and he says: 'I'm sorry, Miranda. I have to. It hurts too much, the way it was. I have to try to survive. I'm sorry, baby—' and he hugs her very tightly, glances once at her damp face as he turns away and takes his coat and leaves.

There will be no sleep tonight. He knows it when he enters his apartment, which is lighted; from the bedroom comes Janis Joplin on the radio. He goes to the kitchen: bourbon started his evening at dusk and brought his night to its dark crescendo, and now perhaps it will allow him to wane. He makes a drink, brings the bottle to the table, sits down, and props his feet on a chair. He is about to drink but instead he pauses and listens to McCartney. He does not want the music coming down the hall from the bedroom. When it does that it only penetrates the spaces near the door, where the sink is. But over there at the refrigerator and there at the stove and here at the cupboard and counter opposite his chair and here beside him at the dark reflecting window and the wide sill where he rests his arm there is no music and when he looks at these places he sees silence. He goes to the bedroom and gets the portable radio, switching to DC when he unplugs it and listening to McCartney as he goes down the hall; on DC the reception is not as good, and he sets the radio on the counter, plugs it in, switches back to AC, and the faint static is gone. He turns out the overhead light so the room is dark except for the light coming from the hall. He sits and swallows bourbon, then lights a cigarette, his first of day. The demons are stirring now, he feels them creeping down the hall, and in another moment they are standing by the sink to his right, and he feels like a colonel with an exposed flank. He finishes the drink and then another, but in his mind there is a relentless dagger of sobriety that will not give in to the booze. What he must do is sleep, and he takes the radio to the bedroom and gets into bed.

Right away his legs tell him it is no use. They will not relax, they will not sink into the mattress, they are restless as they are before he runs. He tries hypnotizing his toes and feet and calves, but by the time he is repeating *My knees are asleep* the calf muscles and feet are yearning again. And he cannot make his mind stop. If he could, then his muscles would follow peacefully and rest like sunning snakes, but his mind is filled with the idea and necessity of sleep, and the more he pushes with his mind the more his muscles and blood push back until the struggle gives him a sensation very much like the need to scratch. Yet still he tries to relax, he closes his eyes and breathes as he would if he were falling asleep, and for a moment it nearly works, his mind has stopped thinking sleep and has begun to drift into a dream when he realizes this and is immediately awake, his heart fast, his arms tight at his sides.

His luminous clock on the chest of drawers tells him it is eight minutes after two, and now he knows he will lie awake till four at the least, but probably five or six, and that he will wake at eight as usual and the day that waits for him will be long, his body tired, his reflexes distorted—he will be easily startled—and as dusk comes his heart and nerves will start again and he will have to devise some way to ease himself into the night, to sneak up on sleep. Angrily he throws back the covers and gets out of bed, his feet strike hard on the floor, his legs take him quickly to the kitchen and he gets ice and pours bourbon and returns to the bedroom where he turns on the radio and lowers the volume on Crosby Stills Nash and Young, then gets into bed, propping himself on two pillows so he can drink. He lights a cigarette and watches his exhaled smoke in the dark.

Before he has half-finished the drink he knows he will call Jo. But he tells himself he won't. It has never worked with Jo and he does not want to hurt another woman, not ever. He does not think he can love Jo, but he is afraid Jo can love him. And he does not want to go to her now, the way he is, for he knows he can mistake relief for love and then it will sour and there will be wounds. He must go it alone, ride out this night, hang on to its neck and mane, and ride. Besides, it is two twenty-seven, she will be asleep (he picks up the phone), he should be tougher than this (he is dialing), he shouldn't disturb poor Jo in all the ways this call will disturb her (it rings), it isn't right, he ought— On the second ring she answers. She has been asleep and there is fear in her voice.

'Jo, I'm sorry.'

'Peter?'

'I'm sorry. You were sleeping, I knew you'd be asleep, but—' He listens to tears coming to his voice, he will not allow them to crest, he stops speaking.

'What happened?' Jo says.

He doesn't answer. He is listening to his silent throat, trying to know if he can talk without crying; but he doesn't have to. Jo takes over, and in a moment which he even trusts he loves her.

'Come on over,' she says.

'I can't do that.'

He has answered without listening first and his voice is all right; or at least it doesn't break into liquid. Jo is working for him.

'Sure you can. Come on.'

'It's awfully late. You won't get any sleep.'

'I'll sleep tomorrow while the girls are at school.'

'Are you sure?'

'Come on.'

'I'll bring some bourbon.'

He turns on the light and blinks, and now his legs are put to good use, they cross the room and take clothes from the closet, he dresses and goes to the kitchen and gets the bottle. Passing his bedroom door again he sees the unmade bed and knowing he is foolishly careful he goes in and makes it, leaving no signs of decline for the demons' morale. He takes a moment to decide it is all right to turn off the radio, turns it off and the bedside lamp too, gets his coat and gloves and heads fast down the hall and out that door into the foyer, dark stairs rising at his left, and goes out the front door into the cold where, on the narrow, icy front porch, he stops.

The apartment's lawn is at most twenty feet wide from the front steps to the sidewalk. If he reaches the sidewalk he will go around the corner of the building, to the garage in back. To reach this sidewalk he must simply traverse the lawn, walking on a shoveled walk between low white banks of snow. But he cannot go down that walk. He stands on the porch looking at the two steps and then at the T formed by the two sidewalks and at the smooth hard snow of the lawn. He starts to step onto the first step, his leg moves, it reaches the step, the other leg follows, he is standing on the step but Peter himself is not really there, whoever Peter is has been driven in panic back into the warm and lighted apartment; he is not on the steps. His body stands spiritless and abandoned, it feels as though it has neither bone nor muscle, it is only shivering flesh inside clothing that doesn't belong to him. He turns away from the dark street and the lawn and goes back into the apartment, where he catches up with himself sitting on the bed and turning on the lamp and taking a shot from the bottle, then corking it and dropping it to the bed and picking up the phone.

'Jo, I can't cross the lawn. It looked huge, it looked like Nebraska. I took a step. Or two of them. I had the bourbon and I had the car key in my hand. I couldn't get down the steps.'

'You want me to come get you?'

'You can't leave your kids.'

'I could leave them for just a minute.'

'No.'

'Don't you want me to?'

'I want to be able to move. Look, I feel better now.' He looks around his room at things he has bought, things which every day tell him he's at home. They seem to be telling him that now. The room is a place he can depart from, Jo's voice on the phone is a person he can go to. He is uncorking the bottle. 'I think I can make it,' he says, and swallows as she says, 'I'll get a fire going. We'll have hot toddies. It'll be nice, Peter.'

Clutching the bottle in one hand, keys dangling from the other, he goes down the hall. He is whistling before he realizes he is. He is whistling 'Summertime.' In the foyer he closes the apartment door behind him, in that closed dark space the demons are so near that he wants to make some sound, not a scream or sob of terror, but a growl, a shout, a sharp command, so they will know they are still dealing with a man in possession of— He is out of the foyer, he is on the porch, and he shuts the door behind him and looks at the dark and minatory sky over dark, white-splotched rooftops; across the street the common is white and smooth; black evergreens rise from it, they are tall and wide, they obscure the sky, they become the horizon until he looks past them at the white church tower with a light in the very top of its steeple, it is nearly a white light in the open, unglassed windows, up where the bell is. Beyond it the sky is without stars. He looks down at his own silent white lawn, and he crosses the porch and is on the top step and without breaking stride he is on the second step and then the walk itself, he is moving, he reaches the sidewalk that parallels the street and he turns right and reaches the corner where there is a streetlight.

He looks to his left-front, lifts his eyes to the light of the steeple, scans the peaceful snow of the common, and then abruptly turns right and is looking down a dark street and sidewalk; as he moves forward he leaves the streetlight behind him, he is passing his living room and now he approaches his bedroom window, but he keeps his eyes fixed on the dark sidewalk before him, he sees that and the huge stump that was a tree until the telephone lines came, he sees the shadowed snow piled between the sidewalk and the apartment and, in his vision to the front and in the corner of his left eye, the dark road. There is no more wind here than there was at the front of the apartment, there is no wind at all tonight, but on this side-walk he is colder, his breath is fast as though he were walking briskly for miles; only a few feet ahead of him is the corner of the building, he will go past that to the driveway and then turn and walk up it and open the door to the garage and then get into his car— He stops. For a second (and in that second his fear stops the clock, he stands within the circle of a pause that threatens to hold him) he knows he cannot go forward but he also believes he can-not retrace his steps, cannot reach the corner he has left, believes he will stand immobile holding a whiskey bottle and car keys until someone comes to save him.

Then he is turning, he is heading fast back to the corner, too re-lieved to feel shame or failure, the streetlight is waiting, now the door, then he is in his warm hall and he goes directly to the kitchen. He takes off his gloves and makes a drink. He goes to the bedroom, drops his coat to the floor, and turns on the radio. Judy Collins is singing, plaintive and sweet. He sits on the bed, drinks twice, drinks again, then he calls Jo. She does not say hello. She says: 'I'll come get you.'

'Wait. Every time you say that I think I can make it. Last time I almost got to the driveway, I got as far as the kitchen. Look: hold on, will you? I'll just go take a look outside and see how things are. Will you just hold a minute?'

'I'll hold. The fire is going. I'm looking at the fire.'

'What do you have on?'

'My nightgown and a robe. They're both pink. My feet are bare. They were cold but now they're warm by the fire.'

'Are you drinking?'

'A little brandy with coffee.'

'Coffee? You'll never sleep.'

'I need to wake up some. You woke me from what they call a drugged sleep. And I just smoked my last cigarette. And you know how coffee and brandy make you want to smoke. So you have to get out of the house so you can bring me some cigarettes. There are all-night service stations with machines.'

Her voice is warm and cheerful, perhaps amused. He knows the game she is playing with him, but he needs it and it seems to be working. He imagines himself in his car, driving.

'I have some here,' he says. 'I'll bring those.'

'Good. Go see how things look outside.'

'Here I go,' he says, and drops the phone to his pillow, not all the way from his ear but lowering it first to a gentle height; he feels he must treat the phone as though Jo were in it. As he goes down the hall past the children's paintings (he averts his eyes from Kathi's happy sun and happy dog and her own happy face at the window in Colorado) he knows he won't make it. The hall itself is too long, already there is too much distance from his bedroom, the only place tonight where he can be, and what will happen if he lets himself be driven there and that room too becomes untenable? He pictures himself huddled on the bed while demons crawl the floor. He looks out the front door, but does not cross the threshold, he does not even take his hand from the doorknob, his look outside is hasty and as he sees the white lawn and dark street with its dirty snowbanks and the swath of yellow sand under the streetlight, the full dark pines and hemlocks, the stripped oaks and maples and elms of the common, and the lighted steeple beyond, he is seeing himself facing the alone and cold passage down the side of his apartment to the garage in the rear, and he is turning away and pulling the door shut behind him. Walking back down the hall he drinks and he drinks again before lifting Jo from his pillow.

'Things are bad out there,' he says. He sits on the bed and looks around him. 'Things are pretty bad in here too, they're coming with bugles. I feel like I'm in the Chosin Reservoir.'

'Peter: listen. Put your drink down.'

'Jesus.' He puts it down.

'Do you have your coat on?'

He looks at it on the floor, shakes his head, then says, 'No.'

'All right. Where is it?'

'It's on the floor. Right here.'

'Leave it there. Leave the drink on the table. Do you have your car keys?'

'They're in my pocket.'

'Take them out and hold them.' To do this he must stand up. He stands and reaches into his pocket and brings out the keys. He lets the other keys fall to the bottom of the ring and holds the ignition key at the ready. 'Now go outside as fast as you can. Don't shut your door behind you. Don't look to the left or the right. Don't wear gloves or a coat. If you stop you'll be cold. You'll be cold anyway. Get in the car and start it and drive it back to your door. Then leave the engine running and come back here and get your coat and tell me you're on your way. You woke me up and now

I'm awake till breakfast and I want those cigarettes and I want to see you. Now go.'

The actor in him is dead but by no means buried and he mutters huskily into the phone, 'All right, baby,' drops the phone, and surrenders to a long glance at the drink on the table but doesn't touch it. He gets a trotting start down the hall and through the foyer, leaves the front door open so light and warmth follow him outside like mute, tactile cheers. He makes it down the walk and turns and walks as fast as he can and when he reaches the corner he is shivering with cold. He turns and heads into the dark, eyes on the sidewalk; as he passes his dark living room he feels its emptiness, but as he passes the bedroom he feels Jo in there on the pillow, she is a wing man in a World War II movie, he is blinded by his shattered cockpit, she is talking him back to the carrier, she is seeing him as he passes the last bedroom window and now the lone kitchen window and he has gone farther than before.

His fingers are stiff and he jams them in his pockets, the right hand still clutching the key, and he has passed the rear corner of the building, he is approaching the driveway, with a sense of victory he turns and goes up the driveway, he knows there are two trials still ahead: stepping into the garage and then getting into the car. But he has momentum and he believes he can make it, his boots are crunching on the packed snow of the driveway, to his right is the dark rising bulk of the building where others sleep, the garage is white before him, the closed door is waiting for his hand. He is there and his cold hand closes on the black handle and he pushes upward, it is good to use his arm and shoulder, to deal with something as direct and physical as thrusting a garage door upward. The door goes up on its rollers and disappears above him. He knows better than to pause. He moves quickly into the dark garage, his teeth are chattering as he slides behind the wheel of the Volvo, his shivering fingers miss the ignition slot, then he finds it and inserts and turns and the engine starts as he notices (wise Jo, she must have gone crazy a few times) that the chill in his back is so severe that it has overwhelmed the other chill he would have felt on a night like this: the chill telling him that if he looks in the rear-view mirror he will finally see the face of a demon.

He has no time for demons now, no warm space in his body where fear of them can live. As he backs out of the garage, twisting to his right to look out the rear window, he is thinking only of the coat and gloves on his bedroom floor. He drives to the corner, leaves the engine idling, and trots up the sidewalk and through the door and down the hall. He puts on his coat and gloves, picks up the phone, and says: 'I'm on the way.'

'Good,' Jo says, and he is down the hall and out the door. He drives through the small empty town, he stops shivering, he warms beneath his coat and in his gloves, the car warms and he turns on the heater. From the radio Joan Baez serenades and celebrates his drive past locked and front-lighted stores and one bundled policeman checking locks.

She hugs him at the door and takes him to the fire in the living room and, still holding him, gives him a maternal and possessive smile that, on a saner night, would frighten him. Looking at her he begins to think that maybe she never has gone crazy, that maybe by instinct she knew what to do with him. the way they always know what to do when someone is sick or hurt. He gives her the cigarettes, she gratefully lights one, and asks if he wants a hot toddy. He says he does. She unbuttons his coat, slips off his scarf, goes behind him and takes his coat off.

'Sit here by the fire,' she says. 'I'll make the drinks.'

She takes the bottle and leaves. He sits and watches the fire and props his feet on a leather hassock. In the warmth and color of the room (it is blue, there are green potted plants, a seascape hangs on one wall, a landscape on another), in its smell of woodsmoke and the sound of burning logs, he feels safe, and when she returns with the drinks he treasures the touch of her fingers as she gives him the glass. She puts her drink on the floor and sits at his feet and unlaces his boots. He gives in to this. At first an instinct tells him he is letting her go too far, that by saving him she will possess him, but he wants his boots off, he wants a woman to take them off, and he watches her fingers on the laces, and when she is done and begins to tug at the boot he pulls his foot out. She takes off the other one and he leans back in the chair and sips. Jo remains sitting near his propped feet, her back to the fire. There are long gray streaks in her brown hair and he fondly takes one in his fingers, then smooths it back into place. Her face is awake, her eyes alert, yet about her mouth and eyes is that weariness she will probably always have; tonight he likes it.

'What was it?' she says. 'Do you know?'

'It was a girl named Miranda.'

'Miranda?'

'Miranda Jones. She's twenty-one years old.'

She lights a cigarette and settles her back against the hassock; her ribs touch his calf, her left arm rests on his knee and thigh.

'Tell me about her,' she says.

'I don't have to. I mean, I've been through this before. I don't have to get it all out anymore.'

'I want you to get it all out. For me. I want to look at it.'

He drinks and tells her; once she rises and brings him another hot toddy and sits again resting her arm on his leg and sometimes she takes his hand, fondles his fingers, and when he finishes his story she says: 'You didn't really love her. You only thought you did.'

'I've never understood the difference.'

'She was only a life jacket.'

'A life jacket is enough, if you're out in the ocean.'

Then he yields to her. He takes her hand and squeezes it with intent, he leaves his chair and lies beside her, this sad woman whom tonight he is learning to love; and as his fingers part her robe he says: 'You and I. We're what's left over, after the storm.'

Still he does not sleep. He gets up and puts another log on the fire, then lies on the rug and she returns her head to his shoulder. She lies between him and the fire, he is warm and peaceful, and his hand moves down her side and settles at her waist.

'What did you do today?' he says.

'What did I do?'

'Yes. What did you do.'

'I gave the girls breakfast.'

'What was it?'

'Oatmeal. Oatmeal and French toast.'

'Good. Then what?'

'I washed the dishes, then took the girls to church. Do you think that's silly?'

'No. No, I think it's good.'

'Do you believe in God?'

'Yes.'

'So do I. Do you know anything about Him?'

'Not much. What church was it?'

'The Unitarian.'

'The old white one by the common?'

'Yes. I looked over at your apartment. That's how I told you good morning.'

'What did you do after that?'

'I went to the supermarket. You made me feel guilty last night, about cooking. Something funny happened at the supermarket.'

'What was it?'

'You'll think I'm weird.'

'No I won't.'

'I left my basket and walked out.'

'Why?'

'The basket was full. I had groceries for a week.'

'Why did you walk out?'

'I was sad. I told you you'd think I was weird.'

'I don't. You said you were sad.'

'I was looking at all the women. They looked sad. Some had little children with them. They were barking at their children. Some were smoking. Some had their coats buttoned and they were hot but they didn't take their coats off. One stood at the meat counter. She was looking around. She wanted something. There was no one behind the counter. There's a button on a pipe, and it calls the butchers out of the room where they butcher the meat. She pressed the button. No one came. I looked at her and I looked through the window where the butchers were supposed to be. There was meat on the tables and meat hanging from hooks. But no one was there. She kept pressing the button. That's when I left.'

'Where did you go?'

'I went to a little market on the corner. Right down the street from here. I probably spent ten dollars more. It's a very small place and people nudge each other while they shop. There's a butcher and a man at the cash register. They knew everyone in the store except me. Everyone was talking. The butcher talked to me while he cut the meat. He told me how good the meat was. He told me he was spoiling me. He's old, and the man at the cash register is his son. I figured that out listening to them. The man at the cash register told me it was going to snow three inches. That's what I paid the ten dollars for. I'll go back.'

'I'll go with you.'

Outside the sky is growing light, the night is almost ended, and inside Peter lies awake. Jo sleeps in his arms, his flesh is warm from the fire, and his heart is a piñata: it bursts and streams invisible colors which he can see: they are the colors of fire, the hopeful rose and gold and red of sunrise, and in the colors he sees Jo, her eyes are a laughing pale blue sky, tonight he will bring wine and flowers, this afternoon between records he will say, once and softly: Hello Jo; and he means that hello, his warm heart pounds with it, he will follow the course of it, for love is time too, and lying here before the fire and looking at her sleeping face on his arm he knows he will love her, and with great relief and new strength his blood runs through his body and he kisses her until she warmly wakes and encircles him with her squeezing arms; he ascends; he is Prometheus; and he pauses in his passion to gently kiss her brightened eyes.

# Miranda Over the Valley

LL that day she thought of Michaelis: as she
packed for school in Boston and con-
firmed her reservation and, in Woodland
Hills, did shopping which she knew
was foolish: as though she were going to some primitive land, she
bought deodorant and bath powder and shampoo, and nylons
and leotards for the cold. At one o'clock she was driving the Corvette past cracked tan earth and dry brush, it was a no smoking
zone and she put out her cigarette and thought: Now he has finished his lunch and they have gone back to the roof, he's not wearing his shirt, he has a handkerchief tied around his head so sweat
won't burn his eyes; he's kneeling down nailing shingles. She saw
them eating dinner, her last good Mexican food until she flew west
again at Thanksgiving, but she could not see the evening beyond
dinner. She saw enchiladas and Margaritas, she saw them talking,
she talked with him now driving to the shopping center, but after
that she saw nothing. And she was afraid. In the evening she
brushed her long dark hair and waited for him and she opened the
front door when he rang; he was tall, he was tanned from his summer work, and he shook her father's hand and kissed her mother's
cheek. Miranda liked the approval in her parents' eyes, and she
took his arm as they walked out to the driveway, to his old and
dented Plymouth parked behind the Corvette. They went to dinner and then drove and then stopped on Mulholland Drive, high
above the fog lying over the San Fernando Valley, and out her window she saw stars and a lone cloud slowly passing the moon. She
took his thick curly hair in one hand and kissed him and with her
tongue she told him yes, told him again and again while she waited
for him to know she was saying yes.

The next day her parents and Michaelis took her to the airport.

She met Holly at the terminal and they flew to Boston. She was eighteen years old.

She lived with Holly in a second-floor apartment Holly found on Beacon Street. It was large, and its wide, tall windows overlooked the old, shaded street. They put a red carpet in the living room and red curtains at the windows. Holly's boyfriend, who went to school in Rhode Island, built them a bar in one corner, at the carpet's edge. Holly was a year older than Miranda, this was her second year at Boston University, and the boys who came to the apartment were boys she had known last year. There were also some new ones, and soon Holly was making love with one of them. His name was Brian. When he came to the apartment Miranda watched him and listened to him, but she could neither like him nor dislike him, because she could not understand who he was. He was a student and for him the university was a stalled escalator: he leaned against its handrails, he looked about him and talked and gestured with his hands, his pale face laughed and he stroked his beard, and his hair tossed at his neck. But there was no motion about him.

When he spent the night, Holly unfolded the day bed in the living room and Miranda had the bedroom to herself. She lay on her twin bed at the window and listened to rock music from an all-night FM station; still there were times when, over the music, she could hear Holly moaning in the next room. The sounds and her images always excited her, but sometimes they made her sad too; for on most weekends Tom drove up from Providence and on Friday and Saturday nights Miranda fell asleep after the same sounds had hushed. Brian knew about Tom and seemed as indifferent to his weekend horns as he was to an incomplete in a course or the theft of his bicycle, which he left on the sidewalk outside a Cambridge bar one Sunday afternoon.

Tom knew nothing about Holly's week nights. The lottery had spared him, so he was a graduate student in history and, though he tried not to, at least once each visit he spoke of the diminishing number of teaching jobs. He was robust and shyly candid and Miranda liked him very much. She liked Holly very much too and she did not want to feel disapproval, but there it was in her heart when she heard the week night sounds and then the weekend sounds, and when she looked at Tom's red face and thick brown moustache and thinning hair. One night in late September Miranda and Holly went to a movie and when they came home they sat at the bar in the living room and drank a glass of wine. After a second glass Miranda said Tom had built a nice bar. Then she asked if he was coming this weekend. Holly said he was.

'I'd feel divided,' Miranda said, and she looked at Holly's long blonde hair and at the brown, yellow-tinted eyes that watched her like a wise and preying cat.

Then it was early October and she was afraid. At first it was only for moments which struck her at whim: sometimes in class or as she walked home on cool afternoons she remembered and was afraid. But she did not really believe, so she was only afraid when memory caught her off guard, before she could reassure herself that no one was that unlucky. Another week went by and she told Holly she was late.

'You can't be,' Holly said.

'No. No, it must be something else.'

'What would you do?'

She didn't know. She didn't know anything except that now she was afraid most of the time. Always she was waiting. Whether she was in class or talking to Holly or some other friend, even while she slept and dreamed, she was waiting for that flow of blood that would empty her womb whether it held a child or not. Although she did not think of womb, of child, of miscarriage. She hoped only for blood.

Then October was running out and she knew her luck was too. Late Halloween afternoon she went to the office of a young gynecologist who had the hands of a woman, a plump face and thin, pouting lips. He kept looking at his wrist watch. He asked if she planned to keep the child and when she told him yes he said that if she were still in Boston a month from now to come see him. As she was leaving, the receptionist asked her for twenty dollars. Miranda wrote a check, then went out to the street where dusk had descended and where groups of small witches, skeletons, devils, and ghosts in sheets moved past her as she stopped to light a cigarette; she followed in the wake of their voices. Holly was home. When Miranda told her she said: 'Oh Jesus. Oh Jesus Jesus Jesus.'

'I'm all right,' Miranda said. She noticed that she sounded as if she were reciting something. 'I'm all right. I'm not in trouble, I'm only having a baby. It's too early to call Michaelis. It's only three o'clock in California. He'll still be at school. I'd like to rest a while then eat a nice meal.'

'We only have hamburger. I'll go out and get us some steaks.'

'Here.'

'No. It's my treat.'

While Holly was gone, Miranda put on Simon and Garfunkel and the Beatles and lay on the couch. The doorbell rang and she went downstairs and gave candy to the children. She and Holly had bought the candy yesterday: candy corn, jelly beans, bags of small Tootsie Rolls, orange slices, and chocolate kisses; and now, pouring candy into the children's paper bags, smiling and praising costumes, she remembered how frightened she was yesterday in the store: looking at the cellophane bags of candy, she had felt she did not have the courage to grow a minute older and therefore would not. Now as she passed out the candy she felt numb, stationary, as though she were suspended out of time and could see each second as it passed, and each of them went on without her.

She went upstairs and lay on the couch and the doorbell rang again. The children in this group were costumed too, but older, twelve or thirteen, and one of the girls asked for a cigarette. Miranda told her to take candy or nothing. When she went upstairs she was very tired. She had been to three classes, and she had walked in the cold to the doctor's and back. While the Beatles were singing she went to sleep. The doorbell rang but she didn't answer; she went back into her deep sleep. When Holly came in talking, Miranda woke up, her heart fast with fright. Holly put on the Rolling Stones and broiled the steaks and they drank Burgundy. During dinner Brian called, saying he wanted to come over, but Holly told him to make it tomorrow.

At eight o'clock, when it was five in California, Miranda went to the bedroom and closed the door and sat on her bed. The phone was on the bedside table. She lowered her hand to the receiver but did not lift it. She gazed at her face in the reflecting window. She was still frozen out of time, and she was afraid that if Michaelis wasn't home, if the phone rang and rang against the walls of his empty apartment, something would happen to her, something she could not control, she would go mad in Holly's arms. Then she turned away from her face in the window and looked at the numbers as she dialed; his phone rang only twice and then he answered and time had started again.

'Happy Halloween,' she said.

'Trick or treat.'

'Trick,' she said. 'I'm pregnant.' He was silent. She closed her eyes and squeezed the phone, as though her touch could travel too,

as her voice did, and she saw the vast night between their two
coasts, saw the telephone lines crossing the dark mountains and
plains and mountains between them.

'It's about two months, is that right?'

'It was September second.'

'I know. Do you want to get married?'

'Do you?'

'Of course I do. If that's what you're thinking about.'

'I'm not thinking about anything. I saw the doctor this afternoon
and I haven't thought about anything.'

'Look: do you want to do it at Thanksgiving? That'll give me
time to arrange things, I have to find out about blood tests and stuff,
and your folks'll need some time—you want me to talk to them?'

'No, I will.'

'Okay, and then after Thanksgiving you can go back and finish
the semester. At least you'll have that done. I can be looking for
another apartment. This is all right for me, *may*be all right for two,
but with a —' He stopped.

'Are you sure you want to?'

'Of course I am. It just sounded strange, saying it.'

'You didn't say it.'

'Oh. Anyway, we'll need more room.'

'I didn't think he'd do that,' Holly said. She was sitting on the
living room carpet, drinking tea. Miranda could not sit down; she
stood at the window over Beacon Street, she went to the bar for a
cigarette, she moved back to the window. 'I just didn't think he
would,' Holly said.

'You didn't want him to.'

'Are you really going to get *mar*ried?'

'I love him.'

'He's your first one.'

'My first one. You mean the first one I've made love with.'

'Yes.'

'And that's how you mean it.'

'That's how. And you've only done *that* once.'

'That's not what it means to me.'

'How would you know? You've never had anybody else.'

'But you have.'

'What's that mean.'

'I guess it means look at yourself.'

'All right. I'll look at myself. I've never had to get married, and I've never had to get an abortion, and nobody owns me.'

'I want to be owned.'

'You do?'

'Yes. The way you are now, you have to lie.'

'I don't lie to Tom. He doesn't ask.'

'I don't mean just that. I don't know what I mean; it's just all of it. I have to go outside for a minute. I have to walk outside.'

She put on her coat as she went down the gray-carpeted stairs. She walked to the corner and then up the dead-end street and climbed the steps of the walk that crossed Storrow Drive. As she climbed she held the iron railing, but it was cold and she had forgotten her gloves. She put her hands in her pockets. She stood on the walk and watched the cars coming and passing beneath her and listened to their tires on the wet street. To her right was the Charles River, wide and black and cold. On sunny days it was blue and in the fall she had watched sailboats on it. Beyond the river were the lights of Cambridge; she thought of the bars there and the warm students drinking beer and she wanted Michaelis with her now. She knew that: she wanted him. She had wanted him for a long time but she had told him no, had even gone many times to his apartment and still told him no, because all the time she was thinking. On that last night she wasn't thinking, and she had not done any thinking since then: she had moved through September and October in the fearful certainty of love, and she still had that as she stood shivering above the street, looking out at the black river and the lights on the other side.

She phoned her parents at nine-fifteen, during their cocktail hour. Her mother talked on the phone in the breakfast room, and her father went to his den and used the phone there. He would be wearing a cardigan and drinking a martini. Her mother would be wearing a dress; nearly always she put on a dress at the end of the day. She would be sitting on the stool by the phone, facing the blackboard where Miranda and her two older brothers had read messages when they came home from school, and written their own. Once, when she was a little girl, she had come home and read: *Pussycat, I'm playing golf. I'll be home at four, in time to pay Maria.* And she had written: *Maria was not here. I feel sick and I am going to bed.* Beyond her mother's head, the sun would be setting over the bluff behind the house; part of the pool would be in the bluff's shadow, the water close to the house still and sunlit blue.

The sun would be coming through the sliding glass doors that opened to the pool and the lawn, those glass doors that one morning when she was twelve she opened and, looking down, saw a small rattlesnake coiled sleeping in the shade on the flagstone inches from her bare feet. As she shut the doors and cried out for her father it raised its head and started to rattle. Her father came running bare-chested in pajama pants; then he went to his room and got a small automatic he kept in his drawer and shot the snake as it slithered across the stones. Sunlight would be coming through those doors now and into the breakfast room and shining on her mother in a bright dress.

'Fly home tomorrow,' her mother said.

'Well, I'll be home at Thanksgiving. Michaelis said he'd arrange it for then.'

'We'd like to see you before *that*,' her mother said.

'And don't worry,' her father said. 'You're not the first good kids to get into a little trouble.'

That night she fell asleep listening to her father's deep and soothing voice as it drew her back through October and September, by her long hair (but gently) dragging her into August and the house in Woodland Hills, the pepper trees hanging long over the sidewalks, on summer mornings coffee at the glass table beside the pool and at sixteen (with her father) a cigarette too, though not with her mother until she was seventeen; in the morning she woke to his voice and she heard it on the plane and could not read *Time* or *Holiday* or *Antigone*, and it was his voice she descended through in the night above Los Angeles, although it was Michaelis who waited for her, who embraced her. When they got home and she hugged her father she held him tightly and for a moment she had no volition and wanted none. Just before kissing her mother, Miranda looked at her eyes: they were green and they told her she had been foolish; then Miranda kissed her, held her, and in her own tightening arms she felt again her resolve.

They went to the breakfast room. Before they started talking, Miranda went outside and looked at the pool and lawn in the dark. Fog was settling; tops of trees touched the sky above the bluff. She went in and sat at one end of the table, facing her father and the glass doors behind him. They reflected the room. Her father's neck and bald head were brown from playing golf, his thin moustache clipped, more gray than she had remembered, and there was more gray too (or more than she had seen, thinking of him in Boston) in the short brown hair at the sides of his head. He was drinking brandy. Or he had a snifter of brandy in front of him, but he mostly handled it; he picked it up and put it down; he ran his finger around the rim; he warmed it in his cupped hands but didn't drink; with thumb and fingers he turned it on the table. He was smoking a very thin cigar, and now and then he cheated and inhaled. Her mother sat to his left, at the side of the table; she had pulled her chair close to his end of the table and turned it so she faced Miranda and Michaelis. Her hair had been growing darker for years and she had kept it blonde and long. Her skin was tough and tan, her face lined, weathered, and she wore bracelets that jangled. She was drinking brandy and listening, though she appeared not listening so much as hearing again lines she had played to for a hundred nights, and waiting for her cue. Miranda mostly watched her father, because he was talking, though sometimes she glanced at Michaelis; he was the one she wanted to watch, but she didn't; for she didn't want anyone, not even him, to see how much she was appealing to him. He sat to her left, his chair was pulled toward her so that he faced her parents, and when she looked at him she saw his quiet profile, his dark curly hair, his large hand holding the can of Coors, and his right shoulder, which was turned slightly away from her. She wanted to see his eyes but she did not really need to; for in the way he occupied space, quiet, attentive, nodding, his arms that were so often spread and in motion now close to his chest, she saw and felt what she had seen at the airport: above his jocular mouth the eyes had told her he had not been living well with his fear.

'—so it's not Mother and me that counts. It's *you* two. We've got to think about what's best for you two.'

'And the baby,' Miranda said.

'Come on, sweetheart. That's not a baby. It's just something you're piping blood into.'

'It's alive; that's why you want me to kill it.'

'Sweetheart—'

'Do you *really* want it?' her mother said.

'Yes.'

'I don't believe you. You mean you're happy about it? You're *glad* you're pregnant?'

'I can do it.'

'You can have a baby, sure,' her father said. 'But what about Michaelis? Do you know how much studying there is in law school?'

'I can work,' she said.

'I thought you were having a baby,' her mother said.

'I can work.'

'And hire a Mexican woman to take care of your child.'

'I can work!'

'You're being foolish.'

Her father touched her mother's arm.

'Wait, honey. Listen, sweetheart, I know you can work. That's not the point. The point is, why suffer? Jesus, sweetheart, you're eighteen years old. You've never had to live out there. The hospital and those Goddamn doctors will own you. And you've got to eat once in a while. Michaelis, have another beer.'

Michaelis got up and as he moved behind Miranda's chair she held up her wine glass and he took it. When he came back with his beer and her glass of wine he said: 'I can do it.'

'Maybe you shouldn't,' her mother said. 'Whether you can or not. Maybe it won't be good for Miranda. What are you going to be, pussycat—a dumb little housewife? Your husband will be out in the world, he'll be growing, and all you'll know is diapers and Gerbers. You've got to finish college—' It was so far away now: blackboards, large uncurtained windows looking out at nothing, at other walls, other windows; talking, note-taking; talking, talking, talking . . . She looked at Michaelis; he was watching her mother, listening. '—You can't make marriage the be-all and end-all. Because if you do it won't work. Listen: from the looks of things we've got one of the few solid marriages around. But it took work, pussycat. Work.' Her eyes gleamed with the victory of that work, the necessity for it. 'And we were older. I was twenty-six, I'd been to school, I'd worked; you see the difference it makes? After all these years with this guy—and believe me some of them have been like standing in the rain—now that I'm getting old and going blind from charcoal smoke at least I know I didn't give anything up to get married. Except my independence. But I was fed up with that. And all right: I'll tell you something else too. I'd had other relationships. With men. That helped too. There—' she lightly smacked the table '—that's my confession for the night.'

But her face was not the face of someone confessing. In her smile, which appeared intentionally hesitant, intentionally vulnerable, and in the crinkling tan flesh at the corners of her eyes, in the wide green eyes themselves, and in the tone of finality in her throaty voice—there: now it's out, I've told you everything, that's how much I care, the voice said; her smacking of the table with a palm said—Miranda sensed a coaxing trick that she did not want to understand. But she did understand and she sat hating her mother, whose eyes and smile were telling her that making love with Michaelis was a natural but subsidiary part of growing up; that finally what she felt that night and since (and before: the long, muddled days and nights when she was not so much trying to decide but to free herself so she could make love without deciding) amounted now to nothing more than anxiety over baby fat and pimples. It meant nothing. Miranda this fall meant nothing. She would outgrow the way she felt. She would look back on those feelings with amused nostalgia as she could now look back on grapefruit and cottage cheese, and the creams she had applied on her face at night, the camouflaging powder during the day.

'You see,' her father said, 'we don't object to you having a lover. Hell, we can't. What scares us, though, is you being unhappy: and the odds are that you *will* be. Now think of it the other way. Try to, sweetheart. I've never forced you to do anything—I've never been *a*ble to—and I'm not forcing you now. I only want you to look at it from a different side for a while. You and Mother fly to New York—' She felt sentenced to death. Her legs were cool and weak, her heart beat faster within images of her cool, tense body under lights, violated. '—the pill, then you're safe. Both of you. You have three years to grow. You can go back to school—'

'To be *what?*' she said. 'To be *what*,' and she wiped her eyes.

'That's exactly it,' her mother said. 'You don't know yet what you want to be but you say you're ready to get married.'

She had not said that. She had said something altogether different, though she couldn't explain it, could not even explain it to herself. When they said married they were not talking about her. That was not what she wanted. Perhaps she wanted nothing. Except to be left alone as she was in Boston to listen to the fearful pulsations of her body; to listen to them; to sleep with them; wake with them. It was not groceries. She saw brown bags, cans. That was not it. She watched Michaelis. He was listening to them, and in his eyes she saw relieved and grateful capitulation. In his eyes that night his passion was like fear. He was listening to them, he was nodding, and now they were offering the gift, wrapped in her father's voice: '—So much better that way, so much more sensible. And this Christmas, say right after Christmas, you could go to Acapulco. Just the two of you. It's nice at that time of year, you know? It could be your Christmas present. The trip could.'

She smiled before she knew she was smiling; slightly she shook her head, feeling the smile like a bandage: they were giving her a honeymoon, her honeymoon lover in the Acapulco hotel after he had been sucked from her womb. She would have cried, but she felt dry inside, she was tired, and she knew the night was ended.

'I was afraid on Mulholland Drive. I was afraid in Boston. It was the most important thing there was. How I was afraid all the time.' Her parents' faces were troubled with compassion; they loved her; in her father's eyes she saw her own pain. 'I kept wanting not to be afraid, and it was all I thought about. Then I stopped wanting that. I was afraid, and it was me, and it was all right. Now we can go to Acapulco.' She looked at Michaelis. He looked at her, guilty, ashamed; then he looked at her parents as though to draw from them some rational poise; but it didn't work, and he lowered his eyes to his beer can. 'Michaelis? Do you want to go to Acapulco?'

Still he looked down. He had won and lost, and his unhappy face struggled to endure both. He shrugged his shoulders, but only slightly, little more than a twitch, as if in mid-shrug he had realized what a cowardly gesture the night had brought him to. That was how she would most often remember him: even later when she would see him, when she would make love with him (but only one more time), she would not see the nearly healed face he turned to her, but his face as it was now, the eyes downcast; and his broad shoulders in their halted shrug.

It was not remorse she felt. It was dying. In the mornings she woke with it, and as she brushed her hair and ate yogurt or toast and honey and coffee and walked with Holly to school as the November days grew colder, she felt that ropes of her own blood trailed from her back and were knotted in New York, on that morning, and that she could not move forward because she could not go back to free herself. And she could not write to Michaelis. She tried, and she wrote letters like this: —*the lit exam wasn't as hard as I expected. I love reading the Greeks. The first snow has fallen, and it's lovely and I like looking out the window at it and walking in it. I've learned to make a snow angel. You lie on your back in the snow and you spread your arms and legs, like doing jumping jacks, and then you stand up carefully and you've left an angel in the snow, with big, spreading wings. Love, Miranda.* When she wrote *love* she wanted to draw lines through it, to cover it with ink, for she felt she was lying. Or not that. It was the word that lied, and when she shaped it with her pen she felt the false letters, and heard the hollow sound of the word.

She did not like being alone anymore. Before, she had liked coming home in the late afternoon and putting on records and studying or writing to Michaelis or just lying on the couch near the sunset window until Holly came home. But now that time of day (and it was a dark time, winter coming, the days growing short) was like the other time: morning, waking, when there was death in her soul, in her blood, and she thought of the dead thing she wouldn't call by name, and she wished for courage in the past, wished she had gone somewhere alone, New Hampshire or Maine, a small house in the woods, and lived alone with the snow and the fireplace and a general store down the road and read books and walked in the woods while her body grew, and it grew. She would not call it anything even when she imagined February's swollen belly; that would be in June; the second of June. Already she would not think June when she knew she would say: Today is probably the day my baby would have been born. So she could not be alone anymore, not even in this apartment she loved, this city she loved.

She thought of it as a gentle city. And she felt gentle too, and tender. One morning she saw a small yellow dog struck by a car; the dog was not killed; it ran yelping on three legs, holding up the fourth, quivering, and Miranda could feel the pain in that hind leg moving through the cold air. She could not see blood in movies anymore. She read the reviews, took their warnings, stayed away. Sometimes when she saw children on the street she was sad; and there were times when she longed for her own childhood. She remembered what it was like not knowing anything, and she felt sorry for herself because what she knew now was killing her, she felt creeping death in her breast, and bitterly she regretted the bad luck that had brought her this far, this alone; and so she wanted it all to be gone, November and October and September, she wanted to be a virgin again, to go back even past that, to be so young she didn't know virgin from not-virgin. She knew this was dangerous. She knew that nearly everything she was feeling now was dangerous, and so was her not-feeling: her emptiness when she wrote to her parents and Michaelis; in classrooms she felt abstract; when people came to the apartment she talked with them, she got high with them, but she was only a voice. She neither greeted them nor told them goodbye with her body; she touched no one; or, if she did, she wasn't aware of it; if anyone touched her they touched nothing. One night as she was going to bed stoned she said to Holly: 'I'm a piece of chalk.' She thought of seeing a psychiatrist but believed (had to believe) that all this would leave her.

On days when she got home before Holly, she put on music and spent every moment waiting for Holly. Sometimes, waiting, she drank wine or smoked a pipe, and the waiting was not so bad; although sometimes with wine it was worse, the wine seemed to relax her in the wrong way, so that her memory and dread and predictions were even sharper, more cruel. With dope the waiting was always easier. She was worried about drinking alone, smoking alone; but she was finally only vaguely worried. The trouble she was in was too deep for her to worry about its surfaces. When Holly came home, short of breath from climbing the stairs, her fair cheeks reddened from the cold and her blonde hair damp with snow like drops of dew, Miranda talked and talked while they cooked, and she ate heartily, and felt that eating was helping her, as though she were recovering from an illness of the flesh.

Her parents and Michaelis wanted her to fly home at Thanksgiving but she went to Maine with Diane, a friend from school. Holly told her parents she was going too, and she went to Rhode Island with Tom. Diane's parents lived in a large brick house overlooking the sea. They were cheerful and affluent, and they were tall and slender like Diane, who had freckles that were fading as winter came. There was a younger brother who was tall and quiet and did not shave yet, and his cheeks were smooth as a girl's. Around him Miranda felt old.

She had never seen the Atlantic in winter. On Thanksgiving morning she woke before Diane and sat at the window. The sky was gray, a wind was blowing, the lawn sloping down to the sea was snow, and the wind blew gusts of it like powder toward the house. The lawn ended at the beach, at dark rocks; the rocks went out into the sea, into the gray, cold waves. Beyond the rocks she saw a seal swimming. She watched it, sleek and brown and purposeful, going under, coming up. She quickly dressed in corduroy pants and sweater and boots and coat and went downstairs; she heard Diane's parents having coffee in the kitchen, and quietly went outside and down the slippery lawn to the narrow strip of sand and the rocks. But the seal was gone. She stood looking out at the sea. Once she realized she had been daydreaming, though she could not recall what it was she dreamed; but for a minute or longer she had not known where she was, and when she turned from her dreaming to look at the house, to locate herself, there was a moment when she did not know the names of the people inside. Then she began walking back and forth in front of the house, looking into the wind at the sea. Before long a light snow came blowing in on the salt wind. She turned her face to it. I suppose I don't love Diane, she told herself. For a moment I forgot her name.

Then it was December, a long Saturday afternoon that was gray without snow, and Holly was gone for the weekend. In late afternoon Miranda left the lighted apartment and a paper she was writing and walked up Beacon Street. The street and sidewalks were wet and the gutters held gray, dirty snow. She walked to the Public Garden where there were trees and clean snow, and on a bridge over a frozen pond she stopped and watched children skating. Then she walked through the Garden and across the street to the Common; the sidewalks around it were crowded, the Hare Krishna people were out too, with their shaved heads and pigtails and their robes in the cold, chanting their prayer. She did not see any winos. In warm weather they slept on the grass or sat staring from benches, wearing old, dark suits and sometimes a soiled hat. But now they were gone, and where, she wondered, did they go when the sky turns cold? She walked across the Common to the State House; against the gray sky its gold dome looked odd, like something imported from another country. Then she walked home. Already dusk was coming, and she didn't want to be alone. When she got home Brian was ringing the doorbell.

'Holly's not here,' she said.

'I know. Are you here?'

'Sometimes. Come on up.'

He was tall and he wore a fatigue jacket. She looked away from his face, reached in her pocket for the key; she felt him wanting her, it was like a current from his body, and she felt it as she opened the door and as they climbed the stairs. In the apartment she gave him a beer.

'Are you hungry?' she said.

'No.'

'I am. If I cook something, will you eat it?'

'Sure.'

'There's chicken. Is chicken all right? Broiled?'

'Chicken? Why not?'

He followed her to the kitchen. While she cooked they talked and he had another beer and she drank wine. She wasn't hungry anymore. She knew something would happen and she was waiting for it, waiting to see what she would do. She cooked and they ate and then went to the living room and smoked a pipe on the couch. When he took off her sweater she nearly said let's go to bed, but she didn't. She closed her eyes and waited and when he was undressed she kissed his bearded face. Her eyes were closed. She felt wicked and that excited her; he was very thin; her body was quick and wanton; but her heart was a stone; her heart was a clock; her heart was a watching eye. Then he shuddered and his weight rested on her and she said: 'You bastard.'

He left her. He sat at the end of the couch, at her feet; he took a swallow of beer and leaned back and looked at the ceiling.

'I saw it downstairs,' he said. 'You wanted to ball.'

'Don't call it that.'

He looked at her; then he leaned over and picked up his socks.

'No,' she said. 'Call it that.' He put on his socks. 'Say it again.'

'What are you playing?'

'I'm not. I don't play anymore. It's all—What are you doing?'

'I'm putting on my pants.' He was standing, buckling his belt. He picked up his sweater from the floor.

'No,' she said. 'I'm cold.'

'Get dressed.'

'I don't want you to go. Let's get in bed.'

'That'll be the second time tonight I do something you want me to. Will I be a bastard again?'

'No. I'm just screwed up, Brian, that's all.'

'Who isn't?'

In bed he was ribs and hip bone against her side and she liked resting her head on his long hard arm.

'What's the matter?' he said. 'You worried about that guy in California?'

'He's not there anymore.'

'Where'd he go?'

'He's still there. Things happened.'

'Have you had many guys?'

'Just him and you. You won't tell Holly, will you?'

'Why should I?'

'How long have you been in school?'

'Six years, on and off.'

'What will you do?'

'They haven't told me yet.'

'Michaelis is going to be a lawyer.'

'Good for him.'

'I used to love him.'

'Figures.'

'He's going to work with Chicanos. I won't be with him now. For a whole year I thought about that. I was going to marry him and have a baby and carry it like a papoose on the picket lines. We wouldn't have much money. That was it for a whole year and I was feeling all that when I made love with him, it was my first time and I hurt and I bled and I probably wasn't any good, but my God I felt wonderful. I felt like I was going to heaven.'

'You better cheer up, man. There's other guys.'

'Oh yes, I know: there are other guys. Miranda will have other guys.'

Her heart did not change: not that night when they made love again, nor Sunday morning waking to his hands. Late Sunday night Holly came home and Miranda woke up but until Holly was undressed and in bed she pretended she was asleep so Holly wouldn't turn on the lights. Then she pretended to wake up because she wanted to talk to Holly before, in the morning, she saw her face.

'How was your weekend?'

'Fine. What did you do?'

'Stayed in the apartment and studied.'

She lit a cigarette. Holly came over and took one from the pack. Miranda did not look at her: she closed her eyes and smoked and felt the sour cold of the lie. Holly was back in bed, talking into the distance of the lie, and Miranda listened and answered and lay tense in bed, for she was so many different Mirandas: the one with Holly now and the one who made love with Brian (balled; balled; she was sore) and the one who didn't want to make love with Brian (b——); and beneath or among those there were perhaps two other Mirandas, and suddenly she almost cried, remembering September and October when she was afraid but she was one Miranda Jones. She sat up quickly, too quickly, so that Holly stopped talking and then said: 'What's wrong?'

'Nothing. I just want another cigarette.'

'You should get out next weekend.'

'Probably.'

'Come to Providence with me.'

'What would I do?'

'I don't know. Whatever you do here. And we can get you a date.'

'Maybe I will. Probably I won't, though.'

Tuesday after dinner Brian came over. He sat on the couch with Holly, and Miranda faced them from a chair. She tried not to look directly at him but she could not help herself: she drank too much beer and she watched him. He kept talking. Her nakedness was not in his face. She felt it was in hers, though, when Holly's hand dropped to his thigh and rested there. She was not jealous; she did not love Brian; she felt as though something were spilled in the room, something foul and shameful, and no one dared look at it, and no one would clean it up. I'm supposed to be cool, she told herself as she went to the refrigerator and opened three cans of beer. She opened Brian's last. It was his because it was on the left and she would carry it in her left hand and she remembered his hands. I am not for this world, she thought. Or it isn't for me. It's not because I'm eighteen either. Michaelis is twenty-two; he will get brown in the sun talking to Chicanos, he will smell of beer and onions, but his spirit won't rise; Michaelis is of the world, he will be a lawyer.

She brought Holly and Brian their beer. I'm supposed to be cool, she told herself as she watched Holly's hand on his leg, watched his talking face where she didn't live. And where did she live? Whose eyes will hold me, whose eyes will know me when my own eyes look back at me in the morning and I am not in them? I'm supposed to be cool, she told herself as she went to her room and felt the room move as she settled heavily under the blankets; she was bloated with beer, she knew in the morning her mouth would be dry, her stomach heavy and liquid. From the living room the sounds came. It's not me. She was drunk and for a moment she thought she had said it aloud. It's not me they're doing it to. I don't love him. She remembered his hard, thin legs between hers and she saw him with Holly and wary as a thief her hand slid down and she moved against it. It's not me they're doing it to. She listened to the sounds from the other room and moved within them against her hand.

In his bed in his apartment Michaelis held her and his large, dark eyes were wet, and she spoke to him and kissed and dried his tears, though she felt nothing for them; she gave them her lips as she might have given coins to a beggar. She could feel nothing except that it was strange for him to cry; she did not believe she would ever cry again; not for love. It was her first night home, they had left her house three hours earlier, left her mother's voice whose gaiety could not veil her fear and its warning: 'Don't be late,' she said, meaning don't spend the night, don't drive our own nails through our hands; already her mother's eyes (and, yes, her father's too) were hesitant, vulpine. How can we get our daughter back? the eyes said. We have saved her. But now how do we get her back? Her parents' hands and arms were loving; they held her tightly; they drew her to their hearts. The arms and eyes told her not to go to Acapulco after Christmas; not to want to go. No matter. She did not want to go. Michaelis's arms were tight and loving too, he lay on his side, his body spent from loving her, and now she was spending his soul too, watching it drip on his cheeks: '—It didn't mean anything. Don't cry. We won't go to Acapulco. I don't think I'll sleep with Brian again, but we won't go to Acapulco. I want to do other things. I don't know what they'll be yet. You'll have a good life, Michaelis. Don't worry: you will. It'll be a fine life. Don't be sad. Things end, that's all. But you'll be fine. Do you want to take me home now? Or do you want me to stay a while. I'll stay the night if you want—'

She propped on an elbow and looked at him. He had stopped crying, his cheeks glistened still, and he lay on his back now, staring at the ceiling. She could see in his face that he would not make love with her again or, for some time, with anyone else. She watched him until she didn't need to anymore. Then she called a taxi and put on her clothes. When she heard the taxi's horn she left Michaelis lying naked in the dark.

# Separate Flights

*The whales, whose periodic suicide instinct has
never been explained by scientists, started ground-
ing themselves yesterday afternoon on the
Florida Bay side of Grassy Key, about seven miles
north of Marathon, in the Florida Keys.*
—New York Times

*for Lynn*

§1    ON the short afternoons of winter Beth Harrison turned on the lights early and started a fire in the living room; when her daughter Peggy came home from high school they sat in chairs facing the fire, Peggy drinking hot chocolate, Beth drinking a bourbon-and-water which she always thought of as her second, though sometimes it was her third. She was forty-nine years old. She did not know—or did not try to know, since there was no reason to—exactly when her before-dinner drinking had slipped into an earlier part of the afternoon. In winter she drank when she turned on the lights and started a fire. But now in May she drank gin and tonic while the sun angled through the kitchen windows, and Mrs. Lester on the corner played golf, and the Crenshaw boys across the street yelled and smacked a whiffle ball. She was usually alone, for Peggy and Bucky ate ice cream cones after school and went driving and Peggy came home in time for dinner, her cheeks warm, her eyes bright as though with images of trees turning green and sunlit farmers plowing their fields.

Today when Lee came home Beth was peeling potatoes at the kitchen table, drinking her third gin and tonic since taking the cleaning woman home at three-thirty. When he saw the drink in her hand his eyes changed, darkened for an instant as in scolding or scorn; then he said hello and moving around the table briefly kissed her lips.

'I picked up the tickets,' he said.

'Who's going first?'

'Mine's at three-thirty and yours is four-forty.'

While he was upstairs changing clothes she made two drinks, and when he came down in sport shirt and loafers he took his and started toward the living room.

'Will I see you in Chicago?' she said.

He turned at the door.

'My connection's right away, so I'll see you in San Francisco.'

'Will I have to wait long?'

'Course not. I'll meet your plane.'

'I mean in Chicago.'

'About thirty minutes. You're on 427 from Chicago, I'm on 502.'

He was turning toward the living room when she said: 'So if 427 goes down—or 502—we've made a mistake.'

'Well, that's true, but it's better to gamble with losing one of us than both.'

'Do you know what you're gambling with?'

'It's for Peggy, you know that.'

'No, she's the stakes. I mean what's holding the other hand?'

He looked at her for a moment; then he half-turned to the living room, standing profiled in the kitchen doorway.

'All I know is it's sound, it's practical. Our company does it, other companies do it—' Then he stopped. 'Anyhow—' he said, and shrugged and went into the living room; she heard him sliding the hassock, then snapping straight the front page of the *Des Moines Register*. She finished peeling the potatoes and went outside to light the charcoal. She watched it until Bucky brought Peggy home, then Lee came outside and the three of them sat in lawn chairs around the grill. Peggy held a small red water pistol and shot at steak drippings that flamed on the charcoal.

'Peggy,' Lee said. 'You know the last thing I did before I came home today? I made a call on a woman who buried her husband last week. He was well covered, so she's better fixed for money than she was before, but the point is she's a widow now. And you know how old she is? Fifty-five. Even it that seems old to you, it's mighty young to be a widow in 1967. She'll probably live another twenty years. And her husband: her husband was fifty-eight—'

Beth sipped her drink and watched two young squirrels darting about in the elm tree whose branches nearly touched the roof, and she wondered if she would ever see seventy-five, or if she even wanted to. Then she looked to her right, at Peggy, her blue eyes made brighter by contact lenses, her cheek concave as she drew on a cigarette, faint downy hair on her face catching the sunlight, and Beth could not imagine this child, her second and last—no: she could not imagine her living through the next sixty years. When Beth was a child the years seemed straight and simple as a road. Yet now they were wide and deep, unbounded as corn fields covered by snow, or in early spring when the fields lay bare as far as you could see and wind blew from the southwest and the sky turned black and yellow; you looked out over the blowing dust and scattered, bending trees and waited for the tornado funnel. Now she heard Lee's voice but not what he said, and the squirrels had left the elm or entered its trunk, and she was thinking of long ago when she lived in the country and spring was like that. Her hand had risen to Peggy's shoulder and was resting there.

'What would I do with a thousand dollars?' Peggy said.

'Two, then. I'll give you two.'

'Oh Daddy, I appreciate it. I *really* do. I mean that you care how I die. But I don't want to quit and you know yourself if you don't really want to, you can't.'

'I did.'

'But you were scared enough.'

'And you ought to be. Haven't you heard your mother, the way she breathes when she carries in groceries or climbs the stairs? The way she coughs in the morning?'

'He's right,' Beth said, and she stood and turned over the steaks. 'How's Marsha?'

'Better,' Peggy said. 'Vic comes home on leave around June.'

'Then he goes over?'

'He thinks so.'

'He will,' Lee said.

'You poor children,' Beth said, and jabbed a steak with the fork, and Peggy shot water into the flames.

That night Beth went to bed while Lee was watching the late news. With her eyes closed she lay in the dark for thirty minutes; then Lee came upstairs and when he turned on his bedside lamp she pretended she was asleep. She tried not to be angry, tried to hold onto the little calm she had gained in half an hour of lying still while he emptied his pockets, coins clicking and ringing on the chest of drawers: if she had been asleep, that light and sound would have waked her. He got into bed, turned out the light, and she listened to his breathing as it slowed and deepened (and yes: oh yes, he was right of course about her: she breathed badly), and she wondered what he thought about in those last conscious minutes. They passed quickly: he shifted a leg, and was asleep. She lit a cigarette, knowing that if she were asleep the scrape of flint, the clicking shut of the Zippo, perhaps even the small flame would intrude as jarringly as an alarm clock or the frightful after-midnight ringing of a phone. She believed any sound would do that: a light rain, a gentle wind rustling the elm leaves, Lee or even Peggy down the hall stirring in bed. Sometimes she woke at night and there was no sound at all; she would lie there in the silence, afraid, as though she had been wakened by the presence of fog outside her window.

She had tried everything she knew of except drugs. She had talked to Polly Fairchild, who couldn't sleep either: Polly had told her that a snack before bed would take blood from her brain and help her relax. If she woke in the night she should get up and read, drink some milk, and she shouldn't smoke. Sometimes you could talk yourself to sleep: *my feet are going to sleep, my feet are going to sleep, my ankles are*—And she mustn't worry: if at nine o'clock or so she started worrying about whether or not she could sleep, she'd only make herself more tense. But none of this worked for Polly: she took a pill every night and slept soundly. She told Beth they were mild, they weren't habit-forming, and though it took her longer to feel really awake in the morning, that was an easy price for a good night's sleep.

Beth said no. When Lee suggested drugs, she said no again; she would not, she said, take a drug so she could sleep. If she couldn't do something as natural and inevitable as sleeping, she wanted to know why. So night after night she went to bed and lay awake or, after sleeping for awhile, she woke again and lay smoking in the dark for an hour and sometimes more. Yet after all this time alone she still didn't know why she couldn't sleep. She knew this much, though: she was not equipped to solve a problem of this sort. Until now she had always dealt with problems that had alternatives and you weighed them and made a choice, like buying one dishwasher instead of another. But now the buyer's instinct was useless: what was needed was a probing insight into herself, and this was a bitter and unprofitable task. For when she did try to explore herself she found—oh God: she found nothing.

Now she got out of bed, went downstairs to the kitchen, and made a gin and tonic. She sat on the couch in the dark living room, lit a cigarette and exhaled quickly before a cough jerked upward from her chest. She knew it was long after midnight, but being awake down here wasn't altogether bad as long as she didn't think of getting up in the morning, and how tired she would be; she never slept in the afternoon, for she was afraid a nap robbed that much more sleep from the coming night. But if she could give up the idea of sleeping, devote herself to the moment at hand, there was an appealing secretive quality about sitting alone in a quiet and darkened house. She knew why too: because upstairs Lee slept like a child, with his clean lungs, his exercised body, and his mind that worked with the precision of numbers.

After another drink she felt sleepy. She was afraid that climbing the stairs would quicken her blood and breath and wake her again; so stretching out on the couch, she slept. She woke to the pounding of Lee's in-place running in their bedroom directly above her. Peggy came downstairs first and sat at the kitchen table with a cup of coffee. When Lee came down, smelling of after-shave lotion, Beth was pouring buckwheat mix into a bowl.

'What did you do, sleep on the couch?'

'I was down here when I got sleepy, so I stayed.'

'You were asleep when I went up.'

'It didn't last.'

He poured a cup of coffee and sat down.

'You don't have to stay awake,' he said.

'I know.'

'There's nothing wrong with taking something to help you sleep.'

'I used to sleep,' she said.

That afternoon she drove Lee to the Cedar Rapids airport, then went back to Iowa City, picked up Peggy at school, and got to the airport in time for a quick drink in the cocktail lounge, a martini for her and a Coke for Peggy. She was not excited about going to a convention of insurance men in San Francisco, but she pretended to Peggy that she was. She told Peggy what food was in the refrigerator, reminded her to leave the back door unlocked while she was at school so the dry cleaners could deliver the clothes, and told her again the name of the hotel in San Francisco. Then she said: 'Look,

I probably don't have to tell you this, but I ought to anyway: don't have Bucky over while we're gone.'

'I didn't plan to.'

'Well, I trust you, and if it weren't for the neighbors I wouldn't care. But you don't want gossip.'

'No.'

'So tell him goodnight on the front porch, okay?'

Peggy did. For the next three nights, after making love in her bed (and they had never had a bed) she told Bucky goodnight on the dark front porch, the living room behind them darkened too, so he could slip out and across the lawn to his car parked down the street.

## §2

'No,' Beth said, on the plane from San Francisco to Chicago, 'I'm really not afraid.'

Her seat was next to the window, and now she looked out, testing what she had just said. They were flying through clouds so thick that she couldn't see the wing behind her. She thought of the pilot flying by instruments, she thought of human error, she imagined a midair collision. Then she turned back to Robert Carini, the silversmith from New York, who a moment ago had lifted his glass in salute and said he was afraid of flying so he was glad he had someone to talk to.

'My husband would get twenty thousand dollars, though. I don't like that.'

'That's not so much. I took out sixty-five.'

'Oh, I don't mean those slot machines. He told me to get some of that, but I didn't. No, he has a policy on me for ten thousand, with double indemnity.'

'That's an expensive funeral.'

'It's not to bury me. He says women are worth more these days, and it'd cost that to hire someone to do what I do.'

Then they were smiling at each other.

'Cooking,' Beth said.

'Where is he now?'

'Flying to Chicago. We took separate flights.'

'Oh, I see. So—'

'Yes. So we won't die together.'

Two hours ago she had been drinking coffee with Lee in a lunch-room at the San Francisco airport. At a table to their left a young soldier and his wife were finishing lunch, talking quietly, their eyes shifting and lowering with that distraction of transitional conversations. In the lobby there were soldiers without girls: at the magazine rack, the tobacco counter, sleeping in chairs; as Beth and Lee walked through she said: 'If I were young and single I'd be a soldier's girl.' Relighting his pipe, he glanced at her. He walked too fast, and she was short of breath when they reached the gate. She went through the lobby with him, to the door. He looked up at the sky, said, 'Still cloudy,' then kissed her and said, 'I'll see you in Cedar Rapids.' She stood in the doorway until he boarded the plane, then she found a bar. There were two men sitting apart from each other at the bar, and a young naval officer with a girl at a small table. Beth sat at the end of the bar and ordered a Bloody Mary.

Waiting for a separate flight made her feel she was involved in a childish ruse. But with her second drink she thought of her plane crashing, a death so much quicker than her actual dying would be. A violent death like that would be an awful shock for Peggy, and now she felt sorry for Peggy and Helen and Helen's two children, Wendy and Billy, who would wonder if it hurt Granma when the plane crashed; and she even felt sorry for Lee, who was sentimental and would therefore believe he was burying something, and next year when Peggy went to college he would be lonely in the house at night. And all this time, sipping her drink and thinking of her own death, there was something else in the back of her mind, something desperately mean, and now with a guilty catch of her breath she let it out: what if *his* plane crashed? She finished her drink in a swallow and left the bar.

She boarded her plane; tall Mr. Carini with his thick white hair and lined dark face was already there, in the aisle seat. The stewardess brought champagne cocktails, and before take-off Beth knew his name and that he was a silversmith.

'Are you really?' she had said. 'I thought only Mexicans and Indians did that.'

He had smiled and said oh no, he did it too, although he mostly just ran things now, and once in a while made something for his wife and daughter. She asked if he had anything with him, anything he had made, and he said no but he'd send her a bracelet, and he wrote her address in a notebook. It had been a long time since she had met anyone whose work was either new or interesting. He ordered martinis and she asked questions about his work, real questions that she wanted answers to, and when he lit her cigarettes she took his hand and guided the flame.

'Your husband's a very practical man,' he said now.

'He sells life insurance.'

'Oh. And what do you do?'

'I don't do anything.'

'Of course you do.'

'A lot of this,' she said, and lifted her glass.

'Really?'

'Yes.'

'Why?'

'I don't know.'

'Do you have children?'

'Two girls. One married, one seventeen.'

'So you're alone most of the time.'

'I have friends: you know, wives of my husband's friends. And Helen—she's my married daughter—she lives in Iowa City, so sometimes after shopping I go see her and we drink beer in her kitchen.'

'It's good you're close like that.'

'We're really not, though. I mean we are but she doesn't really talk to me. You know. But at least she's there and she seems to like it when I go over and I try not to go over too often. Most afternoons I do other things.'

'Bridge?'

'That, and other things.'

'Is it so bad?'

'I hate it,' she said.

She was surprised she had said that; then she was glad.

'Not really,' he said.

'Yes. Really.' Then she turned her eyes from his and looked out the window where still there was nothing but air like wet smoke.

'So many people are like that,' he said.

She looked at him.

'But you're not?'

'No,' he said. 'No: maybe I'm fooling myself, but I don't think so.'

'At least you know about other people. My husband doesn't. He lives on routine like a soldier and that's all he sees.'

'But that can be desperation too, living like that. It's like deep water pressure: take some fish out of it and they turn belly-up and die.'

'I'll have to pull him up some time, and see what happens.'

They had second martinis, then the stewardess brought their lunch, chateaubriand, and poured their first glasses of Burgundy, then asked Robert if they wanted to keep the bottle. He said yes. She spoke to them as a couple rather than fellow passengers, and Beth was amused and also felt pleasingly wicked. She was watching Robert's face; he suddenly squinted and she turned to the window: they had broken through the clouds into a glaring sky that was blue and clear as far ahead as she could see. She looked down at green and yellow and brown squares of earth.

'I wonder what state that is.'

Robert leaned toward the window, his face near her shoulder.

'One of those flat ones.'

'Do you feel safer when it's clear?'

'Better, anyway. Clouds are gloomy.'

'And there I was, having such fun drinking with you in a cloud.'

'It'll be more fun in the blue,' he said, and poured wine in her glass.

'I wasn't put on this plane to have fun. I was put on it so I'd die alone.'

'Are you nice to your husband?'

'I think so. I try to be.'

'That's what I thought. But you're pretty tough on him now.'

'I guess I am. And I guess I shouldn't feel sorry for myself just because what happens to most people has happened to me.'

Then in a low, collusive voice, in their odd privacy that was also public so she again felt illicit, she talked about love. She did not know when she had stopped loving her husband, she said. In a way she was grateful it had happened so late because by that time she had stopped believing in love anyway. No, Robert said, it must have been the other way. She thought about that, lighting a cigarette from the one she was smoking (drinking always seemed to clear her bronchial tubes so she could smoke more) then she said yes, he was probably right. She must have stopped loving him long before she admitted it, then still deceiving herself about Lee she stopped believing in love altogether, thus arming herself to come back full circle and admit she did not love him. That way it was easier to take: you suspected something had died in your house, so you looked around and saw that it was long dead in everyone else's house too; then you were able to return and look under your own bed and find, sure enough, a corpse.

She accepted that death. It was as natural and predictable as a wrinkled face. She would not look under that bed again or anyone else's, for oh she had looked too often, too often. . . . She told Robert of her mother, who was probably content and certainly stupid, for she firmly ignored all failures of the human heart. In her mother's mind everyone lived a life that could be recorded on the obituary page of a newspaper: you were born here, went to school there, were married to a man with such-and-such a job, and you had children. If you asked her about someone she would say: Oh she's doing wonderfully; she has a fine husband and two lovely children.

'She told me that once, about a niece of mine. And I said: I know all that, Mother; what I asked is how *is* she?'

And how could anyone be oblivious to all those signs you could see whether you were looking or not? Give me an hour in a room full of married couples, she said, and I can see their hostilities as plainly as the clothes they wear. Not that she wanted to either. But it was true, all too true, and at least once you understood this, accepted it as commonplace, it wasn't difficult at all to admit that your own life—which long ago you believed was marked for love—had followed the general pattern of humanity. The difficult part was concealing this from your children. At Helen's wedding she had of course cried a little, and for some of the accepted reasons: a daughter had grown, a daughter was leaving, a phase of her own life had ended. But her tears were bitter too, for she knew the rest of Helen's life would never live up to the emotional promise of that day. Like graduation ceremonies where you heard all those words about what lay ahead, then you went out and nothing happened. Helen and Larry would end up, in a friendly way, boring each other, disliking each other. She kept thinking of that during the wedding; in the reception line, when she had to listen to those lecherous old men and tender, hopeful old women, she had to clamp her teeth on ironic replies. And now her seventeen-year-old, Peggy, was in love and she liked to talk about her plans, with this grown-up tone in her voice, and there was nothing to do but listen to her, not as you listen to a child who wants to be a movie star, but to a child whose hope for friends or happiness is so strong yet futile that you know it will break her heart.

'You expected too much,' Robert said. 'Why don't you tell her not to expect too much? Not to stake her whole life on marriage. It's part of her life, but not all.'

'What does your wife do?'

'She's a teacher. Fourth grade.'

'*That* makes a difference.'

They were finishing the wine when the pilot announced their approach to Chicago.

'I've had fun,' Beth said.

'Do you have a layover?'

'An hour.'

'I have two and a half. We can have a drink.'

'We'll be drunk.'

'Well, you like to be and for the flight home I need to be.'

'We'll have a drink.'

'Take-offs and landings are the worst,' he said. The plane had begun its descent; he took her hand.

In the airport they drank standing at a crowded bar. A clock looked at them from above the rows of bottles. Twenty-five minutes before her flight Robert ordered second drinks; she was about to say there wasn't time, but then she didn't. She turned and watched two Air Force lieutenants come through the door and go to the bar. She was looking at their silver wings when her plane was announced. She turned back to her drink. It was half-finished; she picked it up, then instead of drinking she stirred it with a finger.

'Two pilots just came in,' she said. 'All that time with you on the plane I had forgotten the war.'

He turned and looked at them.

'It's not their fault,' he said. 'They're just kids.'

'I guess so, but *pilots*—' Sipping her drink she glanced up at the clock. 'We voted for peace in sixty-four, for Johnson.'

'So did we.'

'For peace?'

'Yes. And my son graduates from college this month.'

She touched his wrist.

'Oh, you poor man. Will they get him?'

'Sure they will, sooner or later.'

'I'm glad I don't have a son.'

'I'd like to keep mine. He's—' Then he frowned and shook his head, his eyes somewhere else now, in New York, on his son's face, in Vietnam. 'Wasn't that your plane?'

'I don't know. What did they say?'

'Two twenty-three to Cedar Rapids.'

'My God, yes.'

She looked at the clock, drained her glass, and they walked quickly down the corridor to her gate.

'Could've missed it,' he said.

'Another couple of minutes.'

They found her gate number and walked faster against a crowd of passengers who had just got off a plane.

'Maybe I did,' she said. 'No one's going this way.'

He looked at his watch.

'Three minutes,' he said. 'I enjoyed it.'

'So did I.'

At the gate the clerk grabbed her ticket and shook his head.

'You almost missed it, lady.'

'She's here,' Robert said. 'Just do what you're paid for.'

Hurrying beside her across the small lobby he took her elbow and said: 'I'll send you a bracelet.'

'Good.'

He pressed her hand and she slowed for a moment.

'If you ever get to New York—'

'Right,' she said, then turned and walked as fast as she could out into the warm sunlight. The uniformed man at the foot of the ladder motioned for her to hurry; at the hatch the stewardess, who was annoyed, smiled and said something, and Beth lowered her face so the girl wouldn't smell gin. She sat in an empty seat at the rear. The plane was small, with propellers; the air conditioning wasn't working and the air was stale. Beth was tight. As the plane took off she wondered if Robert was standing at the door, watching. Then she unbuckled her seat belt and lit a cigarette and looked out the window at the flat earth.

Lee and Peggy were waiting at the airport. She kissed them and asked Peggy if everything was all right. Then Lee said: 'Well, it worked.'

'What worked?'

'The planes.' He was grinning. 'Neither one of them crashed.'

§3 ON the way home they stopped at a restaurant for dinner. In a high, delighted voice Beth told Peggy about the fun they had had in San Francisco (she had not had fun in San Francisco), about the Top o' the Mark and Fisherman's Wharf, while all the time, eating her steak, she sat huddled around her warm secret. That night she took it to bed with her and after Lee was sleeping she lit a cigarette and thought of Robert Carini and a hotel in Chicago; she pulled her nightgown above her hips; she moved slowly so Lee wouldn't wake, and the threat of his waking excited her, and thinking of Robert Carini excited her; she felt wicked, and her fingers holding the cigarette trembled. Then she slept.

It became one of her rituals: at first she told herself she was doing it because her heart was unfaithful and in this way she was having her night with Robert (he did not send a bracelet; after ten days she gave up, with more disappointment than she had expected), but after a few nights she didn't really think of Robert, or of anyone else. Later she told herself she was doing it to help her sleep, though usually she slept just as badly. Then she saw the truth: lying beside Lee, moving and breathing in secret passion, she made her loneliness and dislike for him active: she thought of him beside her, knowing nothing of his own wife, of how little he mattered. Afterward she felt guilty, and she treasured that guilt because it was new. But soon enough guilt faded; next the act itself grew boring; yet she clung to it, forced herself into the only emotions that remained: her heart, beating rapidly toward orgasm, felt mean and vengeful.

Which was not enough. Guilt had been the proper ending for those minutes at night: it had made her feel she was returning home after committing a sin. Now, with the loss of guilt, her nights were changed: her passion took her nowhere, returned her from nowhere. It was merely an extension of the bitterness of her days. She did it less frequently.

What she wanted was not so much to sin but to be able to sin. She started thinking of Robert Carini again. She didn't imagine making love with him. She thought of the guilt: phoning Lee from Chicago to say she had missed connections and would fly to Cedar Rapids tomorrow, then tingling with lies she would have gone to dinner with Robert; after that, in the hotel lobby and elevator and corridor, surely her conscience would have gone to work on her, making her think of Peggy and Helen and Wendy and Billy; and even Lee. And perhaps in the morning she would have opened her eyes to fear and remorse. She might even have returned tender and compassionate to her ordered, disciplined, cuckolded Lee.

But maybe she would have felt nothing except a natural apprehension when she first looked at Lee's face, and when he asked where she had spent the night, was there any trouble finding a room, did she have enough money. Because in order to sin you had to depart from something you believed in, and she had no assurance that being a mother, a grandmother, and a wife would flavor that one night with wickedness. And if that were so, if a night with Robert would have been no more sinful than her private minutes beside Lee, it was better that he had not let her miss the plane.

Yet where had it gone? She had been reared a Catholic, then at some time between starting college and marrying Lee she had stopped being one. She had stopped as unconsciously as your face tans in summer and pales in winter. There had been no iconoclastic teacher, no agnostic roommate: it had been largely a matter of sleeping late on Sunday mornings. Remembering now, she thought there must have been something else, some question on a point of dogma, some dispute with a priest, some book or philosophy course. But there was not, and she was ashamed: not because she had no religion but because she had changed her life without thinking about it. And she had not thought of it since then, except when a friend or relative died (and Kennedy and Marilyn Monroe and Hemingway and Gary Cooper), and for a while she wondered if they were immortal.

But that was all. She assumed there was a God, but maybe there wasn't; worse still, it didn't seem to matter. She didn't know whether Lee believed or not. She could not remember ever talking about God. You didn't do that, sit around talking about God. You talked with frustration about things outside your life, like Johnson and the war; or you talked about the surfaces of your life: the children and grandchildren and school for Peggy and things you had done and things you had to do:—*had all the groceries there and then I looked in my purse and no wallet, I had left it in the other purse, and no checkbook either, so she had to wait while I went to the courtesy counter and used one of their checks; what should we get Peggy for graduation? a watch? you take the VW to work then, and they can pack the wheel bearings on the Lincoln while I'm shopping; a watch, do you think?* You scheduled these things, got them done between the hands of the clock, and at night they gave you conversation. Maybe late some night when Peggy was asleep she ought to make Lee sit down with her and a bottle of gin and she would tell him what she did at night and why, tell him of Robert and how she had waited for a bracelet in the mail, and tell him that on those nights when he made love to her she was eager and hot, but only for herself, and a hand covered her heart and would not yield it to him.

As the summer grew hotter, the idea of such a conversation enticed her. If her belief in God had changed passively, her marriage could change in one violently quick night. The frightening and appealing thing was she could not predict what would happen. Separation, divorce, a marriage counselor—even something new and good, both of them with painful and productive honesty voicing all their dislikes, their secrets (she recalled the moment in San Francisco when she had thought of his plane crashing), and after that maybe they could stand among the fallen roof and exploded walls of what they had called their marriage, and wounded and trembling and alone they could hold hands and start from there. But such a dream was nonsense, and she knew it, and the days of summer went on.

Then one night in mid-July she woke and lay smoking and listened to the hum of the air conditioner in the window. She didn't know what time it was, nor did she want to: she knew she would be awake for at least an hour, probably more. Her hand moved down, then stopped; she didn't want that, it was boring and it took too long and didn't even help her sleep. She got up and put on a summer robe; she would drink gin and tonic in the living room and talk to herself until she was sleepy. Tomorrow was Saturday, so she had no reason to get up; going downstairs she thought of living a nocturnal life when Peggy went to college. She could stay up most of the night until she was truly sleepy, wake up long enough to fix breakfast for Lee, then go back to bed and sleep into the afternoon. Insomnia was only bad if you had to go to sleep and wake at certain times. A bizarre solution, simply to throw away schedules, but you couldn't deny it was a solution; and crossing the kitchen floor in the dark she was pleased, thinking how Lee would despise a life of that sort. He would find several reasons against it but he would never admit his real objection: that people were supposed to be awake in daylight and asleep at night.

She switched on a light and blinked at the clock on the kitchen wall: ten minutes to three. She could hear the air conditioner in the living room; she thought either she had forgotten to turn it off or Peggy and Bucky had come in after their date and turned it on, then Peggy had forgotten it, which was just as well, for already the kitchen was hot and she would go sit in the cool living room and drink gin and perhaps watch the sunrise. She opened the refrigerator and saw there was beer and decided to drink that, because it was simpler and enough of it made her sleepy. She popped open a can and turned off the kitchen light, for she wanted everything dark; she pushed through the swinging door into the living room then stopped, her eyes snapping toward the other sounds which she understood even before she saw the two standing and quick-moving silhouettes at the couch across the room. Her hand darted to the table lamp beside her, but for an instant she squeezed the switch between thumb and finger; her mouth opened to speak but she didn't do that either; then she turned on the switch and stepped back from the sudden light and what she saw in it: Peggy's face hidden inside the dress she was pulling down and shrugging into, and Bucky with his naked back turned, snapping his trousers at the waist. Beth turned out the light before Peggy's face came out of the dress. She backed through the kitchen door and leaned against the sink and took a long swallow of beer.

They would be whispering now. She couldn't hear them, but she moved farther from the door anyway. She finished the beer before she heard the front door closing, then she waited again. She lit a cigarette and was going to the refrigerator for another beer when Peggy came in, standing with lowered head while the door swung shut behind her. Beth hugged her and stroked her long hair.

'Do you want a beer while we talk?'

Peggy nodded against her shoulder. They went into the living room and, avoiding the couch, Beth chose the easy chairs where she and Lee sat at night to watch television or read. The chairs were side by side, with a table and lamp between; when Beth and Peggy sat down, the lampshade hid their faces.

'Has it been—going on?'

'Yes.'

'I won't tell Daddy.'

'Please don't. Ever.'

'No. No, he won't know. He sees things—I don't know how he sees things, but it's different. And now—'

And now what? Instead of turning on that lamp she could have backed out of the room, gone upstairs to bed, and never mentioned it again: she could have pretended to Peggy and gradually to herself that she thought they were only kissing. Which was still another lie: everyone knew that young people did everything short of making love, yet you called it kissing. And she could have done that tonight, but she hadn't, and by turning on the lamp she had committed herself to something more, to the awful risk of forming words and throwing them out into the dark like so many sparks in a dry season. And now that it was time she had nothing to say, and she nearly said, Let's have a good night's sleep and talk about it tomorrow while Daddy's playing golf. But she would not do that, she would *not*. So she decided to talk about those things she did know, to at least deal with and probably eliminate them.

'If I were still a Catholic then you'd be one too and all I'd have to do is send you to the priest tomorrow. I'd tell you it was a sin and he'd tell you it was a sin and you'd believe it. Then he'd tell you to break up with Bucky. But we're not Catholics or anything else, so that leaves us with clichés, and what's wrong with that is a cliché is an out, it just sort of hangs around and waits for someone to use it and when you do use one it saves you from having to think. So now I could say that nice girls make love for the first time on their wedding nights and they never make love with anyone else unless they're divorced first—' The word divorce made her think of Lee sleeping above them, and that she was forty-nine, and that Peggy was leaving for college in two months and during the next four years her need for parents and a home would gradually diminish. 'But you see there's no sense in my telling you all that because you know it's just not so. I mean, do you *feel* bad? Evil?'

'I do right now, but not—' She took one of Beth's cigarettes.

'Not with him?'

'No.'

'Good. I want you to be happy, and I'm not going to ask you to stop seeing him—'

'You're not?'

'Did you think I would?'

'I thought you'd have to.'

'That would be a lie too. Because I don't really have any reason to. Not any good ones, anyway. And you have to believe this: I don't think you're bad, and I love you very much, and you must never feel ashamed. You can tell Bucky I didn't see anything or you can tell him the truth.'

'The truth.'

'All right.'

'He'll be afraid. When he has to see you.'

'Tell him not to be. Is there anything you need to talk about?'

'No.'

'I mean, I've told you what's not the truth about sex, or at least what I think isn't the truth. I suppose now I ought to tell you—I don't know, something else.'

'You don't have to.'

'You're all right?'

'Yes. I love him.'

'Suppose you get pregnant?'

'He's careful.'

'Those things don't always work.'

'Well, they *have* to.'

'No, they don't, I can at least tell you that. I want you to take the pill.'

The sky was dark still; in another two hours dawn would come; two hours after that, Lee would wake to a house that had changed.

'I'll make the appointment and I'll go with you.'

She rose and stood in front of Peggy, who sat with lowered head, her knees pressed together.

'We'll tell him you're getting married.'

'Well, I can, but—' Then she stopped.

'It's all I ask. Will you do that for me?'

After a moment, Peggy nodded.

'I'd do anything in the world for you,' she said.

With arms around each other they climbed the stairs, then kissed. Beth went to her room and shut the door and looked at Lee's face in the dark: an open-mouthed, weary frown. She thought tenderly of how his face had changed. Then she got into bed and slept. She woke up while Lee was doing push-ups on the bedroom floor. She told him she had been awake most of the night and asked if he could fix his breakfast so she could go back to sleep. He said all right, he'd just have some cereal. When she woke after one o'clock she dressed and went downstairs; Peggy was drinking coffee in the kitchen.

'Has Daddy left?'

'Yes.' Peggy blushed. 'Bucky loves you.'

'Oh, you called him?'

'As soon as Daddy left.'

'Good. I'll have a cup of coffee, then take you to lunch. Unless you're doing something else.'

'No, he's still afraid to come over till he picks me up tonight.'

They went in the Volkswagen to a restaurant across the street from the university, then walked in the hot afternoon to several stores and bought Peggy a blouse. They spent the rest of the afternoon talking and laughing about trivial things, and at dinner Lee smiled at them with curiosity and pride. During the next four days Beth was sometimes frightened but always happy: she thought it was a wonderful paradox that Peggy's having an affair made them even closer than they had been before. On the fifth day they drove to a gynecologist in Cedar Rapids. Going there, Peggy was nervous and talked about yesterday's swimming party; coming home she was distant and hardly talked at all.

'He probably didn't believe us,' she said. 'He knows I'm not old enough to get married.'

'It doesn't matter.'

'I guess not.'

'You're safe now. That's what matters.'

That night after dinner, Peggy scraped the dishes, put them in the dishwasher, then went upstairs. After a while Beth went up. Peggy was reading in bed.

'Aren't you going out?'

'No.'

'You aren't having a fight, are you?'

'No.'

'It's so early. Do you feel all right?'

'I'm fine. I just don't feel like going out, that's all.'

'Oh. Well—'

'Don't worry. I'm all right.'

Beth stood in the doorway for a moment, watching her read; then she went downstairs. The next night Peggy went to a movie with Marsha. On the third night Bucky took her to dinner. He was able to look into Beth's eyes again and as she walked with them out on the porch and told them goodbye she felt her collusion was with Bucky, not Peggy. It was almost eight o'clock, but daylight savings time, and the sky was still light. She watched them get into the car. Bucky was talking and Peggy, looking straight ahead, shrugged her shoulders. When they drove off, Beth turned to the door then stopped; she did not want to go in. The dishes were washed, the kitchen cleaned, there was nothing on television, and she did not want to read. She sat on the wooden steps of the porch and watched the night come. When she went back inside, Lee was still sitting in his chair, reading *Time*.

'What were you doing?'

'Just sitting. It's cool, but the mosquitoes got bad.'

She lit a cigarette and sat on the couch, facing him. For a while she watched him read.

'Lee?'

'What,' not raising his eyes.

'Do you believe in God?'

'Sure.'

His eyes lingered, probably finishing a paragraph: then he lowered the magazine.

'Why? Don't you?'

'I don't know.'

'You never told me.'

'No. Will you take me to a movie?'

'Now?'

'If you want to.'

'Can we make it?'

'I'll call and find out.'

The last feature would start in twenty minutes, so they went. When they got home Lee finished whatever he had been reading in *Time*, and Beth had a drink. She was going to the kitchen for another when Lee started upstairs, so she closed the liquor cabinet and followed him up and they made love.

'You didn't want to talk about God, did you?' he said. His voice was sleepy.

'No.'

'Good thing. I don't know any more than you do.'

'Then you don't know a thing.'

'What made you ask me that anyway?'

'Because I question the way we live.'

'How do you mean?'

'Why we do things.'

'What things.'

'I don't know. I wonder about the girls, how we've done with them.'

'We've done all right.'

'It's not that simple, though.'

'What isn't?'

'Everything. Everything isn't that simple.'

She lay awake for another half hour or so, then slept. She woke up when Peggy closed the front door. The next sound was the refrigerator. After a while Peggy came upstairs and went to her room. Beth wanted to go talk to her, but she could not think of an excuse. She lit a cigarette and got up and stood at the window, looking at the streetlight on the corner. Once in a while she looked back at Lee sleeping on his side, and she wished she were like him: believing she knew those things she had to know, and not caring to know anything else. If she were that way she would not be standing here at the window; she might be sleeping or even talking to Peggy now, maybe they would go down to the kitchen for a snack and sit there eating and talking; because above all, if she were that way, she would not have turned on that lamp.

§4     Next day after lunch, when Lee had gone to play golf, Beth asked Peggy if she wanted the car.

'No.'

'I need some things in town,' Beth said.

She was going to see Helen, and lying about it to Peggy made her feel more lonely. On the way she bought popsicles for Wendy and Billy. Helen lived in the country; for the last two miles Beth left the highway and drove on a dusty road through fields of tall corn. When she turned into the driveway Wendy and Billy saw her from the gym set in the backyard and ran to the car. They wore bathing suits. She hugged and kissed them and unwrapped the melting popsicles, and they walked back toward the gym set. Helen was in the kitchen doorway, holding the screen open.

'Beer?'

'All right.'

'Larry went back to bed. There was a party last night, and we got about three hours sleep.'

'Aren't you going to sleep?'

'Tonight. I could put the kids down for a nap, but I don't like to. Wendy doesn't sleep.'

'She could sit in bed with books or something. She'd be all right.'

'I know, but it makes me feel degenerate. Let's go in the living room.'

They sat in front of a large fan and Beth looked out the picture window at the willow tree in the front yard, its branches touching the ground. Across the dirt road there was heat shimmer above the corn that grew as far as she could see. As Helen lit a cigarette her hands trembled.

'You're hung over too.'

'Just tired. I don't get drunk at those parties.'

'That's smart.'

'Next time I'll be smart about leaving too. How's Peggy?'

'Fine.'

'Excited about New England?'

'I guess.'

'Still going steady?'

'Oh sure.'

'Then it's good she's leaving. She's too young for that.'

'You weren't much older.'

'No, I guess I wasn't. Shall we have another?'

'It'll just make you sleepier.'

'As long as I'm suffering I might as well drink.'

'Okay.'

Helen took the empty cans to the kitchen. Beth knew she ought to leave and let Helen rest somehow, at least spare her the effort of talking. But she thought of going home to Peggy and she could not. Helen came back eating a sandwich.

'Peanut butter. You want some?'

'No thanks. Listen: you go up and take a nap and I'll stay with the children.'

'I've made it this far, I can make it till tonight.'

'Don't be silly. Finish your beer then go up and sleep.'

'You're being silly. What kind of visit is that?'

'Well, it's not like I drove a hundred miles. Come on: let me. Don't you know I love to be with them?'

Helen took a long swallow and sank in her chair.

'You're tempting me.'

'Do it, then. Think how nice it'll be to just go upstairs and lie down and sleep.'

'I'll do it.'

'Good.'

'But first I'll put Billy to bed.'

'I'll do that. Just finish your beer and go to bed.'

'Oh, my.' She drank. 'Oh my, you're good to me.'

Now that her favor was accepted, Beth wanted something in return. She wanted very much to talk about Peggy, but she recognized her need for what it was. She didn't want advice: if she did, she wouldn't ask it from her twenty-five-year-old daughter. Nor did she want Helen to speak to Peggy. She merely wanted to talk about it, to share with someone else the burden of her decision. But she couldn't do that: it was cowardly, and it wasn't fair to Peggy. So they made small talk, then Helen said, 'That beer's there to be drunk,' and went upstairs. Beth went outside and carried Billy upstairs; his eyes were closing as she covered him with a sheet and turned on the fan. Going downstairs she wanted another beer but she went past the refrigerator and out into the yard. She could not drink beer all afternoon; the day was too hot and she would drink too fast and go home tight. For a while under the hot sun she pushed Wendy in the swing.

'Aren't you hot?' she said.

'No.'

She pushed her again, then held the chains and Wendy swayed, then stopped.

'I am. What do you do with that willow tree?'

'What tree.'

'In the front yard.'

'Nothing.'

'Come on. We'll have a tea party.'

In the kitchen she made grape Kool-Aid.

'Are there some cookies?'

'Mama hides 'em.'

She looked high in the pantry, found chocolate Oreos, and put some on a plate. Wendy carried it out to the willow tree. Beth brought a beer, the pitcher of Kool-Aid, and a glass for Wendy. Under the willow tree there was shade; across the road the cornstalks were moving with a gentle breeze, and after Beth and Wendy had sat still for a while they could feel it.

'This is a good place,' Wendy said.

'It is.'

'I bet nobody can see us.'

'Not unless they look real hard.'

When the cookies were gone Wendy got restless. She walked

head first through the hanging branches and stood looking into the dust-covered weeds in the ditch beside the road. Sitting on the grass, Beth said: 'Don't you want to stay here?'

'No.'

'Wait. I'll be right back.'

She went into the house. Upstairs in Wendy's room she found a checkerboard and box of checkers: they were all there. She got a beer and went outside.

'Do you know how to play checkers?'

'I forgot.'

Beth parted the branches and went through and sat in the shade.

'Come here and I'll show you.'

For the next two hours, until Helen and Larry came outside with their faces washed and sleepy-looking, she drank beer and played checkers with Wendy. Driving home she opened all the car windows so air blew on her face, but when she parked in the garage she still felt tight. She had also smoked too much: crossing the lawn she wheezed and when she coughed to clear her chest she brought up something. She swallowed and went inside.

She could hear the record player in Peggy's room, and she was about to call upstairs that she was home but she didn't. She ought to eat something. She sliced cheese and ham and ate standing up. As she cut a piece of lime and filled a glass with ice she told herself to get sober before Lee came home; she poured the gin and tonic, her mind detached as though still deciding whether or not to drink it, then she went upstairs. Peggy's door was open, and she lay across her bed, reading a magazine. Beth turned down the volume on the record player and sat on the bed.

'Where've you been?'

'Helen's.'

'You better eat an onion before Daddy comes home.'

She said it in a friendly way, smiling, and Beth winked. It was their first moment like that since going to the gynecologist.

'I guess I better. Is this what you've been doing?'

'Marsha and I played tennis.'

'In this heat?'

'It gave me a headache.'

'Did you take something?'

'Two aspirins. Marsha has a date, and we're doubling tonight.'

'Does she?'

'I finally talked her into it. Vic'll be in Vietnam for a year and I told her, you know, it's just friendly dating to distract her. She needs it.'

'Course she does.'

Peggy closed the magazine and rolled on her back. Beth went to the window and looked past the elm down at the brick street.

'Peggy?' She did not turn from the window. 'Was I wrong?'

'No.'

Now she looked at Peggy on the bed.

'Is that true?'

'Yes.'

'But you're not happy.'

'That's not your fault.'

'Then you're really not?'

'Not what.'

'Happy.'

'No. No, I'm not.'

'Then I was wrong.'

'No, it wasn't that. That was great. Anybody else's mother would have—I don't know, gone crazy or something. No, it's Bucky. I think I'm getting tired of him.'

'Well, that's normal.'

'It doesn't have to be.'

'But it is, honey. You're barely eighteen.'

The record player shut itself off; Peggy got up and turned the records over and started it again.

'I'll be glad when school starts,' she said.

'Because of Bucky?'

'Yes.'

'Then I'll be glad too. But you could just tell him, you know. You don't have to wait till September.'

'No, I'll wait.'

'But be happy. Don't waste time.'

Peggy shrugged and lay on the bed, one arm across her eyes.

'I'll wait till school. Maybe when I get out there I'll change my mind. You know: maybe I've just been with him too much this summer.'

'Well, I'm glad you told me. I thought it was that other business.'

'No. That was right.'

'Do they make you sick?'

'Not so far.'

'Good. I'm going to shower now. Will you—No: never mind.'

Peggy moved her arm and looked at her.

'Will I what?'

'I was going to ask you to start the charcoal, but forget it. You rest and get over that headache.'

'It's about gone.'

She got up.

'No, I'll do it,' Beth said.

'It's done,' Peggy said, and left the room and went downstairs.

Beth left her drink on the lavatory while she showered. She was under the warm spray for a long time, finishing with a few seconds of cold; when she got out she felt better but still tight. She dried and powdered, then finished her drink while she dressed and perfumed in the bedroom. She wore a yellow dress, the color of lemon sherbet, soft and cool and pretty. She stood at the full-length mirror: her face and arms were tan and cool-looking and she smelled good. Robert had thought she was pretty, she knew that. Then why had he let her catch that plane? Not that it would have made any difference. She went downstairs and mixed a drink and went outside where Peggy sat in a lawn chair, watching the charcoal.

'Beautiful,' Peggy said.

Beth went down the steps like a model, and in front of Peggy did a slow pirouette, then forced a short laugh that almost came out as a sob.

'And so are you,' she said. 'And I want you to be *ever* so happy!'

They sat with their legs in the sun, their bodies in the shade; when the shadows of the elm and house had enclosed their legs, Lee came home. By that time Beth was drunk.

Lee knew it, and she saw in his eyes that he knew it, but he didn't say anything. They ate barbecued chicken and baked beans and potato salad; Beth thought the food would make her sober, and she ate second helpings, and wiped the chicken platter with Italian bread. All this only cleared her head, but she still wasn't sober; faced with a waning drunk, she had to prolong it, so while she cleaned the kitchen she had another drink, knowing that behind his newspaper in the living room Lee was scowling at the sounds of ice cubes and stirring. When the kitchen was clean she took her drink outside and sat on a lawn chair. The sun was very low. Across the street beside the house Mrs. Crenshaw was bent over giving scraps to her dog; she straightened and waved. Then Mrs. Crenshaw went inside, and she was alone. It seemed a long time ago she had played checkers with Wendy under the willow tree. She looked over her shoulder at the house: Peggy's room was lighted, the shades drawn while she dressed for her date. The kitchen was lighted. So was the living room where Lee was reading. Beth looked away: everything was shadowed now, and there was a ribbon of deep bright pink over the rooftops to the west. With her back to the house she felt somehow threatened. But nothing was wrong: the kitchen was clean; Peggy's trouble was with Bucky, not her; Lee was sulking, but that was normal.

The sky was nearly dark when Bucky drove up the street. When he opened the door the interior light went on and Beth saw Marsha and a boy in the back seat. Bucky started across the lawn toward the front door, then he saw her and came over and said hello.

'Just go through the kitchen,' she said. She looked up at Peggy's bedroom. 'I think she's downstairs now.'

She watched him go into the kitchen; then she heard him knocking on the wall and calling hello. She went to the car; Marsha rolled down the back window and Beth stuck her head in. She stayed there, talking about the heat and tennis with Marsha and the boy whose name she didn't hear, until Peggy and Bucky got into the car. She stepped back, and as they drove away she called: 'Have fun!'

She went to the back door and into the kitchen. She was dropping ice in her glass when Lee came from the living room.

'No,' he said.

She hesitated. Then, not looking at him, she squeezed lime into the glass.

'Jesus. Did you have to go out to the car too? Couldn't you have just stayed wherever the hell you were?'

'I wanted to tell Marsha hello. What's wrong with that?'

'What's *wrong*. You're so Goddamned drunk you don't even know. How do you think Peggy liked it? Her mother out there bellowing her Goddamned drunk talk all over the neighborhood—'

'I wasn't bellowing.'

She poured the gin halfway up, then the tonic.

'You were. It's what you do when you're drunk, but you don't hear it.'

'Oh. Well, it's a good thing I'm not sober like you because you're bellowing a little yourself, and it's a good thing we're all closed up and air-conditioned or the whole neighborhood would hear *you*.'

'That's your last drink tonight.'

'Ha.'

'I've tried to stay out of this, but not tonight.'

'Ha. *They* can't hear you—' she waved an arm toward the windows '—but I can, and being closed up in a house with you *makes* me drink.'

'Forget about me. I know how you feel about me. I'm talking—'

'Well, I'm glad you know *something*.'

'I'm talking about Peggy. You don't care about me and you don't care about yourself either. You're killing yourself with booze and cigarettes—'

'You're Goddamned right I am.'

'—You don't sleep enough but won't go to a doctor. All right: that's *your* business. But it looks like you could at least stay sober while Peggy's home.'

'Peggy. Oh, you *really* don't know anything, you don't know anything at *all*. You don't know—'

She turned and walked fast to the back door, yet when she reached it the anger and speed of her motion were fake; she didn't want to leave, but when she looked back at him he was standing there shaking his head, his lips tight. So she went outside, where now the sky was dark. She stopped in the backyard and drank, went on to the garage and got into the Lincoln. The key was in the ignition. Holding the glass between her legs, she backed out, looking at the house as she passed it: she did not see Lee at the back door or the kitchen window or living room window. She stopped at the corner, looked both ways, then squealed through the intersection.

Her cigarettes were back there on the kitchen table or on the grass beside the lawn chair. She drove toward a supermarket that was open until nine; in the dark privacy and quiet hum of the car she felt all right; but walking into the fluorescent lights of the store she felt drunk again. The store was nearly empty, and boys were sweeping. She walked fast so she could follow a straight line, took two packs of Pall Malls from the rack and smacked them on the counter; while the girl rang up the sale Beth looked at the clock on the wall, then at her reflection in the glass front of the store. The girl could surely smell her breath but that was all right if you were dressed up and pretty and had a place to go. She picked up the change, told the girl goodnight, and walked out.

Her drink was on the floor near the accelerator, and now she held it down in her lap until she got out of the parking lot. The streets were lighted at every corner, and in the headlights of the spaced yet steady traffic you could see into cars. Just the sort of thing a cop would enjoy: stopping a lone woman on Saturday night. Hiding the cool glass between the steering wheel and her lap, she drove out of town, onto the highway going west to Helen's.

She finished the drink, tossed the ice and lime out the window, and laid the glass on the seat. On the next curve the glass rolled away from her; she lunged for it and the car veered into the opposite lane but it was clear and when she jerked the wheel she almost went onto the shoulder. She slowed to forty. At the white barn before Helen's road she slowed for a turn; she did not plan to stop at Helen's; she would simply drive past and follow the dirt road and see where it went. But she had left her lighter at home, she could go in and ask Helen if it was there and they'd look in the kitchen and living room and with a flashlight under the willow tree, then she could stay and talk. A half mile from Helen's she went up a gentle rise and saw the lighted house. She slowed to twenty, and going by the house she bent over and looked through the picture window: Helen stood in the living room, talking probably to Larry someplace off to the right. She drove on. She picked up a little speed, followed the beige road past dark fields of corn separating lighted farmhouses. She kept turning right, back toward the highway, and finally she came to it and headed for town. The drinks were wearing off and if she went to a movie now she'd get tired and her mouth and throat would dry. It was too late for a movie anyway.

Then, almost furtively, her right foot pressed the pedal while her left hand slipped down to her seat belt, unbuckled it, and returned to the wheel. She did not look at the speedometer: leaning forward, she watched the curves and gentle slopes ahead for the lights of another car. Coming out of a curve she floorboarded; the highway now was straight but narrow and she fixed her eyes on the center line. She must not hit anyone. She felt the dark, flat country zipping past but she was afraid to look; once in a while there was the white blur of a house. A big truck came toward her and she held her breath and stared at the road as the truck crashed by. Now her legs were weak and the muscles in her right one were tight and quivering. Still she kept the pedal to the floor for another half minute, until she saw the close lights of houses. She lifted her foot and placed it on the floor near the brake pedal; when she reached the houses she was driving thirty miles an hour and thinking how pretty she looked in her bright yellow dress and weeping aloud. She drove home.

The lights were on in the living room; she sat in the car, in the garage, and smoked. She remembered the glass and lay on the seat and picked it up from the floor. She was down there when Lee spoke her name.

'Beth?' he said again.

She sat up and looked around at him framed by the garage door. She got out and started to walk past him; when he didn't move aside, she stopped.

'Are you all right?' he said.

She nodded.

'I went for a ride.'

'Oh.'

They walked back toward the house.

'I was worried,' Lee said.

'I just went for a ride.'

In the kitchen he watched her mix a drink, then he followed her into the living room. A movie was on television.

'What is it?' she said.

'*Pal Joey.*'

'Oh, good.'

She sat in her chair; he sat in his and now the lampshade was between them so all he could watch was her hands while she drank. For about five minutes she watched the movie.

'What is it, honey?' he said.

'I don't know.'

'Do you think maybe the change is coming?'

'No. Besides, the pills postpone it.'

'Maybe it's coming, though.'

'No it's not. I'll die of lung cancer, wearing a Tampax.'

He was quiet for a while.

'About the drinking,' he said.

'What about it?'

'Could you cut down if you wanted to?'

Sinatra was singing 'I Could Write a Book.'

'Wait,' Beth said. 'Let's hear this.'

Then there was a commercial for laundry soap.

'Did you ever notice the commercials for Saturday night movies are mostly for women?' Beth said. 'What do they think men are doing on Saturday night?'

'I don't know. Anyhow, what would happen if you told yourself you just won't have a drink till five o'clock? Would it be easy, or would you start climbing the walls, or what?'

'I don't know. I've never had a reason to try it. But since I'm a lousy mother—'

'No, now wait.' His hand gestured under the lampshade, stopping her. 'I'm not talking about that. Forget all that. I just mean that if you can take it or leave it, well, no problem. But if you can't, then you *are* in trouble and we should do something.'

'Why?'

'Because you might be an alcoholic, that's why.'

'Oh, all right. Tomorrow I won't have a drink till five o'clock.'

'Really?'

'Sure.'

'And Monday too? And after that?'

'Yes: Monday too and after that.'

'That's fine. That's the best thing I've heard in a long time.'

She could feel him watching the movie again.

'Is it? Well, you're mighty easy to please. I guess if I quit smoking you'd be so happy you couldn't stand yourself.'

'Why are you talking like that? The fight's over.'

'Okay.' She stood up. 'I guess since I'm going to be so good tomorrow I can have another one.'

'I'll have one too.'

She brought him one. When the movie was over he stood up and cleaned his pipe.

'Coming up?' he said.

'I think I'll read a while.'

He stood there for a moment, then said goodnight and went upstairs. She turned off the television and the lights and sat down again. It took her about fifteen minutes to admit she was hoping Peggy would come home while she was sitting here. Then she stalled for another five minutes, thinking of what she wanted to tell Peggy: that it was all right about Bucky, she was free of him and anyone else, she didn't have to marry until she was twenty-five or thirty, or maybe not at all. Then she went upstairs. When she entered the dark bedroom Lee rolled toward her, awake. She sat on the edge of the bed and touched him, then let him take off the yellow dress and drop it on the floor, and she let him believe the fight was over and everything was fine.

Next day Peggy and Bucky and Marsha and her date went on a

picnic; Lee played golf. At three o'clock Beth started waiting and at exactly five o'clock she mixed a martini. When Lee got home she was sober.

§5     THIS lasted until late August. It was neither difficult nor easy: it was a bother, like being hungry. Sometimes she broke her rule: when she drove out to Helen's or when a friend came over and bored her. Most of them did. She knew some interesting men but she only saw them at occasional parties when usually she was trapped by their wives. Polly Fairchild was good company only when she was troubled or confiding. So on afternoons when Polly came over Beth mixed them a drink and got Polly started on the war or Johnson. Or Beth would remark generally about marriage or changing morality, and Polly usually responded with gossip. She was an intelligent woman who paused to find the right word, the right simile, the psychological term, and she had a way of making gossip feel like an objective discussion of marriage and morality. But after these conversations, when Polly had gone, Beth always felt ashamed.

Most days, though, people did not visit, and she did not go to Helen's, and she did not drink until five o'clock. She spent much time with Peggy, planning what she would need at college, and shopping in town for clothes. They had lunches in town, or Cokes, or ice cream; once, their shopping done, they walked past a movie, looked at the pictures outside, agreed it was the best thing to do on a hot afternoon like this, and went in. Still, since telling Beth she was tiring of Bucky, Peggy had been different. She was friendly again, that was true; but she was like Helen after her marriage. Helen had come home from the honeymoon with a secret, married self that she would not expose to Beth. And now too often Peggy's eyes and smile hid a secret. She never talked about Bucky.

One cloudy morning in late August Peggy and Bucky left for a picnic. They went alone. Lee would not have approved, but he was at work. Beth had slept very little the night before, so when Peggy left around ten she went back to bed. When she woke at noon her room was dark and rain was falling hard. She dressed and went

downstairs to the kitchen; while she was getting Spam and a Coke
from the refrigerator Peggy called hello and came in from the living room. She was wearing her glasses.

'Oh, you came home. Is Bucky with you?'

'Nope.'

'When did it start raining?'

'About an hour ago.'

Beth poured the Coke over ice, sipped it, then handed it to Peggy.

'Here. You want this?'

Peggy took it.

'Why should I drink one of those things when what I really like
after a nap is beer?'

'Drink a beer, then.'

'I will. Now that I've proved I don't absolutely have to.'

She opened a beer and started making a sandwich.

'Did you eat lunch?'

'Sitting in the car.'

'Well, I like rain, but it's too bad.' She went to the window and
looked out at the dark sky and dark green blowing trees and hard
rain washing down the brick street. 'You could have brought him
here, I guess.'

'I can think of better people to be indoors with on a rainy day.'

Beth went to the table and finished making the sandwich.

'Oh, he was full of plans for a rainy afternoon. What he really
wanted—'

'Wait: let's go to the living room. We can open the windows.'

They turned off the air conditioner, opened the windows facing
the front yard, and sat smelling the rain and cool air. Beth was in her
chair and Peggy faced her from the couch.

'A motel,' Peggy said. 'That's where he wanted to go. Can you
imagine anyone letting him into a motel? He hardly even shaves
yet.'

Beth waited.

'What a little rooster he is,' Peggy said. 'His girl takes the pill—
wow.'

'Why don't you stop?'

'And have a little Bucky? I'd rather die.'

'No, I mean stop seeing him.'

'Because—oh because I just can't. I wish—' She stretched out on
the couch and turned her face away from Beth, toward the open
window.

'You wish what?'

'Nothing.'

'No, tell me.'

Peggy was still looking out the window.

'I wish you *had* taken me away. Even if it would've been phony. I wish you had.'

Rain smacked loudly from the gutter near the porch. The windows were under the porch roof, so only the breeze came in; the curtains stirred and Peggy's exhaled smoke drifted back into the room.

'But then you wouldn't have learned anything,' Beth said.

'Learned. What have I learned?'

'That you don't love him. That it wasn't real. If I had taken you away for one of those trips you'd have thought you were heartbroken.'

'I *did* love him.'

'I don't think so.'

'Course I did.' She looked at Beth. 'For God's sake, I *slept* with him.'

'That doesn't mean anything.'

'Then what *does?*'

'I don't know.'

'You don't.'

'No.'

'That's fine.'

'Did you want me to lie to you? Tell you a love story?'

Peggy shook her head. Beth brought her plate and empty beer can to the kitchen.

'Do you want a beer?' she called.

'No.'

She opened one for herself. For a couple of minutes in the living room she sat quietly drinking, looking past Peggy's lowered head at the rain and dark outside. A car passed slowly up the street.

'Why don't you just break up with him. Right now, baby.'

Peggy shook her head.

'Really, baby. Him and his motels. You're right, he's a child. He's not good enough for you.'

'He was good enough to get pills for.'

'They weren't for him. They were for you.'

'So I could *sleep* with him. So now I just can't stop, because—because then—'

She looked up at the high ceiling.

'You've got it all wrong,' Beth said. 'I wanted to make sure you *wouldn't* be stuck with him, that's why, so you'd be free. So you wouldn't have to take sex seriously.'

'*Jee*sus.' She sat up, glaring at Beth. 'It's the most important thing in my *life* right now, don't you see!' Now she stood, leaning forward, waving a hand. 'Don't you see that? Because as soon as I break up with Bucky I'm a girl who *screws*. Don't you see!'

Beth was pushing herself upward to go hold Peggy, but then she stopped, for she knew Peggy would be stiff and captive in her arms, so she sank back into the chair and with one hand over her eyes softly cried.

'Don't,' Peggy said. She was there now, crouched over Beth, squeezing one shoulder. 'It's not your fault.'

'It *is*.' Her hand still covered her eyes. 'But I didn't mean it to be *this* way. I just didn't want you to end up like *me*.'

'Like you?'

Peggy stepped back. Beth flicked tears from her eyes, wiped her cheeks, and looked up.

'Wasted like me. Unhappy like me. *Mar*ried like me.'

'Oh—'

'Don't you *know*?'

'No.' Shaking her head. 'I don't. I didn't.' Shaking it again.

'Well, now you do. I wish it weren't true, but it is. Not just me, everyone. If you don't believe me, ask Helen. Drive out there and talk to her, she'll talk. Not now, the roads are muddy, but before you go to school. Or just look at her. Look at her face that used to be so *ha*ppy, Peggy. Remember? Remember how happy she always was?'

Peggy was nodding, backing toward the couch; when her legs bumped it she sat down.

'Look at her eyes now. It's not just tired, that's not just housework in her eyes. Oh my baby, save yourself—' She crossed the room and sat beside Peggy, hugging and rocking her with both arms. 'You should hear Polly Fairchild, the stories, all these nice people. It's a farce, love, marriage, fidelity—' Peggy jerked tight in her arms. '—No. No, baby, I've never done that. But it doesn't *mat*ter. None of it *mat*ters.'

'But Daddy—'

'Oh, he's all right, baby. He's a good man. It's just natural, that's all. It just happens, and there's nothing anyone can do about it.'

Peggy's face turned away and her body turned with it, pulling against Beth's arms. Beth let go.

'Are you getting divorced?'

'*No*, baby.' Beth held her again but still Peggy was turned stiffly away, so Beth went to the chair and picked up the beer and swallowed with her back turned. 'No, we're not getting divorced. We can live together like anyone else. We don't hate each other. It's just that nothing's there, and this was supposed to be my life. Every woman's life. But it's not. You and Helen are, and now Wendy and Billy too. But you and Helen have to grow up and have your own lives and that's how it should be. But it shouldn't be this way for me. There should have been something else.'

'For *instance*!'

Looking at the wall ahead of her, Beth shrugged; there were tears in her eyes.

'I don't know, and it's too late for it to matter even if I found out. But it's not too late for you. You're young. It's all ahead of you.'

Then Peggy was moving fast, to the kitchen door, stopping there, turning to Beth.

'Oh *why* did you come in that night! Why! Why! Why didn't you just stay upstairs and mind your own ugly *bus*iness!'

Then crying, her head lifted, her clenched fists at her sides, she strode out of the room and pounded up the stairs.

§6 ON the trip from Iowa to Massachusetts Peggy sat in the back seat with her transistor radio. The college had sent her a summer reading list; she was not going to be tested; it was simply a list of books they wanted her to read. She started the first one, *The Great Gatsby*, as soon as they left Iowa City. During most of the trip Lee spoke very little; he did not even object when Beth put an ice chest of beer on the floor behind the front seat, or when three or four times a day she drank one as they drove. He had been sulking since coming home that rainy day nearly three weeks ago. He had come into the living room where Beth was watching Merv Griffin (before that she had watched a movie; Peggy stayed upstairs and did not come down until dinner); Lee had said hello, looked quickly but closely at her face, then her gin and tonic, then the filled ash tray.

'What happened to five o'clock?'

'Just be quiet. I'm not in the mood for that.'

'Mood hell—'

'I mean it.' Watching the screen she motioned at him to be quiet. 'Besides, Peggy's upstairs.'

He started to speak, then shook his head and went upstairs to change clothes. At dinner there was little talk. Peggy and Lee commented on the rain, and Vic's having been in Vietnam for nearly a month now, and Lee said Bucky had better work for grades and stay in school. They knew she was drunk, and she knew they did, but she acted sober anyway. She ate quietly and slowly and carefully. After dinner Peggy went out with Bucky. Then Lee wanted to talk.

'Was it because you had to? You couldn't stop?'

'No.'

'You just wanted to.'

'That's right. I just wanted to.'

That was all she ever told him. Several times he tried to talk again, but she would not. Finally he gave up. It was a problem he could forget most of the time, because she was not drunk again. She simply drank as she had before. Usually she had one before taking the cleaning woman home; by the time Lee got home she was having her third or fourth. But she was all right: her mind and tongue functioned, she cooked, she cleaned the kitchen after dinner, she paid the bills, she kept track of their engagements, and once a week she drove the Volkswagen to a service station and had it washed. Most nights she drank through dinner and on until she went to bed, but she sipped and spaced them and always appeared sober.

Luckily the shopping for Peggy was done, so they had no reason to be together. Peggy spent most of her time out of the house; during the day she swam or played tennis or rode at the stables or just drove about town with the girls she would leave in September. At night she went out with Bucky. When Beth walked them to the door or told them goodnight from her chair, Peggy looked at her with eyes that were at times coldly curious, at others bitterly defiant, at others mirthful and proud. Each day there were times when they had to talk, and they did this in the hollow courteous tones of lovers after a rending quarrel. Beth waited.

Then in early September, Peggy began to mellow. She spent more time with Beth. She did not truly talk to her; instead they did things together. After dinner Peggy helped in the kitchen. One night they went to a movie. On several afternoons they played badminton or croquet. These periods were obviously planned, some of them even timed: if Marsha were picking up Peggy for tennis, she would be ready an hour early and set up the wickets and stakes and ask Beth to play. At first Beth was hopeful. When she realized Peggy was acting from pity she knew she had lost her.

The college was north of Boston. It was a school for girls, it was a hundred and fifty-eight years old, and so was the four-storied red brick building where, on the front steps among suitcases and trunks, daughters and parents, and maintenance men serving as porters, they kissed and hugged Peggy, spoke of Thanksgiving, and told her goodbye. She stood watching as they drove out of the U-shaped driveway; when they stopped at the street for a final look, she waved. Then Lee drove into the street, toward the low autumn sun. With one finger he wiped his eyes, reached across the seat, and took Beth's hand.

'Our baby,' he said.

'I lost her long before now,' she said, and withdrew her hand.

'What's that supposed to mean?'

'She hates me.'

'Beth!'

'It's true.'

'Beth look—that's crazy. Look—'

'Sure.'

He was not angry. He was chewing his lip, and the car was slowing.

'How can you say that about Peggy? What's *wrong*, Beth—'

'Oh, you don't know anything. You know that? You don't know anything.'

She kneeled on the seat to get a beer, pausing first to watch his face. 'Have you ever been unfaithful?'

'My God.'

She leaned over the seat and reached into the ice chest.

'I have,' she said.

'That's a lie.'

She sat down and popped open the beer. They were on the highway now. She looked out the rear window, then took a long swallow.

'Ah, that's good.'

She pushed in the lighter on the dashboard.

'Drink as many as you want,' he said. 'I mean it.'

'I know you do.'

'You need it. Something's happening to you, and we've got to—'

'His name is Robert Carini.'

'Stop it.'

She lit her cigarette.

'He's a silversmith and he lives in New York. He promised to send me a bracelet but he didn't. What's the name of yours? Or is it more than one. It probably is.'

'Beth, stop.'

'You don't believe me, do you?'

'Course not.'

'That's so funny. Because you had everything worked out so we wouldn't die on the same plane. You see? There's all sorts of things out there—' She waved her beer can in front of her, toward the horizon '—*im*pulses, chances, surprises, things nobody understands. But you don't see them, Lee.'

They were driving through rolling wooded hills; the trees were gold and red and yellow, and looking at them with one hand raised to shield her eyes from the sun she felt a sadness like nostalgia.

'Are you telling me that something happened in San Francisco?'

'No. On the plane back.'

'That's silly.'

'Well, you're right about that, I didn't sleep with him. But I would have, so it's the same.'

'Since when is it the same?'

'Since always. And I talked about you.'

'Oh, you did.'

'I couldn't have been more unfaithful. Think about that, Lee: one afternoon last summer your wife was unfaithful.'

'I wouldn't call it that.'

'Call it what you want, but that's what it was.'

She leaned over the seat again, put the empty can in the chest, and brought a full one up through the ice.

'So what about you,' she said.

He didn't answer; with one hand he was filling a pipe from his tobacco pouch.

'All right,' she said. 'We can talk about scenery and traffic.'

He drove quietly. She finished the beer and started another.

There were nine left. Tomorrow she would buy more and she would drink from Massachusetts to Iowa. That amused her: how many people had drunk beer from the Atlantic—or ten miles from it anyway—right into the heart of the country? Now off the highway there were stores and shopping centers and the traffic was heavier. When they got into the country again, Beth looked out her window at colored leaves and green pines and spruce; the sun was setting, and the sky was rose and orange above the trees; she saw stone fences and sometimes a large house built far back from the road; twice she saw a single white boulder in meadows that were light green in the sun and dark green in the reaching shadows of the woods. When the sun went down she said: 'Can you keep driving? Or are you tired?'

'I'm not tired.'

'Good. Cars are nice at night.'

It was dusk now, so she could not see colors anymore, and she wanted dusk to change quickly to night so she could ride in the dark car with only the faint green light of the dashboard and red tail lights far ahead and pale headlights well on the other side of the divided highway.

'Are you hungry?' he said.

'No. Are you?'

'Not yet.'

'We can eat later, then drive some more.'

'All right,' he said.

'I'm going to do it differently now, since Peggy's gone. I'm not going to bed anymore until I'm really sleepy. Then I'll get up and give you breakfast and then I'll go back to bed and sleep till noon or so. I can do that now.'

'I guess you can.'

'It's what I'll do. I'll read a lot.'

'Yes.'

'You were right not to tell me, though. About other women. Because it doesn't matter. That's what no one admits, that it doesn't matter. Course when you didn't answer, that means you have, doesn't it?'

'Yes.'

'Really? I thought so.'

Her voice sounded strange in her throat. Then she was looking out the window at trees that were darker than the sky and she was crying and she could not stop.

'—understand,' he was saying. 'You *wanted* me to say it, so what is it now?'

She was shaking her head, her hands covering her face.

'Because it does matter and it doesn't matter and it does matter. Because I hate you and I hate me. And that's not true either, there's nothing true—' She lowered herself onto the seat, on her side, her head close to Lee. 'Oh Lee,' she said into the leather upholstery, 'when I die—'

'Hush now.' He patted her arm. 'Hush now, don't say that.'

'You take that ten thousand dollars and you and Peggy go on a nice long trip, to Europe or someplace.'

Then, to save them both from having to talk, she opened her mouth and breathed softly and pretended she was asleep. After a few minutes he took the beer can from her loose fingers, drank what was left, and lowered the can to the floor.